MY LOVING HUSBAND

BOOKS BY SHERYL BROWNE

The Babysitter

The Affair

The Second Wife

The Marriage Trap

The Perfect Sister

The New Girlfriend

Trust Me

My Husband's Girlfriend

The Liar's Child

The Invite

Do I Really Know You?

Her First Child

My Husband's House

We All Keep Secrets

Keep Me Safe

One More Lie

MY LOVING HUSBAND

SHERYL BROWNE

bookouture

Published by Bookouture in 2025

An imprint of Storyfire Ltd.
Carmelite House
50 Victoria Embankment
London EC4Y 0DZ

www.bookouture.com

The authorised representative in the EEA is Hachette Ireland
8 Castlecourt Centre
Dublin 15 D15 XTP3
Ireland
(email: info@hbgi.ie)

ISBN: 978-1-83618-295-5
eBook ISBN: 978-1-83618-294-8

For my brilliant readers and all those reader groups out there, for their love of books and wonderful support. It means more than I can put into words while I'm going through some challenging medical issues. Thank you.

A particular mention for Jules, whose passion for reading fired me up while we were out dog-walking. I got home and knocked that plot into shape.

And yes, Jules, you are right – John Marrs is quite brilliant!

Murder is born of love, and love attains the greatest intensity in murder.

Octave Mirbeau, *The Torture Garden*

PROLOGUE

She is beautiful, I have to concede. On the outside. Inside, she's as ugly as sin. She doesn't look very pleased to have been set the task of carrying out an inventory of the storage room, which I assume she feels is beneath her. Standing silently behind her, I watch her huffily opening drawers, muttering to herself as she ferrets through medical supplies. Slamming one of the drawers shut, she turns around and starts when she sees me. 'Oh, it's you,' she murmurs, a hand fluttering to her chest. And then she has the actual temerity to smile.

'It would appear to be.' I don't smile back, but stare stonily at her instead. 'I'm glad I caught you on your own.' I watch interestedly as her eyes, a myriad of browns, from amber to umber, which I'd once found intriguing, kind even, grow nervous, flicking past me to the door. She holds no intrigue any more. She's transparent. A jealous, evil woman who cares for no one but herself, despite her vocation.

Clearly realising she isn't going to get through the door without getting through me first, her complexion pales. 'Look, before you say anything, I'm sorry.' She holds up her hands in a show of contrition. 'I didn't plan for any of this to happen.'

I don't answer. Does she really imagine I'm here to talk to her, to listen to her false apologies, her insane justification for what she's done? Judging by the apprehension I see now in her eyes, I think not.

'I should get back,' she says, her gaze darting again to the door. 'People will be wondering where I've got to.'

I see the swallow slide down her slender throat and realise she's scared. It gives me some small satisfaction that she feels a fraction of the fear she's instilled in others. 'You're not sorry.' I continue to stare at her. 'I don't think you actually know the meaning of the word. You're a liar, aren't you? Delusional and dangerous. You've ruined lives.'

'*I've* ruined lives?' Her eyes widen with indignation. 'Excuse me, but it's *you* who's—'

'*My* life!' I seethe, a toxic mix of hatred and hurt writhing inside me.

She snaps her gaze away from me, her eyes, now terrified, those of a cornered animal, skittering around looking for a means to escape the windowless room she's trapped in. With me. No doubt she's wondering what her fate will be.

ONE

MADDIE

Realising Cole has left me a message saying the hospital has had an emergency pre-alert, I call him back in the hope of speaking to him before he gets tied up in theatre. As his phone rings out, I head to the hall to call my daughter for dinner.

'Two minutes,' Ellie shouts from her bedroom. 'I'm on the phone.'

To her friend Claire, presumably, who she was talking to in hushed tones about some boy or other on the way home. Smiling indulgently, I go back to the kitchen to check the oven. There's no answer from Cole. Guessing that A&E will be chaotic, I'm about to leave a message when he picks up, surprising me. 'Hey, how's it going?' he asks.

'All good,' I assure him. 'How's things on the battle front?'

'Hectic,' he replies wearily. 'There's been a road traffic accident on the Solihull bypass. We have several casualties coming in, one with a suspected skull fracture, so it looks like I'm not going to be home any time soon. Sorry to have left you with all the domestic chores again.'

'It's fine. I can manage. Just focus on what you have to do,' I tell him, aware that he'll be exhausted to his bones. His impossible workload, together with unscheduled procedures, means he's rarely home early nowadays. After a crack-of-dawn start and a full day of surgery yesterday, he was clearly shattered, dark bruises under his eyes as evidence.

'I'll do my best,' he assures me. 'Have I mentioned I love you lately?'

'Once or twice.' I smile, the soft timbre of his voice sending goosebumps over my skin, even after eighteen years of marriage.

'Not often enough then,' he says softly. 'I should go. They're coming in. I'll text you as soon as I have a rough idea what time—'

'Cole, you're needed in resus!' someone yells in the background, cutting him short.

'Duty calls.' He sighs. 'See you later.'

I'm still smiling as he ends the call, pleased that we can touch base through the madness our life can sometimes be with both of us working. Lately, we're mostly too tired once we crawl into bed to do anything but cuddle up and sleep. My job as an agency paediatric nurse, working with acutely ill and dying children, takes its toll, too, but at least I'm able to choose my hours. Being a top specialist in the field of neurosurgery means Cole doesn't have any such luxury. With the NHS in disarray, though, it is what it is. I know he would change it if he could. He hates it that he's missing quality time with the boys and helps out as much as he can when he's not working or on call at weekends. With three children, it's a juggling act sometimes, but I feel blessed to be with a man who gets why I need to work, unlike his father, also a surgeon and the worst kind of misogynist.

After checking the meatballs haven't turned to mush, I head for the lounge, pausing in the hall to straighten the family portrait that hangs there, a beautiful personalised watercolour copied from a photograph a passer-by had taken for us one day in the park. I'm sitting next to Cole, facing slightly away from him, each of us with one of the twins on our laps, Ellie standing behind us, her arms draped around both of us. Cole has an arm around my upper torso and is leaning into me, his mouth brushing my hair. I recall that he whispered, 'Sorry,' just as the photo was taken. We'd argued that morning, because I hadn't been quite so understanding when he'd said he had to go into the hospital to tackle a mountain of paperwork. We'd promised the boys that trip while the sun was shining, and I'd been bitterly disappointed for them. Cole had been tired. I'd guessed he was hoping to clear the decks rather than go in even earlier than the crack of dawn on Monday to tackle the backlog before his clinical team meeting, but I just couldn't say it was fine and make myself smile that day.

He presented me with the watercolour a couple of weeks later, having commissioned it as a surprise. 'I hoped it might convey how much my family means to me,' he said with a heart-melting smile. I'd forgotten about the argument by then, and felt bad that I'd made *him* feel so bad he'd worried about it. He's under so much stress, yet he took time out to preserve this precious memory of us all together for ever. He's not a thoughtless man. He's simply doing what he does to the best of his ability within the time he has available. I do wish he could be home more, but I really wouldn't want to change him. I love him because he's who he is, a fundamentally good man.

Reminding myself to replace the loose picture hook rather than risk the painting I adore crashing to the floor, I carry on to round up the twins. I find them sitting cross-legged in front of the TV superglued to *Minecraft* and feel immediately guilty. Cole assures me that 'brain' games have a positive effect, improving cognitive skills and hand-eye coordination, but still I worry about the amount of screen time they have. I agonised about my decision to pick up my career once they started school. In the end, though, I decided that I love what I do too much to give it up completely. Plus, if I'm honest, being in another environment helps save my sanity.

'Oi, that's cheating,' Jayden says suddenly, elbowing his brother, which brings me back to the predicament of how to get any of my children to the table for dinner.

I decide on the no-nonsense approach. 'Jayden, Lucas. Hands. Wash. *Now.* Both of you.' I clap my own hands behind them, making them jump.

'Aw, Mum,' Lucas moans. 'I was just about to fend off the enemy.'

'The enemy can wait. Dinner can't,' I reply. 'One minute and counting.' I stand aside and point to the door.

The boys sigh in unison and rise grudgingly from the floor.

'It's meatballs, with ice cream for pudding.' I offer an incentive as they trudge past me.

'Cool.' The boys brighten, looking slightly more sprightly as they head for the kitchen.

Smiling, I follow them to find Ellie finally descending the stairs. 'Everything okay?' I enquire.

'Yes. Why?' she asks and carries on to the kitchen.

'No reason. I couldn't help overhearing you mentioning some boy's name when you were talking to Claire, that's all,' I fish a little since Ellie seems to have been moping around lately.

'It's just some idiot at uni,' she replies, plonking herself down at the kitchen island and reaching for the casserole lid.

'Oh dear.' I study her with a troubled frown. Has this 'idiot' upset her in some way? I wonder. 'So what did he do to earn that label?'

Ellie doesn't look at me. 'He's a prat,' she answers without ceremony.

My gaze shoots to the boys, who, with their attention on some transformer toy Jayden has snuck to the table, appear not to have noticed her language.

'Is Dad going to be home soon?' Ellie asks, oblivious to the reprimanding frown I give her.

'Not for a while.' I pass her the ladle, which she appears to be looking for. 'He's having to stay a bit longer at the hospital this evening.'

'Again?' Her expression is somewhere between dejected and annoyed.

'He doesn't have a lot of choice, Ellie,' I remind her. 'There's been an emergency.'

'Isn't there always?' she retorts, taking me completely aback. She's always looked up to her father, and I'm mystified as to why she would be so suddenly down on him.

'He does his best, you know,' I say, watching her carefully. 'People don't conveniently get sick between the hours of nine and five.'

'Yeah, I get it.' Ellie looks contrite. 'I know he's out there saving people's lives,' she concedes, 'but he's doing it at the cost of his family's lives, isn't he?'

'That's a bit harsh,' I respond, now feeling upset – for the twins, who've obviously picked up on her moodiness and are glancing worriedly between us, and for Ellie herself. What on earth has got into her? I watch as, keeping her gaze averted, she dishes out meatballs to the twins, or rather, dumps them on their plates. 'It was a road traffic accident,' I point out. 'He can't just clock off and come home with casualties being brought in.'

'I know.' Ellie sighs lengthily. 'So what time is he going to be back?'

'I'm not sure.' I help the boys to salad, at which there are audible groans and curled lips. 'He said he'd text me. Do you need to talk to him about something?'

She shrugs. 'Not really. I wanted to take up running again, that's all, and I hoped Dad would be able to come with me like he used to.'

I eye her curiously. She does want to talk to him. They

would often go out running together until Ellie hit her teens and possibly thought it wasn't cool or whatever. I know they used the time together to talk, particularly about anything that might be troubling her. *I* need to make time for her, I realise. There's obviously something eating away at her. 'Do you fancy having a girls' night?' I ask tentatively. 'Once the boys are in bed, we could...' I stop as my phone pings. 'That's probably your dad now.'

I climb off my stool and hurry to grab my phone from the worktop. Realising it's not a text but a WhatsApp message, I quickly read it. Frowning, I read it again, and as the words permeate my stupefied incomprehension – *Are you sure your husband is where he says he is tonight?* – I stifle a gasp.

TWO

ELLIE

Curling up on her bed, Ellie stuffed her earbuds in and tried to chill. She shouldn't be so down on her dad. She'd always been really proud of what he did. Now she'd seen what she had, though, she couldn't help it, especially with him coming home later and later. She supposed her view of men had been tainted by the dick she'd been unfortunate enough to lose her virginity to, but she couldn't help that either. Whenever she thought about him, which was constantly, she felt riddled with humiliation and so angry with herself for allowing him to treat her the way he had.

She'd been instantly attracted when she'd met him at Popzone. He was four years older than her, tall and gorgeous-looking. With lush long eyelashes framing ice-blue eyes, incongruous with his dark hair, he actually looked a bit like her dad, who all her mates thought was hot. When she'd learned he was about to start a law degree at the same university where she was doing her undergraduate foundation course in psychology, she'd thought he was smart and sophisticated. Also, out of her league. He'd been way too cool to join his mates giving it their all to cheesy pop tunes on the dance floor. Aware that he was quietly watching her over his Budweiser, though, Ellie had gone for it, as in gone really wild, doing the whole *Men's shirts, short skirts* thing to Shania Twain's classic, 'Man! I Feel Like a Woman!'.

He'd smiled as she'd gyrated, laughed and raised his glass in her direction when she'd scooped up her hair and run her hand suggestively over her torso.

When the DJ had switched to R&B and she'd taken a break to cool off, he'd come up behind her at the bar, sliding a hand around her bare waist and leaning close to her ear. 'I'll get that,' he'd said as she'd ordered a Smirnoff Ice. 'Make that two, mate.' He'd gestured to the barman before Ellie had a chance to object. Not that she was about to. She couldn't believe her luck that he'd chosen her above all the available, ready and willing girls in the club.

'So, how'd you get in?' he'd asked when she'd waggled her fingers at her friends ogling behind her and joined him at a table. 'Not doing one of the bouncers a favour, are you?'

Ellie had felt her cheeks heat up. Not because of the comment particularly, but because he'd clearly cottoned on to the fact that she was underage.

'Forget it. None of my business,' he said, obviously noticing her embarrassment. 'I'm glad you did get in, though. Luke Wainwright.' Extending his hand, he introduced himself – as if she hadn't already made sure to find out his name.

Relief swept through her. She hadn't wanted to let on to him, an upcoming law student, that she and her friends had got their fake IDs online. It was the first time Ellie had used hers and she'd been scared she'd get caught. She dreaded to think what her mum and dad's reaction would have been if she'd ended up at the police station. 'Ellie.' She smiled, goosebumps prickling pleasantly over her skin as she slid her hand into his.

'Nice to meet you, Ellie.' He'd smiled back and held on to it, his striking blue eyes roving over her, pausing at her breasts, which were bursting over her black plunge satin and lace crop top.

He hadn't let go of her hand for the rest of the night, still holding on to it as they'd spilled from the nightclub, her going over on her strappy platforms and almost breaking her ankle. So much for her attempt to be sophisticated. He'd practically held her up as she'd swayed, then hobbled to the taxi. Her ankle had been quite badly bruised, but she hadn't felt any pain. She'd been anaesthetised by alcohol, Luke had said.

He'd kissed her in the taxi. Ellie had felt a bit sick, but she'd gone with it. It was the first time she'd kissed a boy properly. It was okay, quite pleasant up to a point, though she had almost gagged when he'd thrust his tongue deep into her mouth. She'd tried to be cool, not to actually die of embarrassment when he'd tugged down her top and nipped her breasts. She just prayed the taxi driver couldn't see past Luke to where his mouth was – or his hand.

It was when she woke in his single bed at his digs that the pain hit her, her ankle throbbing, nausea grinding her stomach, her insides feeling raw and bruised.

'I take it that was your first time?' he'd asked, frowning curiously as he walked across to her with a glass of water.

Ellie had blinked at him in confusion. She didn't remember a thing about the previous night. After almost falling out of the taxi and him helping her up an overgrown path and through the front door of an old, terraced house into a damp-smelling hall, her mind was blank.

'I have to be somewhere,' he said, placing the glass down on the table next to her.

'Sorry,' she mumbled, uneasiness creeping through her as she realised she was still fully dressed, minus her underwear. Easing her legs over the bed, she attempted to stand, which was like mission impossible with her head still spinning and the walls orbiting in sick-making revolutions around her. 'I think I must have passed out.'

He eyed her thoughtfully. Then, 'Don't sweat it,' he said, an inscrutable smile twitching his mouth. 'Just a thought...' he added. Apprehension tightened Ellie's tummy. 'You might want to dress a little less provocatively in future.'

She'd looked at him in confusion.

'You have to admit, that crop top thing you're almost wearing is asking for trouble.' He nodded towards it, a semi-amused look on his face.

Ellie had glanced down at her top. 'What's wrong with it?' she asked, puzzled.

'Your tits are almost bursting out of it. It screams "shag me", but I'm guessing you're aware of that.'

She'd studied him with a mixture of disbelief and shock. Gone was the sparkle she'd found so attractive in his eyes. Instead, they were filled with icy contempt.

'I've got about five minutes before I have to be gone, so...' He smiled flatly again and let it hang.

Swallowing back the panic and revulsion rising hotly inside her, Ellie scrambled around, grabbing up her bag, not bothering to search for her knickers, and stumbled towards the door. Clutching the handle, she paused. Then, 'Is that why you did?' she asked, tightening her grip.

'What?' He squinted at her, clearly irritated.

'Is that why you *shagged* me?' She spelled it out.

He held his hands up as if warding her off. 'Okay, look, I'm not doing this. I don't have time for your morning-after regrets. Not my problem, so if you could just—'

'While I was too drunk to know what was happening?'

He shook his head. 'You have to be kidding me?' He laughed scornfully. 'You were begging for it.'

'While I was *unconscious*?' she went on, fury sparking

inside her. 'Because that's what you did, Luke, isn't it? Regardless of whether I wanted it or not.'

'That's enough, Ellie,' he said, his face rigid with anger.

'Is it because you think you're entitled?' she pushed on. 'Is that it? Do you think because your dad's a hotshot barrister you can do what you want and get away with it? Or do you just enjoy humiliating women?'

He was across the room before she could blink, his fingers digging painfully into her flesh as he grabbed hold of her arm. 'Do not *ever* repeat what you just said,' he seethed, his eyes now as cold as the Arctic Ocean. 'Or so help me—'

Bringing her knee up sharply, Ellie stopped him dead – and fled. She'd found out days later that he'd done the same to at least one other girl at uni.

Were they all the same? Did men get some kind of kick out of hurting women? Did her dad? *No.* Her dad wasn't like that. He just *wasn't*. Whatever she thought she'd seen him doing, she was wrong. She *had* to be. *God.* Rolling over, she stuffed her face in her pillow. She so needed to talk to someone about it before she went out of her mind.

She'd seen Luke since, at uni. She'd tried to walk past him, but he'd caught her arm again. 'You were using a fake ID, remember?' he'd said, his face right up close to hers. 'I'd keep your mouth shut if I were you. Oh, and if you decide to open it anyway, just to remind you, my father is a powerful barrister, so... Think it through, love. I would if I were you.'

She'd been plucking up courage to try to talk to her mum, but then her mum had gone all weird, being short with the boys when they'd started arguing over some transformer toy or other. Her dad would know what to do. He was calm and measured and she'd always been able to confide in him. Now, though, knowing what she knew, she wasn't so sure.

THREE

COLE

Cole noticed that Dr Hannah Lee looked apprehensive as she prepped to join him in the operating theatre. It was a relatively straightforward procedure to elevate a depressed skull fracture and evacuate a haematoma. She'd completed her neurological training and was now six months into her specialty training, and he considered she was ready. 'Do you fancy having a go at this one?' he enquired.

'You mean now?' she asked, paling somewhat.

'No time like the present,' he said. He supposed she would be feeling daunted since she would be in the driving seat rather than assisting. Also because she was under his tutelage. She'd confessed she was a little overawed by him when she'd first met him during her final-year neuro training.

He had told her she shouldn't be. It was true he expected nothing but the best from his team, which he didn't think was unreasonable considering they walked the tightrope between life and death. The last thing he wanted was for anyone to feel intimidated by him, though. He was exacting, but he hoped he wasn't anything like his father, who would think nothing of humiliating his trainees in front of patients and staff alike. The female trainees weren't intimidated only by his father's bullying, but by his predatory behaviour too, which was largely unchecked by executives of the hospital trust, who valued his expertise as a surgeon above the welfare of junior doctors. The man was a misogynist and a bully by nature. He'd bullied Cole's mother. Humiliated Cole himself as a child, without compunction.

Bearing his father's reputation in mind, Cole had worked hard to put Hannah at her ease. With female neurosurgeons constituting less than ten per cent of the workforce, he wanted her to succeed. She was young, but enthusiastic. Also skilled.

'Nervous?' he asked, glancing at her again and noticing how striking her eyes were. Amber in colour, with an umber limbal ring around the irises, they were unlike any he'd seen before. Quite mesmerising.

'A bit,' she admitted.

'Don't be,' he said. 'You've got this. Just focus on the task. Cut well and sew well, and hopefully you'll get the patient well. Bear in mind that though *you* might be a little apprehensive, this is possibly the scariest moment in your patient's life.'

'I will.' She nodded and smiled appreciatively, though she still looked worried.

'Think of it as a choreographed ballet,' Cole went on. 'If you work with your team and make sure you're in the right place at the right time, everything will flow seamlessly.'

She was definitely gazing at him in awe now, which he had to admit did his ego no harm. His personal life was less than organised, unfortunately. He didn't blame Maddie. They hadn't bargained on having twins so long after their daughter. They'd been ecstatic about the pregnancy after Maddie had had two miscarriages, which had devastated them both. Maddie's grief had been palpable on both occasions, and he'd felt so bloody impotent not being able to make her pain go away. The boys were a handful, though, meaning Maddie was exhausted with the constant demands on her. He'd understood that she'd needed to go back to work – to save her sanity, she'd said – but he couldn't help wishing she'd waited a little longer. Aside from the fact that things between them in the bedroom seemed to have slipped off the agenda due to them both being too tired to do anything but sleep, he'd felt himself getting angry when they'd argued one weekend about his workload encroaching on family downtime. It was a dangerous emotion, one he worked to avoid.

'That's beautiful,' Hannah said, refocusing his mind on the task in hand. 'There's a poetic heart in there somewhere, isn't there?'

'Not too dispassionate after all, then?' He arched an eyebrow.

'Sorry?' Her forehead creased into a puzzled frown. Then, 'Ah. Oh.' She looked as if she would like the ground to open up when the penny dropped and she realised he was talking about the conversation he'd overheard yesterday. She'd been talking to a young male nurse, who'd referred to him as dispassionate because he emphasised that emotions were best left at the door when one went into theatre. 'Sorry,' she mumbled. 'I did defend you,' she added quickly, her cheeks flushing.

Cole laughed. 'Don't worry about it,' he said. 'I'm thick-skinned.'

'You're not going to refuse to mentor me then?' she asked sheepishly.

'No,' he assured her. 'You show great promise. Tell you what, why don't you join me for a coffee once we've finished here? We could have a chat about things going forward. That's unless you have somewhere you need to be?' He had somewhere he needed to be, as in home, but he figured that as he was going to be late anyway, ten more minutes wouldn't hurt.

She smiled. 'No, I don't. I'd like that.'

'Great.' Smiling back, Cole looked her over. She was

undoubtedly an attractive woman. Realising his gaze was lingering, he pulled himself up sharp. He was sending out mixed messages, flying way too close to the flame. Hadn't he done that once before and got badly burned? He'd ended up in a situation he had no idea how to extricate himself from and that might have placed his marriage in jeopardy. What the hell was the matter with him? He sighed with relief when his anaesthetist came through the theatre doors.

'All good?' Alex asked, glancing between them.

'Almost,' Cole answered, and refocused his attention where it should be. 'Hannah, do you want to go ahead and check out the equipment trolley?' he suggested. 'I'll be one minute.'

Watching her go, he turned back to find Alex scrutinising him with semi-amusement. 'Someone looks awestruck,' the anaesthetist commented, nodding after Hannah.

'Naturally,' Cole joked.

Alex rolled his eyes.

'She's impressed with my surgical skills, that's all,' Cole clarified.

'I think it might be a bit more than admiration for your surgical skills, since you're clearly the hospital heart-throb.'

Cole shook his head. 'I'm a respectable married man.'

'Of which I'm well aware,' Alex responded, but though he smiled, Cole noted that there was something behind his eyes.

Regret? he wondered. Alex had gone out with Maddie briefly until she'd found him in a compromising embrace with an attractive colleague at a New Year's party. He had been drinking – far too much, apparently – and had apologised profusely, but it had ended the relationship. He'd never said as much, but Cole suspected he might have felt he'd lost out when Maddie and he got married.

'I'd be careful if I were you,' Alex went on. 'You do tend to be a little overfriendly with female members of staff.'

Cole looked at him askance. 'I'm friendly in order to put

people at their ease, Alex, male or female. I don't want anyone to feel intimidated.'

Alex held his hands up. 'Fair enough. Just be aware of what signals you might be sending out. You don't want people making assumptions.'

That he was like his father, did he mean? Frowning, Cole watched him head back into the theatre. He wanted to ask him, but with a patient prepped and waiting, he hadn't got time to debate it. Alex had known him since medical school and was aware of what kind of man his father was. He was trying to watch his back lest he end up being tarred with the same brush, Cole guessed. He sincerely hoped, though, that Alex, along with everyone else, didn't really think he was like a man whose behaviour appalled him.

FOUR

MADDIE

Hearing Cole come through the front door, I pause in my effort to cram everything in the dishwasher and check the wall clock. It's 10.30. Should I mention the message? It was sent from a blank profile, so it's obviously some crank, but still it is worrying. It's as if whoever it was knew he wasn't here. Straightening up, I turn to face him as he comes into the kitchen, and hesitate. He looks almost dead on his feet. 'I plated a meal up for you,' I say, nodding towards the fridge.

'Ah.' He glances in that direction, a flicker of guilt crossing his face.

'Have you already eaten?' I look at him in surprise. I assumed he would be too busy to even grab a sandwich.

'Sorry.' He looks contrite. 'I had an impromptu meeting over coffee with the doctor I'm training. I decided to grab a bite to eat while we were there.'

'Oh, right. This would be the girl I met when I came in last week?' I ask curiously. I dropped by the hospital to see Kelsey, who transferred from the Birmingham Children's Hospital and now works on the general surgery ward at the same hospital as Cole. We went to the café for a coffee to go with the cake I'd bought her for her birthday – and who should we see there having 'a bite' together but Cole and... 'Hannah, isn't it?'

'That's right.' He smiles. 'She's hardly a girl, though.'

She looked like a girl to me, fresh-faced, young and enthusiastic. 'And is she doing okay?' I enquire.

'She is.' He nods. 'She's talented. Pays attention to detail.'

'Worth your time training, then?' I ask. He doesn't hesitate to tell me when he thinks junior doctors are simply not up to the job. Hannah obviously is.

'I'd say so, yes.' He loosens his shirt collar.

'Good.' I eye him thoughtfully as I pick up my glass of wine and take a sip. 'Do you want a coffee?' I offer, since Cole rarely drinks alcohol. I'm jealous of him spending time with this woman, I realise, and don't like myself for it. Cole and I spend so little time together, though. I can't remember the last time we weren't too tired to make love, something that used to come naturally, spontaneously, lying together afterwards, limbs and bodies entwined, sharing our dreams and hopes for the future, for our children.

'No.' He drags a hand tiredly over his neck. 'Thanks, but I think I'll go straight up and take a shower.'

'Do you want me to have a go at that?' I ask as he rolls his shoulders. He's always liked my shoulder massages, telling me I have a masseur's fingers.

'I'm good.' He smiles. 'Finish your wine. I won't be long. The boys are in bed, I take it?'

'For a good while now,' I answer, careful not to sound pointed. 'Ellie's out. At Claire's house.'

Cole checks his watch. 'Shouldn't she be back by now?'

'I've given her a late pass. Claire's mum's dropping her back,' I reassure him, knowing he worries about her walking home late at night.

Looking relieved, he nods.

'I think something's bothering her,' I confide, because I

know he would want me to. 'I'm not sure what, I haven't had a chance to talk to her yet. That's probably why she's gone to Claire's, so they can have a good natter.'

A concerned frown creases his forehead. 'Boyfriend trouble, do you think?'

'Possibly.'

The furrow in his brow deepens. 'Do you think she might talk to me?' he asks.

I marvel at his intuition. 'I think she would love to, but I know you haven't had much time lately.'

'I'll make time.' He nods resolutely. 'I'll take her for lunch or something, if she's up for it.'

'She'd like that.' I smile, thinking that she needs someone's undivided attention for once. Something tells me that it's Cole's attention she needs, and I'm good with that. I'm certain there are many shared secrets between them I've never been privy to. Cole's always measured and calm in a crisis. A good sounding board for a girl growing up.

'I'll go and grab that shower,' he says, kneading his neck as he heads for the door.

I watch him go. I'd really like to talk to him about the message, but I don't want to pile worry on top of worry. It can wait until morning. After swilling my glass, I take out the meal I made up for him. It's a congealed mess now, not exactly appetising. Heading to the bin to scrape it in, I find it full and, sighing, I heave out the bag to take to the wheelie bin.

I'm on my way back in, thinking I should make us both a hot chocolate, when I hear the hall phone ringing. Wondering who on earth would be calling the landline at this late hour, I hurry to grab it before it wakes the twins, answering with a tentative 'Hello?'

There's no reply.

'Hello?' I repeat, trying to curtail my impatience as I realise it might be the hospital calling with an emergency, having already tried Cole's mobile. Still there's nothing. I'm about to end the call when someone whispers, 'He's lying.'

I feel a chill creep through me. 'Who is this?' I ask shakily. There's no response. Whoever's calling is still there, though. I can hear them breathing. 'What do you want?' I ask, more forcefully.

An interminably long second passes, and then, 'Be careful,' a woman's voice warns me before the phone goes dead.

FIVE

After replacing the receiver, I stand staring stunned at the phone. Then snatch it back up and check the latest call number. It's withheld, unsurprisingly. Anger bubbles up inside me. It's a malicious caller, I tell myself as I head quickly to the kitchen to retrieve my glass. Tipping a hefty measure of wine into it, I take a gulp. *Just like the message was from some random crank?* It's too much of a coincidence, surely? It's almost as if this person – the same person, it has to be – knows his comings and goings. But they didn't mention him by name. Am I reading too much into it?

Leaving the wine, which I actually don't tolerate very well, I head upstairs after Cole. I have to mention it now. He would want to know, and I won't sleep a wink if I don't. As I go into the bedroom, I realise he's already in the shower and that he's left the en suite door open. Going in, I can't help but feel a familiar little dip in my pelvis as my eyes travel over his torso. He looks good, even from behind. Especially from behind: lean-framed, broad-shouldered and athletic, thanks to regular tennis matches and workouts on his home treadmill. I note the water cascading over his skin as he soaps his body, lending it a glistening sheen. If I took a photo and posted it on social media entitled *Behind the Surgical Mask*, it would go viral, I'm sure it would. He's an attractive man. His most attractive feature, though, is that he seems unaware of his appeal, cerebral and physical. He would never do anything to jeopardise his marriage, hurt his children. I know him well enough to know that. His relationship with his own father, brittle at best after the hurt the man inflicted on Cole and his mother, with both his infidelities and his impossibly high standards, made up Cole's mind that he would never follow in his footsteps. His father has curtailed his deplorable behaviour lately, probably because age is catching up with him, but the damage is done. Cole's mother, Lizzie, stays with him only out of duty, I think. Cole could never be anything like him.

I move back as he turns around. He starts slightly as he sees me, and then slides the shower door open and steps out. 'See anything you like?' he jokes, a mischievous smile curving his mouth as he grabs the towel from the rail to wrap around his waist.

'Um?' I can't help but smile back. 'Possibly.'

'Likewise,' he says, walking across to me. 'Sorry my schedule's been so nuts,' he adds, his eyes holding mine, striking blue eyes that reveal his every emotion. 'I've been neglecting you and the kids. I don't mean to.'

'It's okay. I understand,' I assure him. I do understand. It's frustrating, yes, but I've worked in the NHS. And things have only got worse since I left to have the twins.

'Which is one of the things I love about you.' He reaches to stroke my cheek with his thumb. 'I know I'm not here as much as I should be, meaning most of the responsibility for the kids falls to you. I do try, but...'

I silence him, brushing away a trickle of water that spills from his hair to his lips.

He catches my hand, presses a soft kiss to it. Looking back

at me, he hesitates, then leans towards me, seeking my mouth with his, parting my lips so softly with his tongue that something beyond physical dissolves inside me. His kiss is slow, deep and meaningful, and I melt into him. I've missed him, missed this, the closeness between us.

Stopping after a while, out of necessity of breathing, he scans my eyes and then presses his forehead to mine. 'I do love you,' he says throatily. 'You know that, don't you?'

My stomach tightens, a small part of me wondering why he would feel the need to reassure me twice in one night. Easing back a little, I search his eyes in turn, find a flicker of uncertainty there and wonder if he feels the insecurity I do because of the lack of physical contact between us. 'The feeling's mutual,' I whisper.

'Good.' The relief now in his all-telling eyes is palpable. 'I want you, Mrs Chase,' he growls.

I laugh at his overexaggerated attempt at macho. 'You have me,' I assure him, and lean back into him, tracing his damp flesh with my fingertips, tiptoeing my way down his back to the restricting towel.

His kiss is urgent this time, deeper, sensual. Plunging his tongue into my mouth, he kisses me lingeringly, and then stops suddenly, groaning in frustration as Ellie's voice reaches us.

'Hello? Anyone home?' she calls.

Her expression is suspicious as I slip from the bathroom, leaving Cole inside and tugging the door closed behind me. 'You do realise you left the front door open?' she asks.

'Did I?' I look at her in surprise, then squeeze my eyes closed as I realise that in my haste to answer the phone, I obviously did.

'Not interrupting anything, am I?' Eyebrows raised, Ellie looks me over curiously.

'No,' I answer quickly, feeling actually guilty. 'We were just talking.'

'Oh, right. I'll leave you to finish your *conversation*, then.' She pivots around. 'I closed the front door, by the way, so you needn't rush. Night.'

'Night. Thanks.' I cringe and glance back to the bathroom as Cole inches the door open.

'That's spoiled the mood a bit.' He glances after Ellie with an amused eye roll.

'I'll go and check everything's locked up,' I tell him. 'Won't be long.'

'Great. Thanks. I'll have a word with Ellie tomorrow about what you said earlier. See if she fancies some lunch one day next week, if that's okay with you,' he says, heading towards the bed.

'Brilliant.' I smile, glad he's remembered. Seeing him stifle a yawn as he takes his phone from his jacket pocket, I try not to feel disappointed. He's so shattered, and once he's reset his alarm, he'll probably be unconscious in seconds flat. Ah well, we have the weekend ahead. He's on call tomorrow night, but as far as I know, he has nothing on the agenda during the day apart from taking the boys swimming. As I'm only working half a day, with luck we might be able to find some time for just the two of us.

Leaving him to it, I head for the door and then stop, remembering I haven't mentioned the message and weird phone call. 'Cole, there's something else I need to talk to you about,' I start hesitantly. I really don't want him to lose sleep over it, but I can't just ignore it.

He places his phone down and turns to me. 'Sounds serious.'

'I received an odd message,' I go on. 'It worried me a bit.'

'Why?' He eyes me curiously. 'Was it threatening?'

'Not as such.' I waver. 'It seems ridiculous now I think about it.'

'Mads?' Concerned, he walks across to me. 'What did it say?'

'It was more a question,' I answer, wishing now that I'd left it until morning. It's too late to get into this now.

'And?' He clearly notices my reticence. 'Mads, it's not ridiculous if it's worrying you. What did it say?' he urges me.

'It said, "Are you sure your husband is where he says he is tonight?"'

Cole shakes his head in bemusement. 'It's a hoax,' he says. 'Some sick individual trying to get you to engage with them.'

'I know.' I nod. 'It did spook me a bit, though. I mean, how could they know you weren't here?'

He frowns. 'Pot luck,' he says. I can see the apprehension in his eyes, though, as they flick to mine. 'It was random. Possibly someone who knows what I do. Have there been any other messages?'

'No. Just that one, but...'

'But what?' Cole looks wary.

'There was a call on the landline,' I go on cautiously. I don't want to sound as if I'm paranoid, but what if this person – and I really do believe it's the same person responsible for both – calls again when Ellie's here on her own? Or one of the twins picks up? 'Just now,' I add, 'while you were in the shower.'

The furrow in his brow deepens. 'From?'

'I don't know. It was probably just a crank call. I put the phone down, but...'

'Mads, what? You need to tell me. I'm only going to be worrying if you don't.'

I take a breath. 'Whoever it was said you were lying. They warned me to be careful.'

'Said *I* was lying?' His look is now one of astonishment. 'They mentioned me by name?'

'Well, no,' I concede, 'but when they told me to be careful, it really worried me. I can't help but wonder who would say something like that, and why.'

Cole doesn't answer for a moment. 'You don't think there's any truth in it, do you?' he says eventually.

'No,' I answer honestly. 'You have to admit it's a bit worrying, though, the two coming one after the other.'

He nods thoughtfully. 'I can see it would be.' He moves to circle his arms around me. 'I'd never lie to you, though. I would never have any reason to. You know that, right?'

'I know.' I thread my arms around his waist, feeling comforted by the closeness of him.

'Will you promise to do something for me?' he asks, easing back a fraction, the look in his eyes intense. 'You've been tired recently, which is bound to make you a bit more forgetful, but—'

'Forgetful?' I look at him in surprise.

'You just left the door wide open, Mads,' he points out. 'Try to take a little more care of yourself, hey? And make sure to keep the kids safe, will you?'

SIX

Feeling sleep-deprived, I shower quickly and go downstairs in search of Cole. He didn't get much sleep either, probably because what I'd told him was playing on his mind. I wish I had left it until morning now. After tossing and turning next to me half the night, he eventually climbed out of bed and came down early.

'Cole?' I call. He's not in the lounge or the kitchen, but seeing the interior garage door open a fraction, I assume he's out there, working out on his treadmill. Sure enough, I find him running, tuned out with his earphones in.

Going around to the front of the treadmill so as not to startle him, I gesture coffee signs with my hands. He gives me a small smile and shakes his head, and I'm worrying now that he will think I do actually believe there's some credence in what that crank caller said. Sighing, I head back to the kitchen to get the boys' breakfast. Cole will be looking after them this morning. My guilt ramps up as I realise how ragged he will be feeling, and I find myself wondering again whether I should have waited before going back to work. But then I berate myself. My job is hugely rewarding. I've nursed some incredible children who've been through so much treatment, yet still they smile and play in between those treatments. Helping them achieve their best quality of life is a privilege. It makes me feel good, and it also gives me the mental space I need.

As I go back to the kitchen, the twins make their presence known, thundering along the landing from their bedroom. 'Careful, you two. Hold on to the rail,' I yell, my heart missing a beat as I imagine one of them tumbling down the stairs.

'What do you fancy for breakfast?' I ask as they burst into the kitchen.

'Pancakes,' says Jayden, always one step ahead of Lucas.

'I don't have time this morning, sweetheart.' I smile apologetically. 'How about waffles?'

'With chocolate syrup?' Lucas asks hopefully.

I nod. 'And strawberries.'

'Cool,' says Jayden. 'Where's Dad?'

'Treadmill,' I provide. 'Uh-uh.' I stop him as he races across the kitchen in the direction of the garage. The gym area is a no-go for the boys unless under strict supervision. Focused on his running, Cole might not even notice them. I still have palpitations when I recall Lucas trying to climb on the back of the treadmill with him.

'Aw, Mum.' Jayden screws up his face. 'We wanted to ask him what we're doing today, didn't we, Lucas?'

'Yep.' Lucas, who's more laid-back than Jayden, heads for the fridge to fetch the orange juice.

'Thanks.' I smile as he passes it to me. 'The swimming baths,' I tell Jayden. It's become a bit of a weekend ritual, since both boys are keen swimmers.

'And Maccies after?' Lucas asks, now definitely hopeful.

'You'll have to ask your dad,' I tell him. 'And not too much Oreo ice cream,' I add, guessing Cole will indeed take them to McDonald's. For all his efforts at a healthy lifestyle, he can't resist indulging in a quarter-pounder with fries himself.

'Oreo McFlurry.' Jayden corrects me with a sigh that indicates his despair at my lack of knowledge about all things McDonald's.

'Or that.' I wind him up while popping the waffles in the toaster, at which point I get the eye roll, a family trait, it seems. He's soon lost interest, though, his gaze swivelling to the internal door as their father comes in.

'Who's having Oreo McFlurry?' Cole asks, then steps back as both boys charge at him, hitting him full-on mid-torso and wrapping their arms around him, regardless of the fact that he's hot and sweaty. And actually extremely fanciable for being so. I feel a stab of regret about what didn't happen between us last night.

'*We* are!' the boys yell in unison, looking up at him – and I'm struck by how like their father they are. They're miniature replicas of him: the same unruly dark hair that refuses to lie flat no matter how much they smooth it, and startling blue eyes that can communicate their feelings with a stare or an ice-cool glare in an instant.

Cole steers them around towards the kitchen island. 'Breakfast first,' he tells them. 'And then you get dressed pronto and straighten your beds. Trips to McDonald's very much depend on whether your room's tidy, as you both know.'

The boys exchange amused glances as they head for the island. They know their father too well. They're confident they'll be going whatever.

'Do you fancy a coffee now?' I ask him, hoping to touch base before I leave.

Cole reaches for the towel around his neck and wipes the sweat from his forehead. 'I'll make it,' he says, smiling slightly more effusively than previously.

'Thanks.' I smile back as he heads to the coffee machine. I'll call him later. Depending on how my shift goes, I might be able to join them for lunch. The boys will be upbeat after spending time with Cole. They're bound to lighten the heavy mood.

Popping the toaster, I put the waffles in the oven to keep warm and then stuff another batch in. I'm about to call to Ellie, who I can hear descending the stairs, when the hall phone rings. I freeze, actual palpitations in my chest as I wonder who it might be.

'I'll get it,' Ellie calls, jarring me into action.

'*No*. Leave it.' I skid into the hall and snatch the receiver up a second before she reaches it.

'Excuse me, I'm sure.' She huffs indignantly. 'Private, obviously,' she mutters, rolling her eyes and flouncing, arms folded, past Cole, who was quick to follow me.

'Madelyn Chase. Who's calling?' I ask.

There's no answer, and my heart rate ratchets up. 'Who's there?' I demand, glancing at Cole. I note a flicker of something in his eyes, but I can't quite read it. Anger? Probably, if he thinks this is our crank caller.

Still there's silence, and I'm about to slam the phone down when I hear it distinctly: someone breathing, heavy, ragged breaths. My stomach lurches. 'What do you *want*?' My voice quavers and I curse myself. The last thing I want is for this twisted person to imagine they're getting to me.

As Cole steps forward, about to take the phone from me, the caller speaks, her voice tearful. 'Maddie, it's Lizzie.'

'Lizzie?' I frown in confusion.

'Is Cole there?' she asks shakily. 'Can I speak to him?'

'Yes, of course. Are you all right?' I glance at Cole, whose face is wary.

His mother doesn't answer, stifling a sob instead, and I hand the phone quickly to him.

'What's wrong?' he asks tersely.

I'm hovering, wanting to do something but not sure what, when a scream from the kitchen stops my blood pumping.

'Lucas!' I fly straight to my boy, who's on the floor, squirming in pain as he cradles one hand in the other, blood spurting from a wound in his head. 'What happened?' I drop down to him, hastily assessing his wound.

'The waffle got stuck,' Jayden says sheepishly. 'Lucas tried to get it out and he burned his hand, and then he tripped over my remote control car. Sorry.'

Oh no. My stomach lurches as I realise what might have happened if he'd picked up a knife and jabbed that into the toaster.

'What the hell's going on?' Cole is beside me, his face filled with fear and bewilderment, Ellie close behind him.

'He's all right.' I sweep Lucas up and rush towards the sink, where Ellie is already ahead of me, running the cold tap. 'He must have banged his head on the stool. The cut's not too deep, but he's burned his fingers as well. I've got it. Go and talk to your mum.'

Cole drags his hand through his hair, appearing not to know what to do.

'Go.' I wave him away and concentrate on comforting my child.

Minutes later, I leave Lucas with Ellie while I dash upstairs to change my bloodied top and grab my bag and phone. I've decided to take Lucas in with me to the hospital. The gash isn't serious, but he might need a butterfly stitch, and his fingers are already blistering.

I find Cole in the bedroom, pulling off his T-shirt and scrabbling in his drawer for a clean one. 'Is Lucas okay?' he asks as he tugs the shirt on. 'Should I check him over?'

'He's doing fine,' I reassure him. 'I'm taking him in with me. I assume you have to go somewhere?'

Cole nods, and glances agitatedly around the room. 'On the dressing table,' I say, guessing it's his phone he's looking for.

Nodding shortly again, he goes to pick it up.

'What happened with your mum?' I ask as I gather up my bag and phone.

'My fucking father happened,' Cole grates. 'It was obviously her who called last night, obviously *him* who's lying to *her*, back to his old self. I guessed his attempt to be anything but obnoxious wouldn't last. Just a thought, but maybe you should do a dial-back next time the landline rings. You never know, it might help avert a crisis,' he adds, swinging past me to the landing.

'I *did* do a dial-back.' I stare after him in stunned disbelief. Is he saying that *I've* contributed to whatever crisis is going on with his mother? 'It wasn't her!' I shout, hurrying out after him. 'Whoever called last night warned me to be careful. Why would your mother...' I stop as the front door slams.

A second later, there's a crash in the hall. I know what it is without looking, and I feel a sense of cold doom settle deep in the pit of my belly.

'What's happened?' Ellie says behind me, as I crouch to retrieve the watercolour from the floor. The glass is splintered. Our family portrait fractured.

'Nothing,' I answer quickly.

Going back to the bedroom, I try to compose myself, hurriedly pulling off my own top and tugging on the first one that comes to hand. I'm halfway down the stairs when my phone beeps. Thinking it's Cole, I dig it out of my bag. My blood turns to ice in my veins as I read the message: *Do you realise your husband is planning to kill you?*

SEVEN

ELLIE

Watching her mum carefully as she came into the kitchen, Ellie felt her blood boil. She was obviously upset, her cheeks flushed and tears brimming in her eyes. 'So what was that all about?' Ellie asked, swinging her gaze towards the hall, where her dad had stropped out, slamming the door behind him, which had obviously dislodged the painting from the wall.

Her mum kept her eyes averted as she hurried across with a coat she'd fetched to wrap around Lucas. 'It was your nan on the phone. He had to rush over there,' she answered, lifting Lucas into her arms.

'I gathered. I'm guessing that Grandad's reverted to type,' Ellie replied scornfully.

Shooting her a warning glance, her mum nodded towards the boys, meaning she didn't want to discuss it in front of them. Ellie saw the flash of anger in her eyes, though, and knew she was right. Her grandad was horrible. Always vile to her nan, expecting her to jump to his every command, cheating on her throughout their marriage. Ellie had gathered that much from a conversation she'd overheard her mum and dad having after the last time they'd visited. Her mum had put her foot down and said that while she would see his mother, she didn't want anything to do with his father. Ellie couldn't blame her. The man was a bully and a control freak. She'd thought her dad was nothing like him. He hadn't been, despising everything his father stood for, or so Ellie had thought. Now, though, she was beginning to wonder.

'There's been an incident, yes,' her mum said eventually. She met Ellie's eyes briefly, then turned her attention back to Lucas. 'I'm taking Lucas in with me so one of the doctors can have a quick look at him.'

'Like Dad couldn't,' Ellie muttered, not quite under her breath.

Her mum shot her another reprimanding glance. 'Okay, Lucas?' she asked, giving him an encouraging smile.

Lucas nodded bravely, then beamed in surprise as his brother offered him his prized dinosaur transforming toy. 'To keep you company,' Jayden said, with a selfless nod.

Ellie had to smile at that. She was glad that some male members of the family were capable of caring. 'And this *incident* is your fault how?' she asked her mum.

'Leave it, Ellie.' Her mum sighed. 'I can't do this now.'

Ellie took a breath. As much as she wanted to point out that her dad was bang out of order, she refrained from commenting, for now. 'I'll carry him,' she said instead, easing Lucas from her. 'You look shattered.' *Unsurprisingly*, she wanted to add, having also overheard their conversation in the bedroom last night.

Ellie had no idea what was going on. Scratch that. She had a pretty good idea, and she was so furious with her dad, she didn't know how she'd kept her mouth shut. She was glad now that she hadn't spoken to him about what had happened to her, even though if she didn't speak to someone soon, she felt as if she might explode. There was no way she could talk to her mum now either. Piling her problems into the mix was hardly going to help her.

'Thanks.' Smiling wearily, her mum grabbed her bag from where she'd dropped it on the table, then held out her hand, gesturing Jayden across to her.

She was obviously thinking of taking both of them into work with her, which Ellie imagined might not go down well. 'I'll watch Jayden,' she offered as she followed her mum to the hall. 'I'll take him swimming and then meet you guys at Maccies later.'

'Thanks,' her mum said again, reaching to open the front door. 'Have you got some cash?'

'Enough,' Ellie assured her, as they headed out to the car.

'I'll pay you back later,' her mum promised, opening the back passenger door.

'No problem,' Ellie said, lowering Lucas into his booster seat and strapping him in. Straightening up, she gave her mum a quick hug, then, 'You shouldn't let him treat you like that, Mum,' she said, eyeing her meaningfully.

Her mum sighed. 'Don't judge him, Ellie,' she said tiredly. 'He's stressed and exhausted, that's all.'

'Which makes two of you,' Ellie pointed out, as her mum hurried around to the driver's side. 'I'm just saying that whatever his problem is, he shouldn't be taking it out on you.'

'He wasn't. He was just frustrated.'

'Yes, he *was*.' She spoke forcefully. 'Can't you see what's happening here, Mum? He hates the way his dad is, yet he—'

'I think that's enough, don't you?' Her mum gave her a reproving look across the car roof. 'He's *nothing* like his father.'

'Are you sure about that?' Ellie asked her as she climbed in. She guessed from the slamming car door that she'd riled her. She hoped she had – enough to make her think. Ellie desperately didn't want to be right. Her dad had been her hero. She didn't know how she would bear it if he shattered her faith in him. If she *was* right, though, her mum needed to open her eyes.

EIGHT

MADDIE

Once my little boy has been checked over and is in the care of a willing student nurse who offered to take him to the playroom and keep an eye on him, I head for the loos, where I have to steel myself to read the message again. My heart ticks frenetically as I do. This can't be random. It's a threat. And it's petrifying. Does someone *want* me dead? Cole? I press a hand to my mouth, forcing back the sob climbing my throat. I have to face him with this. No matter what's happening in his life, I need him to be aware of it. To be there. For me.

As a cubicle door opens, I spin around, quickly turn on the tap and, with trembling hands, splash my face with cold water.

'Are you all right, dear? You're as pale as a ghost,' someone says next to me. A patient, I realise.

'Yes. Thanks.' I make myself smile as I glance at her in the mirror. 'Just a bit tired.'

'Overworked, no doubt.' She makes sympathetic eyes at me. 'I honestly don't know how you nurses do it. I certainly couldn't.' Tsking, she shakes her wet hands and goes to dry them, while I dab at my face with a paper towel and attempt to compose myself.

I'm dangerously close to tears, though, when she walks back to place a hand on my arm. 'Take care of yourself, my lovely. Sometimes we can give too much of ourselves,' she says sagely.

I heave in a breath as she leaves, holding it to force the tears back. She's right. I do give too much of myself. And right now, I don't feel I've anything left to give. I feel depleted, emotionally and physically. The absolute last thing I need is Cole turning on me as he did this morning. Do I believe this insane message? I scan my eyes in the mirror. No. It's preposterous, but that doesn't make it any less terrifying.

I have to get through my shift. As much as I would like to feign sickness, I can't. There are little patients here who need me. I won't let this perverted individual distract me from doing what I love. My mind made up that I won't buckle, and nor will I take blame where I shouldn't, I draw in another breath and call Kelsey, knowing that she will be there for me if she can. Relief sweeps through me when she picks up. 'You're going to love me,' I say, 'but not a lot.'

'I do love you, but why does that sound ominous?' she asks.

'I need a favour.' I hesitate, feeling awful for asking her when she'll be shattered having already worked two shifts back-to-back this week. 'I know it's your day off, and I wouldn't ask unless I was desperate...'

'If it's money you're after, you should also know I'm already having to sell my body to pay my mortgage. There's not many takers, unfortunately,' she quips.

I smile despite everything. Kelsey always manages to lighten things, even though she has her own problems. She's struggling to make ends meet with only her nurse's salary since she split with her partner – another in a string of bad choices, who it turned out had an addiction to gambling as well as other women. She hadn't realised he was using her credit cards to fund his addictions.

'Ignore me.' She sighs. 'I'm having a woe-is-me moment. What do you need, babe?'

'I was hoping you could look after Lucas,' I start tentatively. 'Just for a few hours. He had an accident this morning. He's here with me at the hospital and—'

'Oh no,' Kelsey gasps. 'Is he all right? What happened?'

'He's fine. Feeling a bit sorry for himself but doing okay. He burned his hand and then slipped and banged his head. Cole was supposed to be looking after them this morning, but…' I trail off, not even sure where to begin recounting the events that led up to my son shoving his hand in the toaster. I can't tell her about the message, not until I've spoken to Cole. Knowing Kelsey, if I do confide in her, particularly about Cole's behaviour this morning, she'll go apoplectic. She might be right to.

'He's been called in to the hospital, I suppose,' she assumes. 'Does the man never get any time to himself?'

'It's a personal emergency this time. He had an urgent phone call from his mum and had to dash off, so I'm a bit stuck.' I confide that much. 'Ellie's taken Jayden swimming, otherwise I could have asked her.'

'I'll come and fetch him,' Kelsey says without further ado.

'Thanks, Kels.' I breathe out a relieved sigh. 'The agency won't have anyone else they can send out at this short notice. I'll pay you, obviously.'

'You'll do no such thing,' Kelsey huffs. 'I don't have anything else on today, and if I can't help out my best friend then I'm not much of a friend, am I?'

'You're a lifesaver. It will only be until lunchtime,' I assure her. 'I'll be off by one, and Ellie and I are meeting at McDonald's. If you fancy joining us, you're welcome.'

'You're on,' she says. 'It's probably the best offer I'm going to get this weekend. No offence intended.'

I smile. 'None taken.'

Kelsey pauses. Then, 'Are you okay?' she asks. 'You sound exhausted.'

'I'm fine.' I assure her. 'A bit stressed, that's all.'

'I'm not surprised.' She sighs. 'I'm on my way. I'll be twenty minutes max.'

After checking on Lucas, who's happily building Lego with another lifesaver, I carry on with my morning rounds, helping with the administration of drugs and injections and preparing little people for procedures and operations whilst making sure to offer them lots of encouragement and supportive smiles.

I'm monitoring a baby's vital signs when I spot Kelsey coming into the ward. She gives me a wave and then chats to one of the nurses she knows.

After reassuring the baby's anxious parents that he's doing fine, I go across to her. 'Thanks, Kelsey.' I smile gratefully. 'You're an angel.'

'No problem.' She gives me a hug. 'Where's our wounded soldier?' she asks, glancing around.

'Playroom.' I nod that way and silently count my blessings. With my mum miles away in Suffolk and my brother having moved there after my dad died to help her run her dog-training business, I'd be lost without my friends and colleagues. I was devastated when my dad died. I feel it even now, the wave of raw grief that crashes over you out of nowhere, leaving you winded in its wake. I miss him still. I was Ellie's age when he was snatched away from me. I suppose that's why I'm worrying there might be a rift opening up between her and Cole.

'So what was the urgent phone call?' Kelsey eyes me enquiringly as we walk.

'A problem with his parents.' I sigh.

'Must be something serious if he just took off and left you stranded?' She frowns.

'I assume it is. I'm not entirely sure what happened, but his mum was really upset,' I tell her. And then wonder how serious exactly, that Cole would react the way he did. I know he carries lot of anger over his father's appalling treatment of his mother. Rarely does he let it surface, though. It's just so not like him.

'It's a good job you're so understanding,' Kelsey says. 'I can't see him being very pleased if you left him with the kids at a minute's notice when he was due at work.'

'No,' I concede. 'He worries about his mum, though, which is no bad thing.'

'I suppose,' she agrees. 'As long as he doesn't make a habit of it. What we do is important, Mads. As crucial to the running of a hospital as what Cole does. You're already fitting your work around him. I'm going on, I know, but as long as he's pulling his weight...'

'He is. At least, he tries. I do struggle to juggle all the balls sometimes,' I admit, possibly also to myself for once, 'but that's not Cole's fault. His work comes with huge responsibilities, emergencies as well as scheduled surgeries. I knew that when I married him. It's simply a case of practicality that I work more flexible hours.'

'As long as it is your choice.' Kelsey looks me over in concern as we pause outside the playroom door.

'Cole doesn't have any more choice than I do, though,' I point out. 'He has so many other responsibilities on top of everything else. He's training someone at the moment, which inevitably takes up more of his time.'

'Ah, yes, Hannah Lee's his latest awestruck protégée, isn't she?' Kelsey comments.

What does she mean? I eye her warily, my mind shooting to the messages and that phone call. *He's lying.* I hear the urgent whisper and my heart misses a beat.

'I'd watch her if I were you,' Kelsey goes on, oblivious. 'You know she had an affair with a consultant while she was doing her final-year neurosurgical training before specialising? I'm surprised the hospital trust didn't... Oh.' She stops, her face dropping as she notes my thunderstruck expression. 'You didn't know.'

'No,' I murmur, stunned. 'I had no idea.' And having transferred from another hospital, Kelsey clearly has no idea that Hannah Lee completed part of her final-year training under Cole's tutelage.

NINE

COLE

'I'm all right,' Cole's mother insisted as she attempted to make tea. She was treating him as she would a guest. Cole guessed that was because he rarely visited now his father was semi-retired, having given up his NHS role to concentrate on his private patients. He wasn't buying her claim that she was fine. When he'd arrived, she'd said she'd overreacted on the phone, that she was upset. Considerably, judging by the fact that her hands were shaking.

'I'll make it. You sit down,' he said, going across to relieve her of the kettle and steer her gently towards a chair at the table before someone else got burned. Recalling that he'd left home without checking on Lucas and wondering what kind of father he was, he felt a sharp stab of guilt. He'd followed in his father's footsteps career-wise, studied hard, attained his degree in medicine, though he'd struggled with his father constantly reminding him that he had high standards to live up to, namely his. He'd done everything that was expected of him in the hope of gaining the man's respect, though never his affection. A heartless narcissist, his father simply wasn't capable of that emotion. Hence Cole's promise to himself never to be anything like him: cold, demanding, indifferent to his wife and his children's emotional needs. Yet here he was, neglecting his responsibilities as a father. As a husband. Cole had never imagined he would be the kind of man who would lie to his wife. He hated himself for doing that, but there was no way to tell her about the abysmal mess he'd managed to get himself into. The irony was that Maddie was the only person he'd ever felt able to confide in. But he couldn't. It was out of the question. She would never forgive him. She would leave him, take the kids. He would never survive that.

He thought back to the many times his mother had forgiven his father, believing his hollow promises that he would never repeat his mistakes, staying with him, supporting him. Look where that had got her. With her confidence whittled away to nil, she was dependent on him financially and emotionally. He'd modified his controlling behaviour since he'd become ill – no doubt because he'd realised he needed her – but up until then he'd made her feel inadequate in every aspect of her life, cheating on her simply because he could. He'd worked to convince Cole he would never get through his neurosurgical training, never secure a surgical post, where competition was high. He wasn't ruthless enough, he'd told him, often comparing him to his brother. Ryan and Cole had been identical in looks, in nature, though, they'd been alike in nothing else. Ryan had been strong, like him, his father constantly pointed out. He hadn't wasted tears over the dead goldfinch they'd found in the garden. He'd been more curious about how the bird had died than upset because it had. Tears were weak, he'd told Cole. *He* was weak. A good surgeon could *never* allow emotion to rule his head.

Had his so-called father allowed emotion to rule his head when he'd climbed behind the wheel of his car dangerously over the limit, crashing it and killing the son he held in such high esteem in an instant? Or had he simply been devoid of emotion?

Cole leaned towards the latter. As the memory flooded back, he clamped hard down on his thoughts, tried not to let his mind go back there, but it did anyway. He felt the impact all over again, like a vicious punch to his stomach, heard the deathly silence before the cacophony of noise hit him, utterly bewildering him: horns blaring, people shouting, petrol spilling, sirens plaintively wailing.

His mother screaming. Her voice high-pitched, hysterical.

His brother silent.

His father had never mentioned the incident since. It was more than Cole or his mother dared do, though the ghost of Ryan haunted every room in the house. After recovering from his own injuries and 'somehow' getting a clear result on his blood alcohol test, his father had picked up and carried on right where he'd left off, directing his anger at his wife for distracting him, at his remaining son for existing.

He'd worked hard to instil discipline into Cole after that. *Character-building*, he called it. Helping him to become emotionally stronger. Recalling one particular occasion, Cole felt his gut tighten. He must have been about seven. He'd been in this very spot, pouring Coke into a glass. He'd spilled it, made the fatal mistake of not clearing it up. He could almost feel his father's fingers digging mercilessly into the back of his neck, propelling him towards the worktop, banging his head against it, then looming over him until he'd cleaned up the mess, the blood from his nose as well as the Coke. It had worked, he thought bitterly. Cole had made sure not to shed a single fucking tear.

Attempting to suppress the anger that had simmered inside him then, and did now tenfold, he made the tea, wiped the worktop, then carried a mug across to his mum.

'Thank you.' She smiled tremulously.

Cole gave her a smile back. He wished she'd had the strength to leave him. That she would now. But she wouldn't. His father had made it so she didn't know how to function without him. Noting the livid bruising under her eye, he nodded towards it. 'Did he do that?' he asked, his anger ratcheting up a notch.

His mother's fingers fluttered to her face. 'It was an accident,' she murmured, protecting the man despite the fact that she'd been crying and clearly terrified when she'd called. 'I wasn't looking where I was going. I fell.'

'Right.' *Against his fucking fist.* Cole felt his blood boil. 'Where is he?' he demanded.

'Outside in the garden.' His mum's face was filled with trepidation. 'But—'

Cole spun around, struggling now to control his overwhelming compulsion to give the bastard a painful taste of his own medicine.

'*Cole!*' his mother called frantically behind him as he strode through the back door. 'Don't do anything rash. I'd had a glass of wine while we were out. I lost my footing. It wasn't all his fault.'

No, it never is. Cole kept going, out into the vast garden of the grand Georgian Grade II listed house his father had *worked his fingers to the bone for*. His mother hadn't contributed, of course. She'd given everything. In return, she got nothing but contempt.

He found him at the end of the garden, lovingly tending the koi carp in his pond. Seeing his back was towards him, Cole had to fight an urge not to shove the bastard in and hope he drowned.

Clearly unaware of his presence, his father started when he approached. 'Well, well, the wanderer returns,' he said, turning to look Cole over languidly. 'So what brings you here?'

Cole stared at him in complete disbelief when he extended his hand as if he were the long-lost son he actually wanted to see. He declined to take it, shaking his head instead. 'You know damn well why I'm here,' he growled.

His father knitted his brow as though he was confused, and then, 'Ah,' he said, 'your mother called you, I suppose.'

Cole gasped with incredulity. Was he really *that* confident? Utterly impervious to the damage he'd caused? 'You're unbelievable, do you know that?' He stared contemptuously at him. 'She should have called the fucking *police*.'

'Language, Cole,' his father reprimanded him, succeeding in ramping his anger up further. 'Before you jump to conclusions, which you're clearly keen to, your mother fell.'

Cole clenched his fist at his side. It was all he could do to keep it there.

'Yes, we argued,' his father went on. 'Badly, as it happened. We were at a dinner function. I was invited to give a talk, you know how it is. Your mother drank too much, got it into her head that I was working to impress a young female doctor who's coming up to the end of her specialty training. No matter what I said, she simply wouldn't accept that I'd taken her aside to give her the benefit of my experience.'

'Really? How annoyingly unreasonable of her.' Cole laughed cynically. Could the man hear himself? But then his conscience pricked him. Wasn't that what he himself had done in inviting Hannah Lee for coffee to discuss her career going forward?

'Regarding her exit exam,' his father added, ignoring his sarcasm. 'I tried to talk to your mother, but as she was getting quite irate, which was embarrassing in front of my colleagues, I decided we should leave. We argued in the taxi, also embarrassing. There was simply no placating her.' He emitted an expansive sigh. 'We were still arguing as we came through the front door. Your mother flounced off and slipped on the rug in the hall.'

'Bullshit.' Cole eyed him stonily.

His father's expression turned to flint. 'Ask her,' he said. 'I'm sure she'll corroborate what I've told you... now she's sober.'

Cole sucked in a breath, studied the man long and hard. 'I'm sure she will,' he said at length, 'now she's been coached.'

His father studied him in turn. 'I know you don't rate me, Cole. I was hard on you, I admit that. For your own good, I hasten to add. You needed to toughen up, become less emotionally involved, if you had any chance of succeeding. I do my best, give my best, I always have. I expect nothing but the best in return from the people around me. I might be a little exacting sometimes, but it's imperative not to be distracted in our field of work, as I'm sure you've come to understand.'

Cole said nothing. He was literally speechless. He'd thought his father had changed. That he might actually have some regret. He hadn't. He was justifying his deplorable behaviour. Still.

'Or do you still let emotion rule your head?' his father asked, his tone challenging. 'Not a good idea, if I may say so.'

Hatred reared up inside Cole as another painful echo of his past crept back: his father berating him for getting drunk at his graduation party. Lashing out at him when he tried to stand his ground. Cole hadn't given in to his emotions. He hadn't fought back. He should have. Right now, he was struggling not to shut the supercilious bastard up once and for all. 'No.' He worked to keep his voice even. 'You're right, you do need to be emotionally resilient to succeed. Just for your information, though, if you ever lay a hand on my mother again, just once, I will most certainly give in to the impulse to break your fingers. All ten of them. Might put you out of action for a while.' He dragged a contemptuous gaze over him, then turned to walk away.

'I see you do,' his father imparted drolly behind him.

Cole about-faced and walked back, and that was when he saw it: a flash of vulnerability in the old man's eyes. He was scared. Of him. The tables had turned. 'Just once,' he reiterated, holding his gaze.

His father looked away first. It was enough. He'd obviously

got the message. Turning away again, Cole left him standing by the pond. He looked smaller, less intimidating. Cole didn't feel any sense of satisfaction. The fact was, his father was right. He did struggle to remain emotionally detached. Finding himself unable to deal with emotions that had surfaced on one occasion recently, he'd given in to them. The consequences of which might well rob him of everything that was dear to him. He should have talked to Maddie. If he hadn't been so scared, he would have. Now that things had spiralled out of control, he had no way to.

Walking back to the house, he felt the knot of panic he'd had in his gut ever since tighten. His heart faltered when his phone beeped in his pocket. Extracting it as he neared the back door, he read the message and his mouth dried. *Ignoring me isn't going to make this go away, Cole. Call me!*

TEN

MADDIE

It's past the boys' bedtime when I hear Cole's key in the lock. I busy myself clearing the kitchen island. He texted me a couple of times to ask how Lucas was. And then to tell me that his anaesthetist had contacted him asking if he could swing by the hospital to offer his advice regarding an operation to remove a cancerous tumour from the spinal cord of a seven-year-old child. Suspicion wormed its way inside me as I considered how easy it would be for him to lie to me if he chose to. Now my mind is running riot, what Kelsey said about his trainee, Hannah Lee, buzzing around in my head like a demented bee. That horrifying message playing endlessly through my mind. Who sent it? *Why* would anyone want to do such an evil thing? To strike the fear of God into me, obviously – they've succeeded – but might there be any basis in it? Might Cole be having an affair and want me out of the way? He's a surgeon. I'm sure he could find any number of ways to engineer my demise.

Realising I'm actually giving this threat credence, I squeeze my eyes closed. I'm going mad, stress and lack of sleep clearly catching up with me. We've been together for eighteen years. I *know* him. Does it really take so little to rock my faith in him?

Shaking myself, I turn to face him as he comes into the kitchen, noticing immediately how drawn he looks.

'Hi.' He smiles cautiously. 'How are you?'

'Reasonable,' I reply, giving him a small smile back. 'How did it go at the hospital?'

'Okay.' He nods. 'Alex was concerned about loss of sensation in the bladder area, but it looks reasonably straightforward. Sorry I was such an idiot this morning.' He sighs apologetically as he walks across to me. 'It was just with Mum being so upset, and guessing what had happened... I don't know. I felt powerless, I suppose. I didn't handle any of it very well, did I?'

I look him over, noting again the dark bruises under his eyes, and refrain from commenting.

'I really am sorry, Mads, about what I said, taking off the way I did. It was thoughtless, immature.' He drags a hand wearily over his neck. 'I should have been more supportive. I know that message must have worried you, the phone call last night, too. I gather Mum didn't tell you it was her.'

'*Was* it her? Did you ask her?' The caller, a woman, had said, *He's lying. Be careful.* I still can't imagine why his mother would have said that. I suppose she could have been referring to his father, who'd often lied to her, but I'm not convinced.

'No.' Cole emits another long sigh. 'I meant to, but I was so wound up by my delightful father, I forgot. And then, when I did remember, I hesitated. I didn't want her thinking that calling here late at night if she needs to might be a problem, so...'

I gather his meaning, gathering also that the reason his mother was so upset is because Robert has been violent again. Cole has tried to convince her to leave him, offering to get her a small place of her own, but Lizzie won't entertain the idea, even though Robert has made her life a living nightmare. She lost Cole's twin when he was aged just five. Cole doesn't talk about it, but he did confide that it was his father's fault, and that the man's violence only escalated afterwards. How did Lizzie get through that? How does she get through her life now? I understand why she stays, to a degree. After so many years being one half of a couple, she's terrified of being alone. She doesn't think she'll be able to function on her own. That's undoubtedly down to Robert's constant undermining of her, making her feel inadequate, as a person, as a woman. He tried to make me feel inadequate once, hinting that I should have the kids tucked up in bed and everything shipshape in the house when Cole came home after a long day at the hospital. I'm sure he thinks I should fetch my husband his slippers and dash off to make him a drink. 'You did see your father then?' I ask.

'Unfortunately, yes.' Cole doesn't bother to hide his contempt. 'I sincerely hope the next time I see him is at the bastard's funeral.'

I'm shocked by that. There's so much suppressed anger. I didn't realise how much. I watch warily as he goes across to the worktop to pour a glass of wine from the open bottle and take a large gulp. That worries me, since he drinks so little normally. I understand why he would be agitated, but he rarely lets his emotions get the better of him.

Is it purely because of his father? The kernel of doubt that's taken root inside me begins to blossom. I hesitate, uncertain what his reaction will be, which in itself is new territory for me, but I have to mention the message. I can't be on my own with this. 'There's something I need to tell you. There's been another message.' I gauge him carefully. 'This morning, just after you left.'

Cole lowers his glass slowly to the worktop. 'What did it say?' he asks, his expression cautious as he looks back at me.

I take a breath, then say it as it is – there's no way not to. '"Do you realise your husband is planning to kill you?"'

'You have to be joking.' His face has visibly blanched. 'Why in God's name didn't you call me?' he asks, walking across to circle me with his arms.

I pull away a little. I need to see his reaction. 'You were dealing with a crisis. And then you were at the hospital.'

'But this was more important.' He searches my eyes, his own a confusion of emotion, from concern to palpable guilt. *'You're* more important. You should have called me, Mads.'

'You went off in a mood,' I remind him. 'I wasn't sure what reception I would get. If you'd been off with me, it would only have upset me more.'

'I am *so* sorry,' he murmurs, resting his forehead against mine. 'I should never have taken my frustration out on you. That was reprehensible.'

'Do you think I should report it?' I ask.

He breathes in sharply. 'Yes. It's undoubtedly some nutjob, but I think you have to.'

'But it's not a direct threat, is it?' I point out. 'I'm not sure how much the police could actually do, assuming they take it seriously. And I've blocked the number now, so...'

'You need to call me if there's another attempt to contact you,' he says firmly. 'If I'm in theatre, ring the department and tell them you need to get hold of me urgently. I should have been there for you. I should damn well be there for you all the time, much more than I am. Can you forgive me?'

I see the sincerity in his eyes, and the fear I've been carrying around inside subsides a little. He's not cheating on me. I would know it. I would feel it. I can't believe I was ready to start checking his phone. I'm not that woman. I've never felt anything but safe with him. And Cole's not that man. Knowing what I know about his father, how Cole feels about him, I'm positive he would rather die than be anything like him.

ELEVEN

'I should have been there for Lucas too,' Cole adds, looking thoroughly disillusioned with himself. 'How is he?'

'He's okay,' I assure him. 'As I said earlier, it was only a minor cut. His hand's a bit sore, but he's fine, revelling in the attention. Even Jayden was sympathetic. He gave him his dinosaur transformer to keep him company at the hospital, *and* he offered him the last triple chocolate sundae this evening while he made do with a plain old vanilla yoghurt.'

Cole smiles, but for a fleeting second I see a flash of deep sadness in his eyes and I feel for him. Having twins of his own must remind him of the part of himself he lost.

'They're still awake if you want to go up.' I nod towards the stairs. 'But don't excite them too much, whatever you do, or they'll never get to sleep.'

'I won't, I promise.' Brushing my cheek with a kiss, he heads for the hall. Then stops. 'I left you completely in the lurch this morning, didn't I?' He glances regretfully back at me. 'Did you manage to sort something out?'

'A colleague watched Lucas for a while,' I tell him. 'And then Kelsey came to pick him up. She took him back to her house while Ellie took Jayden to the baths. We all met up at McDonald's after.'

Cole nods. 'That was good of her.' He smiles distractedly, and I guess his mind is still on the messages.

I hear him on the landing a minute later. 'Evening, how's things?' he says. He's talking to Ellie, I assume, who's been in her room getting ready to meet up with her friends.

'Like you actually care,' is her acerbic reply, which takes me aback.

As it does Cole, judging by his response. 'Ellie? I know I was out of order this morning, but is there something else bothering you? Something I've done? Because if there is, you know you can talk to me, right?'

Ellie doesn't answer, but thumps along the landing and down the stairs instead.

'Ellie,' I look at her in astonishment as she strides moodily into the kitchen, 'your dad was talking to you.'

'I know,' she replies shortly. 'I'm not sure I can be arsed to talk to him, though.'

Bewildered, I hurry to close the kitchen door behind her. 'What's this all about?' I ask. 'If it's about what happened this morning, he's already apologised.'

Ellie doesn't comment, but slopes across to the kitchen island and leans against it, arms folded, face sullen. 'He's taking the piss, Mum. Disrespecting you.'

I shake my head in bemusement. Where do I go with this? Do I admonish her, which will no doubt be me *having a go* at her. Or try for some level of calmness? The latter, I decide. The last thing I need now is a shouting match with my daughter. 'Would you like to tell me why?' I tip my head to one side and wait.

Ellie draws in a breath. 'I heard you,' she says. 'Telling him about that weird message and the call you received. I also saw how he was with you this morning.'

I frown, failing to see how Cole's behaviour translates into him disrespecting me. 'He was upset,' I point out.

'He was disrespecting you, Mum,' Ellie says forcefully. 'He was angry. With *you*, for no reason. And then he stalks off without even checking how Lucas is. He's being a complete dick.'

I look her over in dismay. This is not just teenage belligerence or hormones at play. Ellie worships her dad. Or she did. What on earth's going on? 'There was a crisis,' I remind her. 'His mum was upset.'

'I *know*.' She eyeballs me as if it's me she's angry with. 'And he accuses you of causing the crisis and then walks out.'

'He was stressed. Concerned about his mother.'

'So why didn't he meet up with us?' she asks. 'After he'd been to his mum's, why didn't he come to McDonald's, or at least come back earlier? You'd think he would have, with what happened to Lucas.'

'He was needed at the hospital,' I answer, though I'm aware that sounds as if he had other priorities.

'He's always needed at the hospital,' Ellie mutters. 'He's also coming home later and later, and you just put up with it. I don't get it.'

My patience is beginning to wear thin. 'I think that's enough now. Your dad works extremely hard because he has to. He can't just walk out if—'

'Is he having an affair, Mum?' she blurts.

I feel the breath leave my body. 'Don't be ridiculous.'

She searches my eyes, her own filled with anxiety. 'So why doesn't he come home more?' she asks, her voice small.

'Ellie...' I struggle for a way to reassure her. Despite her Instagram-perfect make-up, she looks more like a frightened seven-year-old than a seventeen-year-old.

As I move towards her, she tears herself from the island, almost pushing past me in her haste to leave. 'I have to go.'

'Ellie, *wait.*' I whirl around to go after her, but she moves like greased lightning. After tugging the front door open, she's out of it, setting off down the road almost at a run.

Hurrying back inside, I grab my phone from the hall table and fumble to pull up her number, then freeze as the phone pings.

Trepidation tightening my stomach, I read the message, obviously sent from another fake profile: *You're sleeping with the enemy*. An almost hysterical laugh bubbles up inside me. *Really?* How unoriginally pathetic. Is this person trying to convince me my husband is coercive now? Ruthlessly manipulating me into believing he cares for me? He's nothing of the sort! 'Who *are* you?' I whisper, then almost jump out of my skin as Cole appears on the stairs.

'Problem?' he asks, looking from me to my phone as he makes his way down.

'No. It's just a work thing.' I lower my phone and clutch it to my side. 'I think I'll take a bath. It might help relieve the stress.'

'Good idea.' He eyes me thoughtfully. 'Would you like me to bring you a glass of wine?'

'No,' I say quickly. 'I'm good. Thanks. You just relax. I won't be long.' I give him a small smile as I move past him.

Ellie's outburst has shaken me. Is there more to it, something she's not telling me?

TWELVE

I wake with a start, my eyes darting to the wall clock. Dread clutches my stomach as I note it's gone two in the morning. *She'll be home,* I try to reassure myself as I jump up from the sofa and fly to the hall. She'll have snuck in and be safely tucked up in bed, while I've been waiting up, worrying myself sick. I'm just thankful that Cole got called back to the hospital before Ellie was due home. He would be beside himself.

Hurrying up the stairs, I creep along the landing so as not to wake the boys. Reaching Ellie's door, I hesitate, then press the handle down quietly. 'Ellie?' I whisper, pushing the door open and going in. Sensing the emptiness in the room, I snap the light on, my gaze pivoting to her bed – and my heart stops dead in my chest. *Dear God, where is she?*

My blood pumping, I spin around and hurry back down. She's never done this before. She's stayed out late, but she's never been *this* late. Never stayed over at a friend's without letting me know. I check the kitchen as if she might magically appear there, and then go back to the lounge to grab my phone and check that, yet again. My stomach turns over nauseatingly as I realise she hasn't texted or called.

Praying he's not in theatre, I call Cole. *Please pick up*, I will him. My breath catches painfully when someone picks up and a female voice trills, 'Cole's phone?'

'Who is this?' I ask tersely.

'Hannah,' she replies. 'Hannah Lee. I'm—'

'Is he there?' I snap over her. 'My husband, is he with you?'

'I, um... yes,' she answers. 'Can I pass on a message?'

'I need to speak to him. It's urgent,' I say, my mind whirring.

'I'll go and find him,' she replies, sounding uncertain. 'Shall I tell him who's calling?'

'His *wife*,' I growl, hot tears of fear and confusion spilling down my face.

What seems like an eternity later, Cole comes to the phone. 'Mads? Sorry, I was changing out of my scrubs. Has something happened?' he asks warily.

'Ellie,' my throat closes, 'she's not here. She hasn't come home.'

I hear him suck in a breath. 'Call all her friends,' he says tightly. 'I'm on my way.'

I feel the shock slam into me as he ends the call, forcing the air from my body. A low moan escapes me, and I squeeze my eyes closed, try to erase the image that scorches itself on my mind. My baby, my strong-willed girl, lying bruised and broken in some dark, friendless place, her beautiful chestnut hair splayed about her face, her eyes, every conceivable colour of the forest and always so spirited and lively, now lifeless. Frozen in terror.

No! my head screams. *She's fine. Safe somewhere.* Blinking hard, I attempt to draw air into my lungs and focus on the contacts I have for Ellie on my phone. I'm about to call her best friend, Claire, who I'm sure she was meeting up with, when the phone rings, jolting me. *Kelsey?* Seeing her number flash up, I hit call receive.

'She's here,' she says quickly. 'Ellie, she's here. I thought I should call you. I knew you would be worrying,' she hurries on as relief crashes through me like a tidal wave.

But... I shake my head in bewilderment. Why is she with Kelsey? 'Is she all right?' I squeeze the words past the parched lump in my throat. 'Has something happened?'

Kelsey hesitates. 'She's been drinking,' she says, her tone cautious. 'A lot. I couldn't get much sense out of her, but I gathered she didn't want to come home. She said you'd argued.'

I breathe in sharply. Try to remain calm. Fail. Why would she have gone to Kelsey's at this hour? Unless... 'You didn't mention what you told me about Hannah Lee when we were at McDonald's, did you?' I ask warily.

'No.' Kelsey sounds confused. 'Why would I?'

'Ellie thinks Cole's having an affair.' My voice quavers.

Kelsey says nothing for a beat, then, 'Have you considered she might have reason to think that?' she asks, astounding me.

'What *reason*?' I ask, staggered. 'He would never even *contemplate* it.' I try to hold on to my conviction. 'I can't understand why she would think it unless someone had put the idea into her head. I hope to God it wasn't you, Kelsey, because if you did—'

'She *saw* him, Maddie,' Kelsey shouts over me.

I feel as if my world has just stopped turning.

'Saw something, anyway, that made her think he was,' she says more quietly.

I don't respond. For a second, I'm incapable of speaking. Then, 'She can't have,' I murmur shakily.

Kelsey draws in a breath. 'She's adamant, Mads.'

My chest constricts. 'What did she see? When?'

'I think you need to ask Ellie. I can't break her confidence, Maddie. I'm sorry.'

THIRTEEN

Opening a bottle of wine isn't a good idea, but I do it anyway. By the second glass, I've made a decision. I'm not going to challenge Cole. I'm not sure how I'll handle Ellie, but I am sure the person responsible for the messages and call is trying to manipulate me into confronting him. They're trying to blow my family apart, to take my husband. Hannah Lee is undoubtedly infatuated with him, probably in love with him. She can't have him. I won't allow it. I won't be scared into creating the very scenario she wants. If I do challenge him, is he likely to admit it? I doubt it. And if he does, what then? I'd like to think I could forgive him, that we could somehow work through it, but the thing that terrifies me is that he might not want to. No, I can't confront him, not yet. Watchful waiting is a term that's often used at the hospital when someone has something that might develop into something terminal. I will watch and I will wait. It's all nonsense, it has to be. But if it turns out to be true, I will find a way to extract the disease that is Hannah Lee from my marriage.

I'm pouring a third glass when Cole comes through the

front door and straight to the kitchen. 'Is she home?' he asks, his voice fearful. 'Did you call her friends?'

As he glances to where I'm sitting at the island, I note his ashen complexion, the palpable worry in his eyes, eyes I once thought conveyed his every emotion. Was I wrong? I take a large glug of wine, attempt to get my rioting emotions under control. 'There was no need,' I answer. 'She's safe.'

Relief sweeps across Cole's features. But then he registers the glass in my hand, the wine bottle parked next to me. 'Safe where?' His gaze is cautious when it comes back to me.

I take another sip of wine. 'She's staying with Kelsey.'

'Kelsey?' He raises his eyebrows in surprise. 'What the hell is she doing there?'

'She's been drinking.' I watch him carefully. 'A lot, apparently.'

Cole sighs and wipes a hand over his face. Then glances again at my glass and frowns. Because of his father, he's wary of people who drink too much. He's wary now of me. He should be. I love him with my whole soul. But I won't let him destroy me, as his father has his mother. I won't let him hurt our children. Not ever.

'So does our daughter make a habit of drinking?' he asks – and I wonder if he realises how that sounds: as if it's solely my responsibility. The fact is, though, while I know Ellie isn't likely not to drink at her age, I should have been aware that something was troubling her enough to make her drink to excess. If a teenage girl can't talk to her mother, who can she talk to? Kelsey, obviously. The realisation hits me painfully.

'We argued,' I remind him. Cole overheard us, but not everything. He was reading the boys an interactive story, keeping them distracted, he said. Unsure where Ellie's anger was coming from, and not wanting to exacerbate the situation, I told him it was because I'd reprimanded her for being so rude to him, but that was all. He must wonder, though, why his relationship with the daughter he doted on, and who once doted on him, is suddenly so fractured.

Squeezing his eyes closed, he draws in a breath. 'Should I go and pick her up?' he asks uncertainly.

'Probably not a good idea at this time.' I glance pointedly at the wall clock. 'Kelsey assured me she was all right. She'll be fast asleep, I imagine. We should go to bed.'

Swilling back the dregs from my glass, I climb precariously off my stool and head for the door, swaying slightly as I do. 'Are you coming?' I ask, glancing back at him.

He sweeps a concerned gaze over me. 'I'll be up shortly. I'll just grab a cold drink,' he says, glancing away.

'Not avoiding me, are you?' I ask him, and then wish I hadn't. I realise then that, for the first time, I'm not sure how to talk to him, and it scares me. Up until now, we've always shared everything.

'I'll only be a minute.' Running his fingers through his hair in that way he does when he's tired or worried, he heads to the fridge.

I leave him to it, rather than blurt something out I haven't thought through. I don't realise how fast the wine has gone to my head until I weave dangerously on the landing. Once in the bedroom, I steady myself and head for the wardrobe, where I have to force myself not to start going through his pockets for any shred of evidence he might have left there. Already, living with the uncertainty is excruciating. But I can't bring myself to do that. Perhaps I'm a coward, I don't know. I do know that if he lies to me, that will be the death of our marriage. About-facing, I go to grab my PJs and start undressing. I hear him on the landing a minute later, note he has his eyes glued to his phone as he comes through the door. 'Anything interesting?' I ask him.

'Not really.' He smiles distractedly, his eyes still on his phone. 'Just had to check there weren't any problems with the patient I left in ITU.'

After a second, he looks up. I hesitate as I notice his eyes travelling over me, and then, needing to feel the reassurance I always do when he holds me, I go to him and thread my arms around him.

He doesn't reciprocate. Doing no more than trailing a hand lightly over my shoulders, he eases away, and I feel it like a slap. 'I should probably shower. It's been a long day,' he says. Stepping away from me, he stuffs his phone in his jacket pocket and nods towards the bathroom.

He's going to wash her off. Suspicion screams loud in my head and my cheeks burn with humiliation and hurt. 'Right, fine. Take your time.' I spin around and head to the bed.

'*Hell*,' Cole mutters as I hurry to hide myself under the duvet. 'Mads, I didn't mean...' He falters. 'I'm just shattered, that's all.'

'As usual,' I mutter, sounding like a petulant child and not caring.

He sighs wearily as I twist onto my side, away from him. 'I won't be long,' he says.

I wriggle back around. 'I'm tired too, you know.'

'I know. You're bound to be.' He studies me for a long, searching moment. 'Christ, Maddie, what's really going on? What's this all about?'

'I would have thought that was obvious,' I mumble.

'You've been drinking.' Despairing, clearly, he tugs off his jacket, drapes it over the chair at the dressing table, then comes across to me. 'You're emotional.'

'Am I not supposed to be then?' I snap, cursing the tears that spring to my eyes. 'You've just as good as pushed me away.' I *am* growing emotional, extremely. I'm trying to hold things together here. I'm trying to believe in him. Surely he must realise that?

'I wasn't *pushing* you away.' He laughs, incredulous. 'I'm sorry if it seemed that way. I'm exhausted, Mads. That's all it is.'

Giving me a small placatory smile, he lowers himself to sit on the edge of the bed and reaches for my hand.

'Don't.' A vivid image of him holding his pretty little protégée's hand flashing into my mind, I snatch it back.

Cole eyes the ceiling. 'I don't believe this.'

'Nor do *I*.' I glare at him. 'I don't mind that you rejected me. You're too tired, fair enough. But you could have done it a little less obviously.'

He squints at me as if perplexed, then shakes his head. 'Look, Mads, can we just rewind this? I wasn't rejecting you. I just... It's gone three in the morning. We'll wake the boys at this rate. Can we not just go to bed? Cuddle up under the duvet and get some sleep?'

Where you can't see me, I think childishly. Because I'm not twenty-something like awestruck bloody Hannah Lee. I feel the tears plop down my face and feel like a complete idiot. I must look like one. I *have* been drinking. After worrying myself sick about Ellie, what Kelsey told me, I'm confused and frightened, filled with anger I have no idea what to do with.

'I'll go and take that shower,' Cole says. 'I'll be two minutes.' He hesitates. Then, 'I don't not want to be with you,' he says quietly. 'I love you, Madelyn. I wouldn't know how to be without you. Please don't ever doubt that.'

My eyes shoot back to him. Why did he say that?

He smiles again and reaches to stroke a tear gently from my cheek with his thumb. I search his eyes, find such sadness and sincerity there, I feel my heart wrench. 'Always,' he adds, leaning to press a soft kiss to my forehead.

I can't do this. Desperation rears up inside me. I can't lose him. I just can't. Fighting back my tears, I lean into him, needing him to hold me. I want to know what's going on. I want to be able to forgive him, however weak it might make me. I can't just stop loving him. How does that work?

'Two minutes.' He brushes my lips with his, then eases

himself from the bed. 'Snuggle down,' he says, encouraging me back under the duvet and drawing it over me as if I really were a child. 'Back soon.'

I feel my head swim as I hear him go into the bathroom and I know I've no hope of staying awake. I can't handle alcohol in quantity. I never could. My eyelids are suddenly so heavy, I feel I could sleep for a week. I close my eyes, then snap them open again. *His phone.* I yank myself up to see his jacket still draped where he left it. There won't be anything damning on it. He wouldn't have left it where I can access it if there was.

My gaze on the bathroom door, half expecting him to come out again, I ease myself woozily off the bed. The door remains closed. The shower goes on – and I'm across the room, steadying myself on my feet, fumbling in his pocket and extracting the phone.

Glancing again at the bathroom door, I key in his code – Ellie's birthday, unless he's changed it. Finding he hasn't, I'm reassured, briefly. As I read the last message received, though, my heart lurches violently. *You need to tell her. You have no choice. Do it, Cole. You know there'll be consequences if you don't.* My husband is cheating on me.

FOURTEEN

COLE

Cole turned his face to the flow of cold water raining down on him like a thousand needles, as if it could wash his guilt away. Why was she doing this, sending threatening messages, not just to him, but now to his *wife*?

Fuck! Bowing his head, he pressed his hands against the wall tiles and tried to regulate his breathing. Staying like that for a moment, he regained some control over his emotions. She wouldn't do it. There was no way she would tell Maddie outright.

Yes, she would. Christ. What should he do? Maddie knew... something. It was right there in her sharp green eyes. She wasn't stupid. She would guess he was lying to her. He'd lied to her about where he was the night this whole thing started. He'd told her he was in theatre performing an emergency craniotomy on a malignant oedema. She'd believed him. She always believed him. He'd sworn then that that was it. That he wouldn't lie to her again. Yet he had, every untruth that fell from his mouth digging a bigger hole, which would eventually swallow him whole. What was the woman thinking? Did she truly believe that he wanted to be with her?

He didn't *want* her. Wouldn't. Ever. He didn't love her, as she seemed to imagine he did. He loved his *wife*. He pressed the heels of his hands hard to his eyes. Why had he been such a fucking *idiot*?

Did Ellie know something? She'd changed. She was different around him. He could feel the hostility emanating from her, and it was crucifying him. He'd loved her with every fibre of his being since the moment he first saw her. Looking down at her delicate features as he'd cradled her in his arms, marvelling at her softly curled eyelashes, her perfect cupid lips, he'd sworn he would kill to keep her safe. He'd meant it: emotionally safe, physically safe. He was failing her, failing in his fundamental obligations as a father. Why had she drunk so much tonight? And how the hell had she ended up at Kelsey's.

He would lose them. His family. He didn't know how he would survive that.

Wiping away the salty tears that mingled with the water cascading down his face, he turned the shower off, stepped out and towelled himself quickly, then braced himself to go back to the bedroom. He found Maddie sleeping, her soft chestnut hair splayed across the pillow. She was beautiful; he didn't tell her that often enough. He would have liked nothing more than to have felt the comfort of her soft body close to his tonight. He couldn't do it. Make love with her while lying through his teeth to her. His chest catching, he reached to smooth her hair away from her face, then pressed a light kiss to her forehead.

Leaving quietly, he walked along the landing to the boys' room. They were both fast asleep, looking angelic, like peas in a pod. They even slept in the same position, one arm thrown over their heads, the duvet kicked to the bottom of their beds. Burying a sharp reminder of the empty bed he'd stared at as a kid, listening to the muted sobs of his mother in the bedroom next door, he went across to Lucas. Guilt weighed heavier in his chest as he noted the sterile dressing on his wound. He hadn't been called to the hospital this afternoon. He'd been meeting with *her*, begging her to please just stop all this. Trying desperately to find some sort of compromise. *Sorry, Lucas.* He swallowed and reached to pull up his duvet.

Jayden stirred as he went across to him. 'Is it morning?' he asked sleepily.

'No, not yet. Go back to sleep.' Cole smiled and ruffled his hair. He couldn't bear to contemplate the hurt and confusion they would feel, Ellie would feel, if their family fell apart.

Leaving the room before he disturbed them further, he went back to the main bedroom, doubting very much he would get any sleep. He was certain he wouldn't when he retrieved his phone from his jacket and read the message that flashed up. *Tell her. Do it tomorrow, or I will.*

He sucked in a breath, glanced at his wife, and then messaged back. *We need to talk more. Meet me tomorrow evening.*

OK, she shot back. *When and where? XX*

FIFTEEN

ELLIE

Ellie kept her eyes glued shut as someone trilled merrily, 'Good morning,' dragging her from the heavy slumber she'd been desperately trying to hang on to. 'How are you feeling?'

'Like death,' she croaked, her throat parched and the sour taste in her mouth reminding her she'd thrown up last night, spectacularly.

'Oh dear. Not so good then?' Kelsey asked sympathetically.

'Uh-uh,' Ellie answered, and then winced as the small shake of her head caused her brain to jar excruciatingly against the inside of her skull.

'I brought you some coffee,' Kelsey said, placing a mug on the bedside table.

'Thanks,' Ellie mumbled, but she doubted she could drink it. Even the smell of it made her stomach heave. 'What time is it?'

'Early. Seven-ish,' Kelsey answered. 'I'm on shift at the hospital.'

Ellie suppressed a groan. *Seven o'clock. On a Sunday?* That was obscene. 'Sorry, Kelsey,' she said, prising her grainy eyelids open and then snapping them shut again fast as the blinding early-morning sunlight filtering through the gap in the curtains sliced through her vision. Kelsey should have been annoyed with her turning up the way she did. Instead, she'd been really kind, holding her hair back for her when she'd been sick. Ellie wasn't sure her mum would have been so understanding if she'd rolled up at midnight and proceeded to puke all over the show. Her dad would have been disillusioned with her. He didn't approve of people who drank too much. How disillusioned would he be if he knew she'd got so drunk she'd ended up losing her virginity and didn't even remember it? That she had been dressed provocatively? Dancing to attract a man's attention? She had gone home with Luke Wainwright. And she *hadn't* said no. But that was because she'd hadn't been *able* to. Would her dad see it that way? Would her mum if she reported it and it went to court and Luke Wainwright and his barrister father made out she was 'gagging for it'? Or worse, if the police didn't even believe her? Had it been her fault? She so needed to talk to someone, but how could she when her dad seemed to be showing as little respect for women as that bastard Luke Wainwright had, and her mum was running herself ragged and worrying herself sick while he did?

'No problem. We've all been there,' Kelsey assured her. 'There are painkillers in the bathroom cabinet,' she offered, as Ellie gingerly eased herself up onto her elbows. 'Have a shower when you feel up to it. You can help yourself to anything else you need.'

'Thanks, Kelsey.' Managing a small smile, Ellie pushed the duvet back, swung her legs over the edge of the bed and attempted to stand. Then plopped heavily down again as the merry-go-round room revolved nauseatingly around her.

'Take it slowly,' Kelsey advised. 'There's no rush. Leave when you're ready.'

'Thanks. Kelsey...' Ellie stopped her as she walked to the door. 'What I told you about Dad, what's your take on it?' she asked. Kelsey had known him as long as her mum had. Ellie figured she would know what he was like. She needed to know. Was she being paranoid, imagining her dad was having an affair? She so wanted to be wrong, but what she'd seen, together with the fact that he was never home, told her she wasn't. She recalled how, when she and her dad used to go running together, they would talk about everything from the different species of birds they would see in the trees to climate change. His work, which fascinated her and made her feel dead proud of him. How things were for her at school. She'd confided once that she thought a girl who was supposed to be her friend was telling lies behind her back, but that she didn't know for sure and felt bad for thinking she was.

Her dad had furrowed his brow in that way he did when he was deep in thought. 'You know, I try to live by two maxims, Ellie,' he'd said at length. 'Look before you leap – as in, think before you act or speak, because you might end up really hurting someone with no real justification – and trust your gut feeling. If your instinct is telling you something, then it's probably right.'

Kelsey was looking pensively at her from the doorway. 'Honestly, Ellie, I don't know.' She sighed, crossed her arms over her chest and walked back towards her. 'Your dad can be quite approachable. People tend to confide in him.'

Ellie eyed her questioningly. 'Women, you mean?'

Kelsey said nothing, and Ellie drew her own conclusions. 'It would kill Mum if he was having an affair.' She sighed miserably. It would kill her too.

Kelsey lowered herself to sit next to her. 'I know, sweetheart,' she said kindly.

'They've been a bit distant,' Ellie went on, relieved that she'd been able to confide about her dad at least, instead of bottling that up too. There was so much churning around inside her, some days she felt as if she might explode.

Kelsey reached to give her hand a squeeze. 'It happens in marriages sometimes.'

'Especially when one half of the marriage is missing,' Ellie added acerbically. 'They were all right the other night, though. You know, getting intimate. And then all of a sudden, *boom*, they're poles apart again.'

Kelsey looked awkward. 'I don't think your mum would want you sharing details,' she said with a small frown.

She was right. Ellie probably shouldn't be talking about that kind of stuff, but then Kelsey was her mum's friend. She would want to look out for her. 'Mum's been getting messages,' she confided, eyeing her worriedly.

Kelsey's frown deepened. 'What kind of messages?'

Ellie shrugged. 'I'm not sure. Warnings, I think. I heard them talking the other night and then again last night. And Dad's been acting really weirdly. He got so angry with Mum for no reason. I've never seen him like that before. And he's always coming home late.'

'I see.' Kelsey looked perturbed.

'I think they're from the woman he's seeing. Do you?' Ellie scanned Kelsey's face carefully.

Kelsey didn't say anything for a second, but Ellie could tell from her troubled expression that she was thinking the same. 'Kelsey?' she urged her.

Taking a breath, Kelsey looked her over cautiously. 'I think we might be jumping to conclusions,' she said. 'Women do tend to be a bit awestruck by him. Your dad is a renowned surgeon, and he's a good-looking guy, after all. It's possible some woman's become infatuated with him, hoping for a relationship with him, but...' She stopped diplomatically.

'Not if I have anything to do with it,' Ellie growled, shooting off the bed. 'I'll tear her bloody hair out.'

'Ellie, hold your horses.' Kelsey jumped up, catching hold of her arm. 'Tearing her hair out is a bit drastic, don't you think?'

Ellie breathed in deeply. She wanted to strangle the woman, whoever she was. She wanted to punch her dad and knock some sense into him. What was the matter with him?

'You need to get yourself together and go home. Your mum will be worried sick,' Kelsey advised. 'And I think you should talk to her about what you told me.'

Ellie nodded, but she wasn't sure she would be able to reassure her. She seemed to be burying her head in the sand rather than confronting him. Her mum was strong. She supported her dad because she wanted to, because she loved him. It was obvious every time she looked at him. If he was cheating on her, she would fight for her marriage, but to do that she would need the scales peeled from her eyes.

SIXTEEN

MADDIE

Startled by the sound of a car door slamming, I snap my eyes open, then squeeze them closed again, my stomach lurching as I recall the events of last night. My drunken neediness. Cole seeming so distant. The message. A mixture of fear and simmering anger churning inside me, I turn my head to look at him. He's sleeping, one arm thrown over his head, his brow furrowed, even in sleep. Is his conscience troubling him? I wonder. I have to confront him, I realise. I can't go on like this. But not now. I need to get up, get my act together and see to my children. *Ellie*. My thoughts flying to her and what kind of state she will be in, emotionally as well as physically, I push the duvet back and climb determinedly out of bed. Cole stirs, but he doesn't wake. Not ready to face him yet, I leave him to sleep and go to the bathroom to shower.

He's up and dressing when I go back to the bedroom. Hurriedly, it appears. 'How are you?' he asks, pausing halfway into his shirt.

I feel a pang of guilt. I know he worries when people drink excessively. I know why. I shouldn't have opened the wine. I can't afford to be overemotional. If I have a battle ahead – and I do, because I will fight for my marriage – I need to be in control. 'Fine,' I assure him, faking a smile. 'You?' I glance at him as I head to the wardrobe to pull out a clean T-shirt.

He frowns, looking unconvinced – as he would be, I suppose, considering how things were left between us last night. My chest squeezes painfully as I recall his fingers tenderly brushing my hair from my face as I feigned sleep, the featherlight kiss he pressed to my forehead. Were they the actions of a man who loves me, or of a man stuffed with guilt? Something akin to grief crashes through me at the thought of what I might have lost, my soulmate, the person I thought I would spend the rest of my life with. The man I've loved with all of myself, and still do. I don't think I can bear it. Already I feel as if my heart is splintering inside me. But I have to be strong. My children need me standing upright, not broken. I feel broken, though, hollow inside, as if a vital part of me is missing.

'Tired,' he answers, 'but that's nothing new.'

'You're bound to be,' I say, slipping out of my dressing gown with my back to him. I've never been embarrassed in front of him before, but try as I might, I can't get the image of him making love with another woman out of my mind, doing all the things with her he does with me. I doubt her lithe young body will bear the scars of childbirth.

My breath catches sharply and I hurry to cover the scar from my Caesarean T-incision. I felt broken after the birth of the twins, partly because they'd come so early and I was so worried they might not survive, partly because of the physical and emotional trauma. Cole said I should be proud of my scar, that it was a reminder of the power of my amazing female body. He traced the raised flesh gently with his fingertips, brushed my tummy so softly with his lips, I felt tears slide from my eyes. In that moment, I think I loved him as much as it was possible for a woman to love a man. Will I ever be able to forgive him for betraying not just me, but our children? The two children we lost? They were early miscarriages before I finally got pregnant with the twins, but still I considered them our children, tiny human beings I grieved over. I thought Cole did too.

My heart twists painfully as my mind goes again to the message. I didn't read any more. After stuffing the phone back in his jacket, I only just made it to the main bathroom before the wine came up much faster than it had gone down. She said there would be consequences. She was forcing his hand, obviously. What should I do? Should I wait it out in the hope it will go away? But will the internal scars he's knowingly inflicting on me with his lies and deceit ever go away? This is all assuming he's not in love with her. That he doesn't want to be with her.

I start as I realise he's behind me. He reaches to free my hair from the back of my T-shirt and I feel like sitting down and weeping. 'You're angry with me,' he says softly.

'No.' Goosebumps prickling my skin as his fingers brush my neck, I step quickly away and turn to face him. 'I'm angry with me,' I answer, meeting his gaze briefly, then walking past him on the pretence of applying some make-up. I don't feel like titivating. I doubt any amount of make-up is going to help me compare favourably with Hannah Lee anyway.

'For?' Cole asks as I apply a slick of under-eye concealer in the hope of making myself look half human.

'Drinking too much,' I answer, glancing at him in the mirror. 'I was upset.'

'About Ellie?' He moves closer. 'You were bound to be.' As he leans to glide his hands over my hips and kiss the nape of my neck, panic grips me and I twist away from him. I can't do this. Not now I feel I can't be natural with him. Deep sadness envelops me as I consider that this might be the start of the end of our marriage. He catches my arm, and suddenly I'm face to face with him and utterly destabilised as I see the flicker of bewildered hurt in his eyes. Because I've rejected him? Or because he can't understand why I would? No. Cole might be an eminent surgeon, but he's not a conceited man. I recall how I once went to meet him at the hospital for lunch. He was delayed, inevitably. I quashed any irritation I might have had as I watched him talking to the tearful mother of a ten-year-old child whose life he'd saved after a head injury had required urgent surgical intervention. 'I'm just doing my job,' he assured her, smiling warmly as she thanked him. 'I'm thinking your job will be the harder one once he's up and running around again thinking he's Spider-Man.'

I watch him now as he drops his gaze and a conflict of emotion rages inside me. I can't reconcile that caring man with someone who would destroy the lives of his own children. I have to say something. I can't not. I won't mention checking his phone, though. That will only put him on his guard. Isn't he bound to change his PIN if I do? What would that tell me? I take a breath. 'And I'm worried about the messages,' I tell him.

He nods. 'I get why you would be,' he says with a sigh. 'Someone does appear to be targeting you. I have no idea why.'

I study him, try to read what's in his eyes. There's nothing but concern there. 'But that's the point, isn't it?' I ask. 'Why would someone target me? It's as if they're trying to drive a wedge between us, and I can't think why anyone would want to do that, unless...'

He eyes me questioningly as I falter.

'Are you having an affair?' I ask, my heart thundering against my chest.

'*What?*' He stares at me, staggered. 'You're serious, aren't you?' He emits a disbelieving laugh.

'I'm asking you to tell me the truth, Cole.' I hold his gaze. 'Are you having an affair?'

His gaze doesn't flinch. 'No,' he states categorically. 'I never have and I never will. I thought you knew me well enough to know that I would never even consider doing what my father did to my mother. He destroyed her, Maddie. I would never do that to you. I *love* you. Will you please just believe me?'

Guilt rises inside me as, his look one of bitter disappointment, he tears his gaze away. 'I should go,' he says quietly. 'I have a clinical team meeting.'

I want to reel the words back, but I can't. I had to ask. Surely he must realise why I would. My chest fills up as I watch him agitatedly fastening the rest of the buttons on his shirt and fetching the phone I wish I could smash into smithereens from his bedside table. I can hear the twins in their bedroom – squabbling about their Box of Frogs it sounds like, horrible slimy, sticky things I'll no doubt find suctioned to the tiles in the bathroom – and I'm torn. I should go and intervene, but I don't want Cole to leave, not like this. 'Can you not call in? Tell them you're going to be delayed?'

He runs his fingers through his hair. I note the frown crossing his face, and my heart sinks. 'I wish I could. We clearly need to sit down and talk,' he says tightly, 'but—'

'Right. Fine.' I swallow and head quickly for the door.

Cole follows me. 'Mads, wait. It's not that simple. You know it isn't. I can't let everyone down at such short notice.'

'No.' *Just me.* I don't meet his gaze.

'I'll do my best not to be late this evening,' he promises.

'Don't rush on my account. I know you have to prioritise,' I retort, hating the facetiousness I can hear in my voice. When did we arrive at this place in our relationship? *How* did we?

'Mads.' He sighs as I pull the door open. 'Please don't be like this. We clearly do need to talk. I know I haven't been around much, but I'll make time this evening,' he says, as if suddenly he magically can. 'I have a late-afternoon procedure, but I'll get someone to cover.'

Hannah Lee. I've no doubt she'll be falling over herself to support him, whereas I appear to be putting him under pressure.

I see red. I can't help it. We're not talking about him not being around more to help out. We're talking about where he might be when he's *not* around. 'You're not the only one who's under pressure, you know,' I respond tearfully. '*I'm* tired, Cole. Completely frazzled with Ellie being so unpredictable lately and the twins needing so much attention. I'm sorry if that makes life complicated for you, but we do have children.'

'I know. I do know, Maddie,' he says. 'And you're doing a brilliant job. I just wish I—'

'Don't, Cole,' I warn him, a combination of anger and humiliation rearing up inside me. 'Just don't.'

He squints at me in confusion. 'Don't what?'

'Don't patronise me.' I look at him steadily. 'You're better than that. Or at least I thought you were.'

'For *Christ's*...' Breathing in hard, he eyes the ceiling. 'I was *not* patronising you. I was actually trying to compliment you, because I do think you're doing a brilliant job, despite my not being as hands-on as I—' He stops as his phone rings. '*Shit!*'

I swear I see the blood draining from his face as he fumbles it from his pocket.

He glances at it and back to me, then turns away to take the call – and my heart slides icily into the pit of my belly. I try to tell myself it means nothing, that it's just what people do. I don't believe it, though. He's shutting me out. Again. It's *her* calling.

I'm through the door onto the landing when I hear him behind me. 'It's okay,' he says quietly. 'I'm on my way. I'll be there soon.'

He's out of the bedroom in a second flat.

'Cole?' My heart catches as he almost pushes past me. 'Cole!' Following him down the stairs, I call after him, 'Where are you going?'

He grabs his car keys from the hall table and heads fast for the front door. It opens as he reaches it, and Ellie walks in. '*Cole*,' I shout as he attempts to manoeuvre past her. 'For God's sake, what's going on?'

'I can't talk now. I have to go,' he says tightly, and swings out of the door.

SEVENTEEN
COLE

His mind on Maddie and how to tell her what he knew he was somehow going to have to, Cole mounted the kerb, careering his car haphazardly to a stop on the pavement a few yards from his parents' house. His gut twisting violently as he wondered who the paramedics from the ambulance parked out front were attending, he rammed his car door open and scrambled out to set off at a run.

Finding his mother outside the house, relief swept through him on some level. She was clearly distressed, tears streaming down her face and mingling with the blood from an open gash on her forehead.

'The paramedics are with your father.' Her neighbour, Mrs Matthews, nodded towards the open front door and tightened her hold around his mother's shoulders, preventing her going back inside, which she appeared to want to. Cole was grateful.

'He's not well,' his mother said, as he quickly checked her injury.

'Did you lose consciousness?' he asked, scanning her eyes. The wound would need taping and she would possibly need a

CT scan, but her pupils were normal and she seemed alert and coherent, which subdued his anger a little.

'No,' she assured him. 'I'm fine, but I'm so worried about your father. He couldn't see properly,' she went on shakily. 'He was clutching his head, vomiting and screaming with pain. I tried to help him, but he wouldn't let me. He pushed me away.'

As in physically, obviously. Cole felt his jaw tense.

'I didn't know what to *do*.' Fresh tears springing to her eyes, his mother looked beseechingly between him and her neighbour.

'It's okay, Lizzie,' the woman assured her. 'You did everything you could.' She glanced at Cole. 'Should I drive her to the hospital? They said something about another ambulance, but...'

It would take for ever. And it wasn't really necessary. Cole felt like taking her himself and leaving his father to it, but something deep down inside him wouldn't let him. He nodded his thanks. 'Go with Mrs Matthews, Mum,' he said gently. 'I'll be there soon.'

'But I don't want to leave him,' his mother fretted. 'I know he hasn't been good to me, Cole, but I can't just abandon him. Not now. He's so sick.'

'He's in good hands.' Cole gave her a reassuring smile. 'Once he's been checked over, we'll be right behind you, I promise. You need to get that head looked at meanwhile. It's important, Mum. Please go, will you? For me.'

His mother searched his eyes, eventually nodding, and Cole breathed a relieved sigh. As the neighbour shepherded her off, he turned to go and see what was happening with his father. He had to force himself to go into the house. Old habits. Ever since he was old enough to leave the place on his own, he'd had to brace himself to go back inside. Taking a breath, he pushed through the front door.

One of the paramedics pulled herself up from where they

were assessing his father on the kitchen floor. 'If you could give us some space, sir,' she said. 'We need to—'

'I'm a neurosurgeon at the General,' Cole interrupted. 'Cole Chase.'

The paramedic glanced at her partner, who recognised Cole and nodded him on.

'What's your thinking, Mike?' Cole asked, his voice tight with conflicting emotion as he crouched down next to the man.

'From the symptoms described – severe headache, nausea, sensitivity to light, together with weakness down one side and slurred speech – we're thinking subarachnoid haemorrhage due to ruptured aneurysm.' Mike brought him up to speed. 'We were concerned about a drop in systolic blood pressure so used rapid intubation and intravenous lidocaine sedation to blunt intercranial pressure.'

Cole quickly assessed the situation. All the symptoms fitted, and his father had had high blood pressure and cholesterol for years. With his diabetes diagnosed a few years back, he'd been at risk of atherosclerosis, but Cole guessed he wouldn't take the advice he offered his own patients, that being to give up cigars and whisky. Fat building up on his artery walls would definitely increase his risk of developing a fusiform aneurysm. As he looked into his father's eyes, he saw nothing but confusion there, as if he didn't know what day it was, where he was, who Cole was. And then, for the briefest of seconds, palpable fear as he clearly did.

Cole looked away. 'He'll need surgical intervention asap,' he said, telling the crew what they would already know.

'On it,' Mike said. 'Sorry, mate,' he added. 'I hope he makes it.'

Cole smiled tensely. What would Mike think, he wondered, if he knew what his thoughts were? That far from hoping he made it, he prayed that the bastard who'd killed his brother, made his mother's life an utter misery and done his damnedest to ruin his, wouldn't survive.

EIGHTEEN

Are you sure about this?' As he monitored his father's vitals, Alex questioned Cole's choice of microvascular clipping over coiling. He was obviously wondering why he would go for the more intrusive surgery bearing in mind the patient's age. His father was possibly unlikely to outlive the need for the less durable coiling procedure, which would have to be repeated in the event of recurrence of aneurysm.

'It's a large one, not easily accessible,' Cole answered, glancing at Hannah. With no other surgeon available and due to his close relationship with the patient, he'd elected to stand back and let her take the lead. Quietly, he thanked God for protocol. He very much doubted he could have remained as focused as he should be, given the true nature of their relationship.

'Take a look.' He made room for his anaesthetist to peer into the microscope inserted through the window they'd made in the cranium, which confirmed what the CT and MRI scans had revealed: that the aneurysm, twenty millimetres in size and located in the frontal lobe of the brain, might prove difficult to access via the less intrusive option. 'It's wide-necked. See?

While both options are available to us, in this case I think clipping is the way to go, particularly as there's a possibility of a rebleed before we can get to it. Do you agree, Hannah?'

Hannah nodded, and Cole moved back to give her access.

'You're the expert,' Alex said, frowning fleetingly as he looked him over.

That he was, in the field of surgery. Making clinical decisions based on physical symptoms came naturally. Emotionally, he was out of his depth and had no idea how to negotiate what was happening in his life.

'Think of it as a choreographed ballet,' he reminded Hannah as she appeared to hesitate, causing him a stab of panic.

She nodded again, tightly, but still she hesitated, and Cole's gut twisted. 'Okay, I've got it,' he said, stepping quickly forward.

'Cole?'

He heard the warning in Alex's voice, but this was a decision he had no choice but to make. It was clinical, clear-cut. Hannah was struggling, possibly also because of who the patient was. Despite his conviction that he could remain detached, though, he felt his heart banging as he went back in. He was way too hot under his mask and he guessed Alex would notice his hands were shaking. He needed to focus, locate the blood vessels feeding the aneurysm and get the clip in place to stop the blood supply as soon as possible. He glanced at Alex for confirmation that he was happy with the patient's sats.

Alex double-checked the heart, blood pressure and oxygen levels. Then, 'Right, we're all good,' he said, giving Cole the green light.

Nodding firmly, Cole drew in a breath and positioned the spring clip ready to pinch the aneurysm off… then faltered. Every second counted, and yet for the first time since his junior days, he'd frozen. *Do it, for fuck's sake!* Sweat dripping from his forehead, he blinked hard, trying to erase the image that, out of nowhere, had scorched itself on his mind, instantly transporting him back to his formative years. He blinked again, but it was still there. He could feel the impact, like a punch to his solar plexus, taste the petrol fumes thick on the air.

'Cole?' Alex's voice permeated the cacophony of noise playing too loudly in his head: horns blaring, his mother screaming, hysterical, 'Ryan! Oh God. Oh God. *Ryan!*' His father retching in the gutter. Not from shock, but because of the booze. Cole could still smell it.

'Cole! For *fu*— Hannah, take over!' Alex shouted. 'No, wait. Shit. The patient's convulsing. Cole, get out of the *way*.'

His heart slowing to a dull thud, Cole moved away. Then staggered another step back as a rich crimson fountain spewed upwards, spattering the front of his scrubs and his face. His father's blood, salty, metallic, reminding him the man was human.

As he stood there stupefied, Hannah pushed her way in. 'It's ruptured again,' she said tersely, 'bleeding into the brain. A tear in the neck of the aneurysm, I think. Jesus, Cole, I can't find where it's coming from.' She glanced desperately at him. '*Cole?*'

The urgency in her voice filtering through the thick fog in his head, Cole felt his near-dormant heart kick back hard. He couldn't let this happen. *Wasn't* going to let this happen. *No* fucking way. He'd taken an oath, lived his life by it. He was not going to let the man who'd constantly told him he would never secure a surgical post take it away from him. 'Give me some room,' he said, moving purposefully back to the table.

'I can't find it,' Hannah repeated shakily. 'I think it's the blood vessels close to the base, but—'

'Hannah, you need to give me some *space*,' Cole shouted. 'Live, you bastard,' he grated, his gloves slicked stark red as he tried desperately to stem the flow. He was struggling in vain. He knew it before Alex warned him the patient's sats were dropping dangerously low.

Hour-long seconds ticked by, the deathly silence punctuated only by the jarring beep of the monitors. Then, 'He's asystolic,' Alex announced grimly, and hissed out a curse.

Christ. Wiping the back of his hand across his forehead, Cole moved to the chest area. He knew it was pointless before he started pumping, willing the man on the table to live. He knew that was pointless, too. His father would probably die just to spite him.

'It's too late, Cole.' He felt a hand on his arm. Kept pumping.

'Cole, he's flatlined. There's no point,' Alex said, attempting to pull him away. 'It's too late.'

NINETEEN

MADDIE

Leaving Cole's mother in the relatives' room, where it was deemed she was well enough to wait, I step into the corridor to look for someone who can tell us what's happening. Nearing the nurses' station, I move back into a side ward as I see Alex and Hannah Lee coming through the swing doors ahead of me. They're still in their theatre scrubs, I notice. Also that the woman's scrubs are covered in blood. She's clearly upset, as indicated by the arm Alex places around her shoulders. 'Don't blame yourself, Hannah,' I hear him say, giving her a reassuring smile as they slow in front of the desk. 'You did your best under the circumstances.'

I feel my stomach tighten as I see her wipe a tear from her face. 'I know,' she murmurs emotionally, 'but I feel so awful for Cole. Do you think they'll blame him?'

Oh God, no. My hand flies to my mouth. His father has died, hasn't he, on the operating table. I swallow back a lurch of fear as I recall Cole saying he hoped the next time he saw him would be at his funeral.

'The patient's case record will be reviewed,' Alex replies, dragging a hand tiredly across the back of his neck. 'They're bound to check for omissions in care, but I doubt it will go to investigation. Given his father's age, his medical history and the difficult location and size of the aneurysm, his chances of survival weren't great.'

'I know, but...' Hannah looks Alex over cautiously. 'He just seemed to freeze and I should have carried on with the surgery,' she says wretchedly. 'I didn't feel confident, but I should have pushed through it. Cole shouldn't have had to step in. His emotions were bound to be all over the place, considering his relationship with the patient.'

'Possibly,' Alex concedes. 'I didn't see anything that might have significantly contributed to the patient's death, though,' he adds.

I close my eyes, filled with gratitude for Alex, who's obviously answering carefully, but also with sudden vitriolic hatred for this woman. What is she implying? More worryingly, will she repeat what she's just said to the review team? Does she want Cole's future ruined? Aside from that, does she realise that he will carry this for the rest of his *life*?

'You should go and clean up,' Alex says kindly.

She nods, looking tearful and vulnerable and concerned. About *my* husband. Anger rears up like a viper inside me, and I have a sudden almost overwhelming urge to go and confront her. Stilling myself, I watch Alex place a hand on her back as they resume walking, guiding her gently towards the doors into the corridor that leads to the locker rooms and the showers. *Oh, Alex.* Even in her scrubs, Hannah is undeniably pretty, and clearly knows how to use her womanly wiles. I can see why he would be protective of her. Why Cole would. Does Alex know there's something going on between them? I wonder. I recall how he guessed that Cole and I were dating before we'd made it public. *I couldn't help noticing the furtive glances between you*, he enlightened me when I looked at him in surprise. *He's a good bloke. Thoughtful, despite his father trying to knock any feeling out of him. He won't mess you about,* he added with a regretful smile, and then wished me luck. Alex is a good man. He and I weren't right together, but he and Cole have a relationship that has stood the test of time. They've known each other since medical school and would have each other's backs if the need ever arose. Clearly he has Cole's back now.

Jealousy and fear squirm inside me as my gaze travels back to Hannah, and I have to stop myself from following her into the showers, which might give me an opportunity to corner her and question her. I daren't. Not because I'm concerned about how she might react. But because I'm concerned about how *I* might react once I'm face to face with her.

TWENTY

COLE

Numb with shock and disbelief, Cole stayed where he was, the world seeming to stop turning as the machines plaintively beeped end of life. As realisation hit him, physically forcing the breath from his body, he backed away from the operating table, stumbling over equipment, until he met the far wall of the theatre. Standing there, he stared at the shell of the man who'd once been his father. A cruel, sadistic man who'd taken pleasure in humiliating him. Disciplining him. He half expected him to move. He emitted an almost hysterical laugh as he actually saw him sit up, his skull wide open, his eyes as cold as the Arctic Ocean and filled with palpable contempt. *Didn't I say you were too weak to make a good surgeon?* He could hear the words as the dead man spoke, see the scornful smile curving his mouth. *Perhaps you can see now where allowing your emotions to rule your head gets you. There's no place for emotion in the operating theatre, Cole. Is there?*

Cole laughed again, a laugh that turned to a sob that died in his throat as the man lowered himself silently back to the table. *Jesus.* He wiped his arm under his nose, then slid to his haunches. He was hallucinating. Was that why his life was falling apart? Was he losing his mind? No. He had a blank in his memory, hours he couldn't fill no matter how hard he tried, but in this room, he'd been present, aware of his responsibilities as a surgeon. Yet his father had died. The man had been right. He had let his emotions surface. He'd had his life in his hands. That had been power. Real power. As much as Cole would like to deny it, he couldn't. For a split second, his impulse had been to kill him. He'd struggled to get a grip on himself, and he'd thought he had. So why the fuck had this happened?

Alex, his friend through med school and the one person other than Maddie who was aware of his toxic relationship with his father, who'd witnessed his father belittling him, even right here in the hospital, had seen him falter. He'd been the one to pull him away. Cole should have stepped away before he'd had to do that. Alex had guessed he might struggle. Cole had heard the warning in his voice. Seen the sympathy in his eyes. Alex hadn't said anything, though, turning his attention to reassuring the team instead. Cole owed him for that.

What was happening to him? He breathed in hard. Held it. What the hell was he going to do? Pressing his hands over his face, he stifled a moan that seemed to come from his soul. His world was disintegrating. One single evening he couldn't even remember most of had kicked off a chain of events, and suddenly his life was spiralling out of control.

He *was* giving in to his emotions, each and every one of them hitting him so hard he couldn't breathe. He didn't know how to deal with it. Any of it. Exhaustion seeping through him right down to his bones, he stayed where he was. He wasn't sure how long he sat there, his hands still shaking, his whole body shaking. He wasn't aware of anyone coming into the theatre until he felt a hand on his shoulder and snapped his gaze up to find Alex looking down at him.

'Okay?' his friend asked, his look a mixture of pity and concern.

Cole nodded, sucked in a breath, and then shook his head hard.

'You need to clean up,' Alex said. 'Go and be with your family. I'll take over here.'

Cole followed his gaze to his father. 'I killed him,' he murmured past the jagged knot in his throat.

Alex hesitated before answering. Then, 'It was doubtful he would have made it,' he said. 'The odds were stacked against him. You did nothing wrong. I can vouch for that. Right now, you need to pull yourself together and go and talk to your family.'

Cole studied him, read what was in his eyes and knew Alex would have his back if he needed him to. 'Thanks,' he said hoarsely, then took hold of Alex's outstretched hand and heaved himself to his feet.

He had to break the news to his mother, be there for her. For Maddie and his kids too. They would feel the impact of this, despite never having warmed to the man who'd only ever treated them with disrespect.

'Move on, Cole,' Alex advised as he reached the theatre doors. 'There's nothing to be gained from dissecting it. Put it behind you and get on with your life.'

Nodding again, Cole pushed through the doors. He'd barely gone two yards when his phone signalled a message. After scrabbling to find it under his scrubs, he checked it, knowing in his gut who it was. *I hope we're still on for this evening. XX*

He cursed. *Christ*, why couldn't she just back *off*. She wasn't going to, was she? He had to find a way to make her. If he didn't, he would have no life, no family, no career, no future.

TWENTY-ONE

As he headed for the relatives' room, he sent a short reply. *Can't make it. Will message back.*

There was a beat, then, *Make sure you do,* she responded.

Cursing silently again, Cole paused outside the relatives' room door, then took a breath and pushed the handle down. His mother rose from her chair as he went in. He noted her fearful expression and his gut clenched. He couldn't remember a time when his father had ever treated her with anything but disdain, but he guessed from how upset she'd been when he'd arrived at the house that on some level she must have cared for him. 'Sit down, Mum,' he said softly, walking across to place an arm around her.

Maddie was with her. Leaving Ellie looking after the twins, she'd come straight away when he'd called her. She'd never liked his father, unsurprisingly, but she'd always got along with his mother. As she walked across to them, he met her gaze. He could see in an instant that she knew something had gone wrong in theatre. It was right there in her eyes, the same sharp perception that told him she also knew there was something fundamentally wrong between the two of them, something he wasn't telling her. Christ, how he wished he could find the courage to.

'Cole?' his mother said tremulously, drawing his attention back to her.

Cole hesitated. 'He had a bleed. We did everything we could, but...' He faltered, the trepidation he could see in his mother's eyes cutting him to the core. 'He didn't make it, Mum.' He wanted to add he was sorry, but the words wouldn't come.

His mother stared at him uncomprehending for a second, and then it hit her and the blood drained from her face.

'Come and sit down, Lizzie,' Maddie urged her, wrapping her arms around her. She glanced tearfully at him as she did. She knew he would struggle to come to terms with this, that though he'd hated the man, there was a part of him that had craved his affection, his respect. She knew him. And he was going to lose her. And he had no idea how he was ever going to deal with that.

As if rooted to the spot, his mother remained standing, her eyes a kaleidoscope of emotion: shock and disbelief, but most of all fear, as she processed the news. 'What will I do now?' she murmured, looking bewildered, and Cole felt sick to the pit of his stomach.

He wouldn't grieve for his father, not in any way that could be considered normal. But his mother would. She would wonder how she was going to function without him. She'd had no life outside of the marriage, no identity other than the great Robert Chase's wife.

'We're here for you, Lizzie,' Maddie whispered. 'We'll help you sort everything out,' she assured her, intuitive as always. Cole was reminded too of how caring she was as, seeing the tears roll down his mother's face, Maddie eased her closer. 'I could come and stay with you for a while if you like,' she offered. 'Or maybe Cole could.'

As her gaze flicked to his, Cole felt a surge of panic. He wasn't sure he could read her look now. She was devastated for him, clearly, but there was something else there. Doubt? Anger? Did she want him to go? 'I can take some compassionate leave,' he said, looking back to his mother. 'Stay with you for...' He stopped as the door opened behind them.

'Sorry,' Kelsey said, stepping tentatively in. 'I just came to check your mother's dressing and let her have her prescription before she's discharged. And to offer my condolences.' She looked between Cole and his mother, but her gaze didn't linger on him.

'Thanks,' he said awkwardly. 'Will you be okay here, Mum?' he asked. 'I should probably go and find out what the situation is.'

Gathering his meaning, his mum nodded. 'I'll be fine,' she murmured. 'I'm just sorry to be such a nuisance.'

'You're not being a nuisance at all,' Kelsey assured her, going across to her.

Cole took the opportunity to leave. Aside from the fact that he needed to make sure his father's body was ready for viewing, should his mother want to see him, his emotions were far too close to the surface for him to be able to trust himself.

He was a few yards along the corridor when Maddie called after him. 'Cole, hold on.' She hurried towards him. 'Are you all right?'

He took a breath. 'Not great,' he answered in the only way he could.

She nodded, eyeing him thoughtfully. 'I'm sorry,' she said.

He swallowed. 'It's no loss,' he assured her, his voice tight.

She studied him for a long, searching moment. Then, 'I'm worried about you,' she said.

'I'm okay.' He shrugged. 'I will be.'

She narrowed her eyes. 'Are you sure about that, Cole? I can't help thinking you're keeping everything stuffed inside.

You were upset when you left home. And with the things you said about him…'

Cole eyed her quizzically. 'What things?' He tried to recall. He had been upset, terrified his marriage might be falling apart, and this was without him revealing something he thought would blow it apart anyway. Blind with fury at what he believed his father had done, he barely remembered the drive to his parents' house, let alone anything he might have said.

'The last time you went there.' Maddie hesitated. 'You said you hoped the next time you saw him it would be at his funeral. You were obviously upset then, too, and I thought… I don't know…' she paused, dragging her hair from her forehead and looking extremely uncomfortable, 'that you might be feeling guilty, blaming yourself in some way.'

'I was angry. He'd bloody well hit her.' Cole stared at her in astonishment. 'And of course I feel guilty. Because he died at my hands in there. Also because his behaviour of late might well have been as a result of a slow bleed on the brain and I had no way of knowing that because I kept as far away from him as possible. I didn't mean I *wanted* him dead. Is that what you think?'

'*No*. Of course not,' Maddie refuted, but the uncertainty in her eyes told him otherwise.

'Do you think I engineered his death in some way? Is that it, Maddie?' His emotions now way off the scale, he squinted hard at her. 'That I would actually have…' He stopped, the words wedging in his throat.

Maddie said nothing, and Cole felt his heart sink without trace. Did she honestly have that low an opinion of him? Clearly she did. Because he'd lied to her and she knew it, and he had no way to undo it without telling her the truth, and he simply couldn't. 'You actually do, don't you?' he asked. 'You think I killed him.'

Still Maddie didn't answer, which spoke volumes.

'I see.' He raked his fingers through his hair. 'Right. Well, thanks for that,' he said throatily. 'At least I know where I stand in your estimation.'

'Cole, *wait*,' she called after him as he turned to walk back to theatre. 'That's *not* what I meant. I was just concerned for you. Please don't go off like this.'

Cole didn't respond. He couldn't do this. Not here. She was right. He did keep everything stuffed inside. So *much*. Too much, including the fact that he did think he was responsible for his father's death. And now it was all in danger of spilling over.

Wiping his hand over his eyes, he kept walking. He didn't see Alex approaching from the opposite direction until he almost collided with him.

'Everything okay?' Alex asked, glancing past him to Maddie.

'As much as it can be.' Cole breathed in tightly. 'It seems my wife doesn't have quite the faith in me she once did.'

Alex surveyed him thoughtfully. 'Maybe you should work on restoring her faith,' he suggested.

Cole frowned, unsure what he meant.

'Pay her a little more attention, maybe?' Alex went on with a shrug. 'Be honest with her.'

'About?' Cole asked warily. Alex couldn't know anything. There was no way he could.

'How you're feeling. I don't know. Whatever,' Alex answered with another vague shrug. 'From the look on Maddie's face, though, it seems you two need to do some talking.'

He was right. After today, Alex would know something was going on with him, if not what. It would be obvious, too, that there was a problem between him and Maddie. If he was to have any hope of regaining her trust, he had to find the strength to do as she'd asked and tell her the truth, pray she would believe him. Even as he thought it, he knew it was impossible. She would never believe him, simply by virtue of the fact that it wasn't believable. His only alternative was to find a way to make the threat that was hanging over him go away.

TWENTY-TWO

ELLIE

Hearing a car on the drive, Ellie flew to the window and was relieved to see it was her mum arriving home. She still didn't know what was going on. Her mum had had a call from her dad and then dashed off, saying his father had been taken to the hospital. Ellie had heard nothing since, but she guessed it must be serious. She couldn't help feeling for her dad, but she had no idea what she would say to him when he came back.

'Stay here, guys. Won't be a sec,' she instructed Lucas and Jayden, who were glued to the TV watching *Inside Out* 2. Going into the hall, she met her mum coming through the front door. One look at her ashen face told her things weren't good.

'What's happened?' she asked. 'Is Nan all right?' She couldn't muster up much sympathy for her grandad – after being treated the way she had by that shit Luke Wainwright, she had no time for bullies – but she loved her nan.

'She's fine,' her mum answered with a tired nod. 'Where are the boys?'

'Lounge, watching a film. They've had their tea and got their PJs on,' Ellie assured her, guessing she would be shattered. 'Mum, what's wrong?' she pressed her. 'Is Dad okay?'

'Yes, he's okay,' her mum reassured her. 'I think,' she added, her expression troubled as she headed past her to the kitchen.

'What do you mean, you think?' Frowning worriedly, Ellie followed.

After dumping her bag on the worktop, her mum drew in a breath and turned to face her. 'Come and sit down,' she said.

'I don't want to sit down.' Ellie eyed her warily. 'Something has happened, hasn't it?'

Her mum hesitated. Then, 'Your grandad died,' she said softly.

'*Died?* But...' Ellie stared at her, stunned. 'How?' She scanned her mum's face, her heart banging manically as her mum's eyes skittered away. 'Mum, *talk* to me,' she begged her. 'You need to tell me. What *happened*?'

Her mum clamped her hands over her face, drew in another sharp breath, then looked back at her. 'He had something called an aneurysm,' she explained. 'He needed urgent surgery. Your father had to step in and...' she faltered, 'your grandad died on the operating table.'

Oh no. Ellie's heart lurched as she recalled her nan's phone call before Lucas burned himself, how furious her dad had been with her mum when he'd stormed out. Most of all, though, he'd been furious with his father. He hated him, the way he was, the way he hurt her nan, everything about him. 'Did he do something, Mum?' she asked, her stomach churning with sick trepidation. 'Dad, was it his fault?'

Her mum didn't answer – and Ellie's heart stopped beating. 'Mum!' she shouted, causing her to jolt. 'Did Dad do something? Did he do it on purpose? *Talk* to me.'

'No,' her mum answered firmly, but she was scared. Ellie could see it in her eyes.

'He *didn't*,' she cried, her tears exploding with frustration and anger. 'He would never do something like that. He *wouldn't*. He's a good surgeon. If he made a mistake it will be because he was distracted by that *bitch*,' she seethed, growing terrified now for her dad.

Looking bewildered, her mum moved towards her. 'Ellie, you need to slow down. Just stop and breathe.'

'Why is he doing this? *Why* would he do it?' Ellie couldn't stop. Couldn't breathe. 'I don't get it. What the *fuck* does he see in her?'

'Ellie.' Her mum caught hold of her shoulders. 'Slow down,' she urged her, clearly frightened for her.

'She's manipulating him, that's what she's doing,' Ellie went on feverishly. 'Turning on the tears, playing on his emotions. Is he blind? Stupid?'

Her mum pulled her close. 'Who are you talking about, sweetheart?' she asked, her voice strained. 'What did you see? Was your father with someone? Is that it? You can tell me.'

Ellie froze, her chest booming. She hadn't meant to blurt it all out like this. But she had to tell her. Her mum needed to know. She dragged a hand under her nose, tried to stop crying like a child. 'He was in the bar, the one close to the hospital. I was in there with some friends, and I know I shouldn't have been, but I was, and Dad was there too, and...'

'Breathe, Ellie,' her mum said softly. 'It's okay.'

But it *wasn't* okay. Ellie swallowed back the huge stone in her throat. 'He was with someone. I've only seen her once, but I think it was that woman he's training. He was holding her hand. She started crying, and he was looking at her like... Is he going to leave us, Mum?' she asked, her voice small.

'Oh, Ellie.' Her mum wrapped her arms around her and pulled her back to her. 'Why have you been bottling all this up? Why didn't you talk to me?'

'She's trying to take him away from us, isn't she?' Ellie cried into her shoulder.

'It's all right, sweetheart.' Her mum stroked her hair soothingly. 'It's all right,' she murmured. 'She's not going to take him away from you. I won't let her.'

Ellie heard her mum's tone harden and felt a little better. 'Promise?' she asked tremulously.

TWENTY-THREE

MADDIE

'I promise.' Forcing back the turmoil of raw emotion roiling inside me as I try to process what she's just told me, I squeeze Ellie close. I want to scream. I can't do this. I just *can't*. I knew he was having an affair, and who with. I didn't need the knowledge that Ellie, his own *daughter*, had seen them together to confirm it. His constant late arrivals, his excuses, along with those damn messages, was enough. Cole, a man who never allows his emotions to rule his head, is giving in to his most basic instinct. My heart constricts excruciatingly as I acknowledge it would have to be more than the thrill of illicit sex that attracted him, that he must actually love her if he's prepared to destroy his children's lives for her. Ellie is distraught, frightened. My anger intensifies, hardening to hatred as I imagine the bewilderment my boys will feel as their safe world crumbles around them. I felt so guilty questioning him after his father's death, a tiny part of me imagining that he might have done the unthinkable. If he could do this, though, something I didn't think he had in him, what else might he be capable of?

'It's okay, sweetheart,' I whisper, holding my shaking daughter tight.

Ellie draws in another tremulous breath. 'You need to tell him,' she murmurs, pulling back to look up at me. 'You need to make him stop seeing her.'

I have no idea how to respond. How can I tell her that if he loves this woman, no ultimatum in the world can make him fall out of love with her?

'You have to, Mum, or *I* will,' she seethes, her eyes sparking fury. 'He can't do this to you. To us. *She* can't.'

'I will talk to him, Ellie,' I assure her, though I have no idea how or when, with all that's going on. 'He's with his mum right now, but...' I stop, glancing towards the hall as someone knocks on the front door.

'Tonight?' Ellie asks, frowning uncertainly.

Ignoring the door, I look hesitantly back at her. 'I think I should see how things are first,' I answer cautiously. 'It's been a stressful day. It might be quite late when he—'

Ellie pulls sharply away. 'Oh well, that's a given, isn't it?' she growls. 'When is he ever *not* late?'

'Ellie...' I try to close the gap that's sprung up between us, but Ellie's arms are now folded defensively across her chest. 'He's just lost his father,' I remind her. 'He'll be exhausted and emotional. It's not a conversation we can have tonight.'

'He doesn't give a shit about his father,' Ellie retaliates. 'He doesn't give a shit about you either.'

My heart drops. She's right. He can't care if he's doing this. *If* he is. Even now, I'm holding on to the hope that he's not. 'Ellie, stop. You need to calm down.' I say shakily.

'And you need to stop looking for excuses to bury your head in the sand.' She eyes me furiously. 'He *doesn't* care about his father. You *know* he doesn't. He'll just use his death as another excuse to...' She stops, her gaze swivelling towards the kitchen doorway, where Lucas is standing, his gaze travelling cautiously between us.

'There's some eyeballs looking through the letter box,' he murmurs.

Swapping worried glances with Ellie, I hurry past him to the hall, where I find Jayden lifting the flap, about to peer back through it. 'Jayden,' I hiss, gesturing him away. 'Kitchen,' I instruct, catching hold of him as he comes towards me and steering him that way. Then, bracing myself as I worry who it might be, I reach to pull the door open.

Relief sweeps through me when I find Kelsey standing on the doorstep with her back to me and her phone pressed to her ear.

'Mads.' She swings around, looking as relieved as I feel. 'I've been trying to call you. I was getting worried about you. Are you all right?'

'I'm fine.' I stand aside to let her pass. 'Sorry, my phone's in my bag. The battery must be dead.' I follow her through to the kitchen.

Kelsey bends to hug the boys and then delves into her bag, extracting two Kinder Surprise eggs and presenting one each to Jayden and Lucas, to their delight.

'Can we open them now, Auntie Kelsey?' Lucas asks, looking hopefully up at her.

'You'll need to check with your mum,' Kelsey tells him, giving his hair a ruffle.

The boys' gazes swing simultaneously to me. 'Can we?'

'I'll take them up and keep an eye on them,' Ellie offers, clearly wanting to give Kelsey and me some space.

'Thanks, Ellie.' I smile gratefully.

Kelsey moves to give her a hug. 'Are you doing okay?' she asks, easing back to scan her eyes carefully.

'Not great,' Ellie answers with a despondent shrug.

My heart squeezes. I watch as she takes hold of the boys' hands and walks glumly past me.

'She's upset, isn't she?' Kelsey sighs sympathetically as they disappear up the stairs. 'Was she close to her grandfather?'

'No. It's shaken her, obviously, but it's not that,' I reply. 'She told me. About Cole. What she saw.'

'Ah.' Kelsey nods. 'Bound to be upset, then. She dotes on him, doesn't she, poor thing?'

'I do know that, Kelsey,' I respond irritably, and regret it immediately. She's come here out of concern for me, and I bite her head off. 'I'm sorry.' I blow out a breath. 'I didn't mean to snap. I just...'

'Feel crushed,' she finishes, coming across to squeeze me into a hug. 'Don't worry, I understand. What I don't understand is what on earth has got into Cole. I can't believe he wouldn't consider the effect all this would have on the children, let alone on you. I'm sorry.' She apologises in turn. 'That doesn't help much, does it? Would you like me to make some tea or coffee?' she asks kindly.

'Coffee. Thanks.' I muster up a smile.

'Was she all right when she got back?' Kelsey asks as she goes across to the kettle. 'She was in a bit of a state when she arrived at my house. She'd had an awful lot to drink, Mads. I was scared for her, in all honesty.'

'I gather.' I sigh wretchedly. 'I wish she'd felt able to talk to me.'

'She probably didn't know how to,' Kelsey offers in Ellie's defence. 'It's a huge dilemma for someone her age, after all, whether to tell her mum... Well, you know.'

'She's clearly been carrying it around inside her.' I feel cold suddenly to my bones. 'It certainly explains why she's been behaving so oddly around Cole.'

'Do you think maybe you should give yourself some space?' Kelsey asks as she makes the coffee. 'Take some time and go to your mother's for a while?'

'It's an idea.' I consider it. I'd like nothing better than to touch base with my mum, but, 'I can't just take off, though, Kelsey. The children have school and Ellie has her uni course. I think Cole might stay with his mum for a while anyway, but, even so, I can't just go. I have to at least try to talk things through with him.'

'I'm not suggesting you leave permanently,' she clarifies. 'He might come to his senses. You never know, there might even be an innocent explanation, though I think your instinct is telling you otherwise. You owe it to the kids to get them away from all of this, though. Especially Ellie. She needs some space to heal. You all do.' She turns around, a mug of coffee in each hand – and the caring smile she's wearing slides from her face.

'Finished?' Cole says from the doorway.

'Cole.' Kelsey laughs nervously. 'I didn't see you standing there.'

'Clearly.' My husband simply studies her. 'You were just leaving, weren't you?'

Kelsey looks from him to me, frowning in confusion. 'No.'

'I think you were,' he says quietly. His eyes drilling into hers are as dark as thunder, I note, and my stomach tightens with wary trepidation.

Kelsey's expression hardens. 'And *I* think that's up to Maddie, don't you?'

'Now!' Cole yells, causing her to jolt.

Shakily, Kelsey turns to place the mugs down, then turns back. 'And what about your *wife*, Cole?' she asks, eyeing him defiantly. 'Does she not have any say in the matter?'

His eyes flint-edged, dangerous, he studies her for another blood-freezing second, and then he moves, striding across to the island picking up her bag and shoving it at her. 'Get the fuck *out* of here,' he seethes.

My heart slams against my chest. 'Cole, stop!' Seeing he's

about to take hold of her arm, I fly across to place myself bodily between them. 'Don't you *dare*,' I warn him.

Cole's jaw clenches as he stares past me at Kelsey. 'Just go,' he grates, snapping his gaze away and turning to the hall.

My heart sinks as I see Ellie standing in the doorway.

TWENTY-FOUR

'It's all right. Not your fault.' Kelsey assures me as I go with her to the front door.

She swipes her hair from her face, the tears from her cheeks, and fumbles for the door latch. 'Call me,' she whispers, her gaze darting to the kitchen door as she turns to give me a hug, and it's obvious she's scared for me.

As she eases away, her gaze travels to Ellie, who's sitting at the foot of the stairs, fiddling with the 'I Love You Unconditionally' charm that Cole bought for her Pandora bracelet. With her face drained of colour, she looks bereft – and so young suddenly I want to hold her and never let go of her.

'You know where I am,' Kelsey tells her, clearly offering my daughter the space she thinks she needs. Is she right? Should I just pack some things, take the kids and go?

Kelsey looks back to me. 'Speak later,' she says, eyeing me worriedly as she leaves.

Once the door's closed behind her, I turn to Ellie, who stands to face me, her eyes searching mine as if looking for reassurance, and it grows painfully obvious to me that I can't let this situation go on.

As I struggle for a way to offer her that reassurance, she turns away and heads to the kitchen. Scared of what she might be about to say, of how Cole might react, I follow her. He's just suffered a bereavement. He will have so many mixed emotions, anger undoubtedly being his overriding emotion, given his relationship with his father, but if he can't contain it around our children, then one of us does have to go.

Ellie casts him a scathing glance as she walks across the kitchen to the fridge. 'I'm going up to my room,' she mumbles to no one in particular as she extracts a Coke, then spins around to head back to the hall.

'Ellie, hold on.' Cole starts towards her. 'Please don't go off like this. I didn't mean to—'

'You two need to talk.' She cuts him short.

He breathes in and studies the ceiling. 'Will you at least let me apologise?' he asks, looking back at her.

Ellie stops and faces him. 'For?' she asks, her eyes guarded.

Cole drags a hand over his neck. 'Losing my temper,' he says regretfully. 'It's been a stressful day, and then finding Kelsey here, overhearing what she was saying to your mum, I... She appeared to be trying to stir up trouble between us,' he says wearily. 'I overreacted. I'm sorry.'

Ellie furrows her brow. 'Right, so the problems you two are having are all Kelsey's fault then?'

'No, that's not what I meant,' Cole answers with a frustrated sigh. 'I suppose she's right not to be impressed with me, to a degree. With the pressure at the hospital, I haven't been home as much as I would like to be, but it's actually between your mum and me and absolutely nothing to do with Kelsey.'

'I see.' Ellie nods slowly. 'So you're apologising for the way you treated Kelsey, but not for the way you're treating Mum?'

Cole looks at her uncertainly.

'For the fact that you're cheating on her,' she clarifies bluntly.

My heart jolts.

Cole's face has drained of all colour. 'That's not true, Ellie,' he responds shakily. 'I have no idea where this is coming from, but I would never do that.'

'*Liar*,' Ellie growls, facing him full-on.

Closing his eyes, Cole presses his thumb hard against his forehead, then looks back at her. 'Who told you this?'

Ellie doesn't answer but continues to stare defiantly at him.

'It's not true,' he states emphatically. 'Whatever anyone's told you, it's wrong.'

'Liar!' Ellie repeats furiously. 'I *saw* you!'

Slowly, as if trying to comprehend, Cole shakes his head. I see the shocked bewilderment in his eyes as his gaze swivels to mine. Also fear – and my blood freezes. 'When?' he asks, his voice less strident. 'Where?'

Wrapping her arms tightly around herself, Ellie drops her gaze.

'For Christ's sake, Ellie, *when* did you see me?' Cole barks – and Ellie flinches. Staring at him in confused disbelief, she stumbles away from him, and then whirls around and races to the kitchen door.

'Ellie, wait.' I move towards her, try to catch hold of her, but she shrugs me off.

'*Dammit!*' Cursing, Cole goes after her to the hall. 'Answer me, Ellie!' he shouts as she flies up the stairs.

'Cole, leave her,' I warn him, a short step behind him.

His gaze flicking to mine, he hesitates briefly at the bottom of the stairs, and then goes up after her. '*Did* you see me, Ellie?' he asks tightly as he reaches the landing. 'Or is someone filling your head with this rubbish?'

Grinding to a halt outside her bedroom door, Ellie whirls around. 'I'm not the liar here, *Dad*,' she seethes, her fists clenched at her sides and her face white with anger. 'Yes, I saw you. I was in Joe's Bar. But that's kind of the point, isn't it? You were so busy with her, *you* didn't see *me*.' Poking herself in the chest, she eyes him with sheer contempt, then shoves her bedroom door open, strides inside and slams it shut behind her.

'Ellie,' Cole calls shakily through it, 'please open the door.'

'You don't see Mum either,' she yells. 'Or you would realise what you're throwing away!'

Cole doesn't respond. He's completely motionless for a second. Then, 'It's not true,' he says, his face ashen as he turns to face me. 'Whatever she thought she saw, it wasn't how it looked.'

My heart splinters inside me as he comes out with the classic cliché, each piece piercing my chest like a knife. 'No, Cole, it never is, is it?' My throat closing, I wrench my gaze away from him and head towards the main bedroom. I stop short as I hear a plaintive voice behind me. 'Daddy, what's wrong?'

Lucas. Spinning around, I see Cole crouching to talk to him. 'Nothing,' he says throatily, beckoning to Jayden, who's hovering at their bedroom door. 'It's just a silly argument.' Looking between them, he attempts a reassuring smile.

'Are you and Ellie not friends any more?' Jayden asks.

Cole draws in a sharp breath. 'God, yes, of course we are. Don't worry, we'll figure it out.'

Lucas studies him for a long second, then reaches out to brush his cheek gently with his fingertips. 'Why are your eyes leaking, Daddy?' he asks, his voice a worried whisper.

TWENTY-FIVE

After promising the boys that everything's going to be fine, promises I pray are not hollow, I finally manage to settle them down, then brace myself to go and talk to Cole. I can't leave it. He seems like a different man, angry and defensive. Aggressive. I've never seen him like that before. I have to give him a chance to explain, but I can't allow our children to be affected any further by all of this. Whether we can stay under the same roof very much depends on what he has to say.

Stepping out onto the landing, I close the boys' bedroom door quietly behind me, then pause as I hear Ellie's phone ringing from her room. Thinking it might be Kelsey calling to check on her, I can't help but feel hurt. My daughter's refusing to talk to me, snapping, 'Go away,' when I tapped on her door. That she feels she can talk to Kelsey is almost breaking what's left of me.

Feeling guilty and helpless in turn, I stay where I am. I shouldn't be eavesdropping, but I can't be locked out of any conversation Ellie is having with Kelsey. I'm taken aback when I realise it's actually Cole who's calling her, from our bedroom. 'Ellie, please listen to me,' I hear him say emotionally. 'You don't have to say anything, but please let me explain. I won't lie to you, I promise.'

There's a pause, and I'm sure Ellie must have cut the call. I realise she hasn't when Cole continues, 'You know who the woman I was with is, right?'

Ellie doesn't respond.

'It was Hannah Lee, the doctor I'm training,' Cole confirms anyway, and the knot of fear tightens inside me.

Again he pauses. Still Ellie says nothing.

'This is possibly going to sound like a lie, but it's the truth, Ellie. I swear it is.' He pushes on. 'She was struggling with some personal issues. She'd just heard that her mother had died. She doesn't have anyone else, no relatives here, no partner or husband. She was upset because she won't be able to go home for the funeral. She says her parents gave up everything to put her through medical school, that her mother, in particular, was so proud of her achieving so much.'

There's another long pause, then finally Ellie speaks. '*Is* that the truth?' she asks.

'It's the truth,' Cole says, his voice flooding with relief. 'She was considering going anyway. As her family's in China it would mean she would be gone a while, though, which might mean her training would be disrupted, and that would be a shame as the trust suggested there might be an opening coming up for her.'

'What did you tell her?' Ellie asks.

'That I thought she would regret it for the rest of her life if she didn't go,' Cole says. 'I said I would speak to the executives of the trust on her behalf.'

'So she will go?' Ellie asks.

'I hope so, yes.'

'Good,' she says.

'I should go and speak to your mum,' Cole says, then hesitates. 'I just need you to know I love you, Ellie,' he adds softly.

'More than my life. I would never knowingly do anything to hurt you. I love your mum, too. I do see her. I see how much she supports me, all of us. I wouldn't know how to be without her. I wouldn't want to be.'

Ellie appears to consider. Then, 'Okay,' she replies, her voice tremulous, and my emotions collide. I know he would die before deliberately hurting his children, but still suspicion gnaws away at me. He's just explained his reasons for being in a bar with a woman, holding her hand. It doesn't explain away the messages, though. The knot in my stomach twists itself tighter as I recall them. *Are you sure your husband is where he says he is tonight? Do you realise your husband is planning to kill you? You need to tell her. You have no choice. Do it, Cole.* It doesn't explain away the phone call. *He's lying. Be careful.* The warning whispers insidiously in my head.

When I go to our room, I find Cole sitting on the bed, his head buried in his hands. Looking up as he senses me, he drags an arm quickly across his face and gets to his feet. He doesn't speak, but scans my eyes nervously, as if trying to read what's going through my mind. I wish I could tell him, scream and shout at him, demand to see his phone, which if he has nothing to hide he won't object to. I can't, not yet. I won't instigate an argument, not in front of our children. 'How's your mum?' I ask instead, postponing the confrontation we inevitably have to have – for now.

His expression changes to one of marginal relief – because I don't appear to be about to scream and shout, I suppose. 'Not good, obviously,' he says. 'Her neighbour's staying with her tonight. I said I would be there first thing tomorrow. I need to start helping her sort her affairs out, talk about the funeral arrangements, although we can't set a date until the body's released, obviously.'

I look him over, worried for him despite everything. 'There's going to be an inquest, then?'

'I imagine so, yes.' He sighs. 'The coroner will want to assess whether action could be taken to prevent future deaths.'

A conclusion that might be reached, I realise, if it's deemed there was a fundamental error in the procedure being carried out, which it might well be if this Hannah Lee, who he appears to think so highly of, repeats what I heard her telling Alex. Aware that it wouldn't be helpful to comment, I simply nod.

'I didn't kill him, Maddie. You have to believe me,' he says, his voice ragged. 'Trust me, if I'd wanted to get back at him for a fraction of the cruelty he's dished out, I would have made sure he lived – minus his dignity.'

A chill prickles my skin as I assume that by that he means he would have ensured his father had an impaired quality of life. That he has it in him to even entertain such a thought frightens me. 'I think that might have had more of an impact on your mother, though,' I point out, eyeing him carefully. 'Don't you?'

Cole closes his eyes. 'I know.' He nods and looks back at me. 'I wouldn't be capable anyway. To do that I would have to be like him, someone who enjoys making the people he's supposed to love suffer, for whatever warped reason.' He laughs with a mixture of scorn and hurt, and I can't help but feel for him, for the childhood innocence lost, for the young man growing up who I know suffered horrendously.

'I could go and see her,' I offer. 'When I'm not working. Take Ellie and the boys over. It might help take her mind off things, at least for a while.'

He looks surprised. 'That would be great,' he says with an appreciative smile.

I answer with a small nod. 'I should go and check on Ellie.'

'Maddie.' He stops me as I head back to the landing. 'I'm sorry.'

I turn back, interested to hear what it is exactly he's apologising for.

'About the way I reacted,' he clarifies. 'It's no excuse, I know, but my emotions have been all over the place. I had no idea that Ellie... It makes more sense now why you were so freaked out by the messages, but why didn't you just tell me she'd seen me?'

I study him cautiously, questions immediately pinging through my mind. Yes, his emotions have been swinging wildly, but they were doing that before his father died. Is he using his death to cover that fact? Using what Ellie revealed to dismiss messages that were worrying enough to freak anyone out?

'I didn't know,' I answer. 'Not until recently.'

He tugs in a breath. 'I see,' he says quietly. 'I spoke to her, you might have gathered. Explained. Tried to. She's clearly imagining I've been elsewhere when I've been at the hospital. I'll try to get back more. Maybe we could all...' He stops as his phone rings.

I watch warily as, a flicker of irritation crossing his face, he picks it up and checks it. 'Sorry, I should get this,' he says, glancing quickly to me and then turning away. 'It's Alex.'

TWENTY-SIX

His eyes were guarded before he turned away. Why would that be? And why would he turn away to take a call from his anaesthetist? *Can you not see that I can see?* I feel like shaking him. Begging him to stop all of this and go back to being the man he used to be. He's crushing me. Surely he must realise that?

My heart stalled in my chest, I listen from the landing, trying to glean who it actually is calling him. He doesn't speak for what seems like an eternity. Then, 'That wouldn't be a good idea,' he says, clearly agitated. 'I'm on my way.'

Hearing him coming towards the door, I go quickly to the airing cupboard, extracting a towel I don't need. He looks distracted as he emerges from the bedroom.

'Problem?' I ask.

'A road traffic accident,' he says. 'There are no available surgeons, so they're talking about transferring a patient with a blunt-force head trauma to Birmingham Children's Hospital. I don't think she'll make it.'

'Oh no.' I look at him aghast. 'You should go.'

He scans my eyes, indecision now in his, and I wonder whether he's feeling guilty, or whether he's assessing how gullible I am, how much he can get away with. 'Are you sure?' he asks. 'It's not great timing, is it?'

'Go.' Squeezing the word past the hard lump in my throat, I stand aside to let him pass.

'I'll be back as soon as I can,' he says, heading to the stairs and hurrying down them.

'Make sure to drive carefully,' I call after him.

I wait for the front door to close, then go to Ellie's room. I don't want to bring her into this, but there's no one else I can ask to watch the boys at short notice, apart from Kelsey. After what happened this evening, though, I can't imagine she would be in a rush to come back here.

I'm poised to knock on Ellie's door when she opens it. 'I heard,' she says before I can speak. 'Do you need me to stay with the boys?'

She's gathered that I don't trust him to be going where he says he is, and I'm grateful for her intuitiveness. Also deeply concerned for her. I can't cover for Cole if I find conclusive proof he's lying to me. I won't lie to her. 'Thanks.' I smile tremulously and squeeze her into a hug.

She squeezes me back hard. '*You* make sure to drive carefully,' she tells me, her forehead creased into a worried frown as she eases away.

'I will.' I swallow back a lump of emotion, then hurry down the stairs. He'll be long gone by now, so I can't follow him. My only option is to go to the hospital. And if he's not there, will I challenge him when he comes home? I don't know. I'm not sure I can contain my anger enough not to. If I do, though, and he lies, how will I contain my anger then?

Grabbing my bag and keys, I fumble the front door open and race to my car. After plugging my phone in to charge and starting the engine, I attempt to slow my erratic heartbeat and pull off the drive. I can't believe I'm doing this, following my husband for what I imagine is some sordid sex tryst. I've never doubted him before now. He's always been caring and loving, the polar opposite of his father. I trusted him with my heart.

Even as I'm thinking it, wondering how naïve I've been, my hands-free alerts me to a message. Quickly I accept it. *Do you really trust him to be where he says he is?* a monotone voice asks me, and I gasp out a stupefied laugh. She's playing with me. *He* is. I tighten my grip on the wheel. She wants me to catch him in the act. And I intend to. I need to know who this woman he would sacrifice his family for is. I need to find out who my husband is, once and for all.

Twenty minutes later, I arrive at the hospital and, with nerves churning inside me, drive around checking car parks and spaces. I can't see his car parked anywhere. My throat closes, and though I try to fight them back, the tears come anyway, hot, fat tears of hurt and humiliation. Pulling into an empty space, I give myself a moment to compose myself and try to decide what to do. I should probably just go home. If I need to be two parents to my children, I will be. My mum did it for my brother and me. She stayed upright when her world crumbled. If I have half her genes inside me, I can be strong too. I don't feel it, though. Right now, I feel confused and powerless and utterly defeated.

Wiping my wet face, I pull out and swing back towards the exit. Can I really have been so wrong about him, living with him all these years, making three children with him while being completely oblivious to the fact that, underneath his caring facade, he's every bit as cruel as his father? More so if, knowing he had the power to end a man's life, he actually did. *Do you realise your husband is planning to kill you?* The message that sent my world spiralling out of control slams again into my mind. No. It's preposterous. Spouses cheat. It's a fact. I'm painting him as a monster because I'm hurting. *Please don't let him be.*

As I drive around the one-way system, past the main entrance, my stomach lurches. It's there. Cole's car, a white Audi A6 with his personalised number plate, is in one of the emergency spaces at the front of the hospital. It's parked askew, as if he abandoned it in a hurry. My blood pumps, kick-starting my heart into beating again. He wasn't lying. He's here, and he obviously *is* attending an emergency.

Driving past, I pull up in one of the spots just along from the ambulance bays, where I debate for a second and then decide to call him. I know he can't pick up if he's in theatre, but even so, when he doesn't, I ring the A&E desk. I have to know he's in there. I recognise the voice of the nurse who picks up; her soft Irish lilt is unmistakable. 'Tara, hi. It's Maddie,' I say, trying to sound casual. 'Is Cole around?'

'Hi, Maddie. Afraid not. Is everything okay?' she asks.

'Yes, all good,' I assure her. 'I just wanted to check something with him. Is he...' I stop as I hear someone shout, 'Tara, we need you in resus.'

'On my way,' she replies. 'Sorry, Maddie,' she comes back to me, 'got to go. I'll catch up with you soon.'

Frustration bubbles up inside me as she ends the call. I still don't know my husband is where he says he is, not for sure.

TWENTY-SEVEN

COLE

Seeing Kelsey sitting on one of the comfy sofas in the central café area as he walked along the main corridor, Cole slowed his pace. Should he go across to her? She looked up as he debated, staring right at him. Even from where he was standing, he could see the hostility in her eyes. Guessing that, as much as he would like to, he couldn't avoid her, he headed towards her.

'Coffee?' she asked as he stopped directly in front of her. 'The café's closed,' she added, as if he would be unaware of this fact. 'The vending machine stuff's not too bad, though.'

He studied her for a long, cold moment. 'No. Thanks. I'm good,' he answered shortly.

'Debatable,' she replied drolly.

Ignore it. Cole warned himself not to react.

'Well at least sit down if we're going to chat. You're making me feel uncomfortable, standing there glowering down at me.' To Cole's astonishment, she patted the seat next to her.

Was she serious? After all she'd done, she really expected him to sit and have a coffee and a cosy chat with her? 'What is it you want to chat about, precisely, Kelsey?' he asked, feeling jaded to his bones.

She ran her eyes slowly over him, then picked up her coffee cup, took a leisurely sip from it and swirled the dregs around. 'I would have thought that was obvious,' she said, looking back at him, her dark hazel eyes as bitter as the black coffee she was drinking.

'It's not,' he said, a toxic mix of anger and frustration simmering inside him. 'Enlighten me.'

Kelsey placed her cup back down on the table in front of her, twirling it around, taking her time, apparently enjoying the game she was playing. A dangerous game. Did she realise, Cole wondered, with his marriage under threat, his competence as a surgeon possibly about to be questioned, just how dangerous?

'Actually, don't bother,' he said, turning away. 'I have more important things to do.'

'You have to stop seeing her,' she blurted.

Cole turned back. 'Who?' he asked, eyeing her curiously.

'You know damn well who.' Kelsey's eyes narrowed to icy slits. 'Your little fucking protégée,' she hissed. 'It's obvious she's fangirling you. Hoping that sucking up to your ego and opening her legs will open up doors for her.'

Cole looked her over, hard pushed to hide his disgust. Now he understood why Ellie had been so distraught. It was obviously Kelsey, the woman his wife trusted as a friend, who'd filled her head with all this, careless of the fact that she was just seventeen years old. What perverse kick was she getting out of trying to alienate him from his daughter? 'Really?' He smiled sardonically. 'Thanks for the heads-up. I'll make sure to be aware of it.'

'Ha.' She spat out a scornful laugh. 'As if you're not aware. I've seen the way you look at her, smiling encouragingly, as if she needs any bloody encouragement. I've seen the way she looks at you, blinking her big brown doe eyes at you,' she went on, hissing venom.

He shook his head in despair, wondering what it was

Maddie saw in her, a woman who would be so openly vile about someone who'd done her no harm.

'The whole hospital can see it,' she fumed, her eyes sparking fire.

Cole dragged his gaze away. 'I'm leaving,' he said. 'Don't choke on your coffee, will you?'

'Maddie knows.' She stopped him dead in his tracks.

He looked sharply back at her. 'Knows what?'

Kelsey's mouth curved into a laconic smile. 'I think you know the answer to that too.' She eyed him with semi-amusement.

Cole felt his jaw clench. He didn't speak. He couldn't trust himself to. He simply stared at her.

'Don't you think it's about time you showed her a modicum of respect and came clean with her?' she went on, obviously goading him to react. 'It's going to end very messily if you don't. Your children will be stuck in the middle of it, remember? You don't want to end up traumatising them further, do you?'

Cole's anger tightened like a hard fist inside him. 'I have *never* cheated on my wife,' he seethed, eyeing her steadily.

'Bullshit,' Kelsey sneered. 'You're as guilty as sin. You *know* you are.'

Biting back his fury, he continued to stare at her. Her gaze didn't flinch, until he moved towards her – making sure as he did not to appear threatening in this public space where anything he did might be witnessed. It was enough. She retreated as he sat down next to her.

Clasping his hands in front of him, he looked down at them for a long moment, then picked up her coffee cup and examined it as if it were infinitely interesting.

Her pupils dilated as he looked back at her. She was scared. She should be. Locking his gaze hard on hers, he studied her coldly for a moment longer, and then slowly crushed the cup in his fist. 'It has to stop, Kelsey. Your obsession with me, your determination to ruin my marriage, it has to stop. Now.' His eyes never left hers as, careless of the dregs that dripped from it, he dropped the cup into her lap. 'Or this will most definitely end messily.'

TWENTY-EIGHT

MADDIE

I feigned sleep when I heard Cole come into the bedroom last night. Not wanting to call the hospital again for fear of alerting him to the fact that I was checking up on him, I eventually texted him, asking how it was going. *Good*, he replied after a while. *Shattered. Back soon.* He arrived two hours later, and I had no idea how to talk to him without looking for the lies in his eyes. After lying awake watching the digits on the clock click over, I finally drifted into a fitful sleep, only to be jolted awake by a phone alert. Desperately not wanting to check it, but knowing I had to, I slipped out of bed and crept down to the kitchen. As I stared at the message I'd received – *Do you still trust him?* – sent by someone who's clearly playing psychological games with me, a jolt of pure rage shot through me.

When Cole spoke behind me, wondering if there was a problem, I quickly blanked my phone and told him I'd had a text from the agency asking me to cover a shift as someone was off sick. He didn't question me, even offering to take the twins to school before going off to his mother's. I didn't mention which hospital I would be covering at. It apparently didn't occur to him that it might be his. Because he had nothing to hide and was therefore unconcerned? If only I could believe that.

As I walk along the hospital corridor towards the neurosurgical department, hoping to catch Alex before his first procedure, my anger intensifies. Whoever is sending these messages is drip-feeding me poison in order to get me to push the button that will blow my marriage apart. I won't allow them to. Aside from the fact that he's *my* husband, not hers, with my children's futures to consider, the stakes are too high. I will fight. If I give up, it will be because *I've* decided to.

Going onto the surgical ward, I find Alex is with a patient and I wait for him to finish. Minutes later, he appears from behind the curtain, smiling reassuringly back at his patient. His smile widens when he sees me. 'Hey, how are you?' he asks, walking across to me.

'Good,' I lie. 'Juggling, as usual. You?'

'Hectic, as usual.' He rolls his eyes semi-amusedly. 'Apart from that, fine. So are you working here today? We could have a quick coffee and a catch-up later, if you fancy it?'

'I'd love to, but I'm at the private hospital,' I lie again, out of necessity. A quick check of the rota on the children's ward will soon reveal I'm not covering here.

Alex looks disappointed and, sensing he's lonely, I feel for him. He's had a few relationships since we dated years ago, one long-term relationship that ended six or so months back, which must have been quite traumatic considering they had to sell the property they'd bought together. He moved back to his mother's cottage, and stayed there after his mother sadly passed away, which must also have been devastating for him. Situated on the Grand Union Canal just outside a remote little village, I gather that the old, beamed cottage is still as run-down as it was when we were together. He must be so isolated stuck out in the middle of nowhere. When I subtly asked him why the relationship had broken down, he said she'd accused him of being a commitment-phobe, meaning they'd discussed marriage and presumably Alex wasn't keen. 'And are you?' I asked him, recalling why we'd split up, which did indicate he might struggle to commit.

'My heart belongs to another,' he joked, and gave me a mischievous wink.

I glance at him now, noting his glum expression, and decide to make a bit more of an effort to be a friend to him. 'I'll catch up with you next time I'm here,' I promise, as we walk on. 'I've just swung by to pick up Cole's jacket. He forgot it, thinks he might have left it in the staff room.'

'I'm not surprised,' Alex says. 'It was pretty full-on last night.'

'I gathered.' Relief surges through me as I realise that although I don't know what his movements were the whole time Cole was out last night, he was definitely here. *Is* he having an affair? The sender of those messages is malicious, clearly, but might whoever it is be doing it out of resentment or anger? A colleague who feels Cole has wronged them in some way? A patient or relative who thinks he's somehow been neglectful? It's possible. 'Also a late one.' I fish a little, hoping I don't sound too obvious. 'He was shattered when he finally got home.'

Alex glances at me. I note the frown crossing his face and my heart falters. 'I imagine he would have been.' He nods. 'Especially after losing his father the way he did. How's he doing? I did ask him, but you know how stoical he can be.'

Oh, how I do. 'Upset, despite the relationship he had with him,' I confide, aware that Alex knows how toxic their relationship was. 'He's with his mum today.'

'That's good.' Alex nods thoughtfully again. 'I just hope he takes the time out he's entitled to. I'm guessing that with so much going on here at the hospital, though, he probably won't.'

'No.' I hesitate, wondering whether to broach the subject of his father's procedure, and decide I have to. 'He's also feeling guilty. As I suppose he's bound to be, considering the circumstances around Robert's death.'

Alex draws in a breath. 'He shouldn't be. He was emotional in theatre, as he was bound to be, but the old man would have died anyway.' He shrugs and reaches for the ward door, holding it open to allow me through it before him.

Is he saying that Cole might have hesitated during the procedure, as Hannah Lee suggested he had? How do I question him without sounding as if I'm doubting my husband?

'How's the seven-year-old boy?' I ask instead. 'The one with the cancerous spinal tumour,' I remind him, as he looks blank, sending a ripple of apprehension through me. 'You were after Cole's advice, I think. You texted him on Saturday and asked him to drop by the hospital.' I look at him expectantly.

Alex knits his forehead. 'Er, fine,' he says, glancing away. 'He's doing well. Should be transferred from ITU soon.'

'Good.' I nod. The child was definitely assessed urgently for surgery on Saturday – I've checked. From Alex's reaction, though, I'm doubting that Cole was part of that assessment.

'I should crack on,' he says, coming to a halt near the operating theatres. 'I need to get ready for my first patient. Take care, Maddie, and give my best to Cole's mother.'

'I will,' I assure him. 'You too.'

He hesitates. 'Maddie, if there's ever anything you want to talk about...' He trails off as, hearing my phone ping, I reach to scramble it from my pocket.

Holding my breath, I check it, then exhale in relief when I find it's just a routine reminder from my dentist.

'Everything okay?' Alex asks, clearly having noted my unease.

'Fine,' I lie, and manage a small smile. 'Just a routine thing.'

Another frown crosses his face, as if he's not quite

convinced, and then he nods. 'You know where I am if you want to chat. Any time,' he says, his eyes lingering on mine for a second before he turns to go.

Watching him push through the swing doors, I feel more confused than ever. *Did* Cole hasten his father's death? Guilt twists afresh inside me as I recall his expression when he suspected I thought so. He looked as if I'd plunged a knife through his heart. I still don't know. I don't know for certain that he's having an affair, even with the vitriolic messages being sent to me. What do I do? Can I trust Alex enough to confide in him? From his reaction just now, I'm sure he knows something.

My emotions see-sawing, I turn to head back towards the main entrance. Then stop, my heart jarring, as I see the woman I suspect my husband to be having an affair with hurrying towards me. Breathing deeply, I take my courage in my hands and sidestep in front of her. Hannah Lee looks preoccupied, and then startled as she sees me. 'Hi.' I smile to put her at her ease. 'I don't think we've met. I'm Maddie.' I extend my hand.

A flicker of confusion crosses her face as she tries to place me.

'Cole's wife,' I enlighten her. Is it my imagination, or is that a flicker of panic I see in her eyes? 'I've heard a lot about you,' I add, interested to see her reaction.

'Really?' She looks flustered and surprised in turn.

'Cole's quite impressed with you, I gather.' I scrutinise her carefully.

She drops her gaze and reaches to tuck her sleek ebony hair behind her perfect petite ears. 'That's a huge relief,' she says, looking back at me after a pause, during which my suspicion has gone into overdrive. 'He's a good surgeon. A good man, too.'

I widen my eyes at that.

'Some doctors at his level can be a bit superior,' she adds quickly. 'You know, a bit...'

'Full of themselves,' I finish, seeing she's struggling.

'Yes, that.' Her taut body language relaxes a little. 'How is he?' she asks, her Bambi eyes filled with such concern I can see how they could melt a man's heart in an instant.

'Coping. It's not easy for him,' I reply, and try to quash the jealousy squirming inside me. Is my suspicion unfounded? She seems awestruck, yes, but not embarrassed or awkward as a woman standing in front of her lover's wife might.

She nods and sighs. 'No. It's hard losing a parent,' she says. I see a dark cloud skitter across her eyes, and I feel another stab of guilt as I remember what Cole told Ellie about her recent bereavement. Was it true?

I take a breath. 'You recently lost your mother, of course.' I smile sympathetically. 'Cole mentioned it,' I expand when she looks confused. 'I'm sorry.'

'Oh. Right. Thank you,' she mumbles, glancing down as her phone sounds a timely alert. 'I should go.' She nods past me. 'I'm needed in theatre. It was lovely meeting you, Maddie. Please give my best to Cole.'

Giving me a small smile, she carries on past me, leaving me in turmoil. There was nothing in her expression but nervousness, no spark of resentment as I expected to see. She didn't appear to be measuring me up, and that flummoxes me.

With my mind still on Hannah Lee and whether I might be horribly wrong about her, I'm so distracted as I reach the car park I don't notice Cole's car until I'm almost on top of it. But he shouldn't be here. He's supposed to be with his mother. My heart banging a frantic drumbeat against my chest, I spin around and race back to the neurosurgical department. I grind to a halt at the relatives' room, the very same room in which he broke the news of his father's death to his mother – and in which he now has his arm around another woman. Frozen to the spot, I stare in disbelief through the viewing pane, then thrust the handle down and bang the door open.

Cole shoots to his feet, his pretty protégée standing quickly beside him. *I'm needed in theatre*, a little voice in my head mimics. The lying bitch. She's shocked, as she would be. Also upset. I can see that clearly from the tears welling in her deceitful eyes. I recall what Ellie said: *Turning on the tears*. Why? I wonder. Has someone else in her fucking family suddenly dropped dead? Hence her need to fly to my husband for comfort. More likely because now she's met me, she perhaps realises the promises he will undoubtedly have made her might be hollow. He has no feelings, does he? My gaze pivots to him. No guilt. No grief. No compassion. Nothing.

I don't speak. If I did, the anger that is way too close to the surface would explode. Looking him over with utter disdain, I turn and walk out instead.

'Maddie.' I hear him behind me. I keep going. '*Maddie*,' he calls more urgently, catching up with me and grabbing my arm.

I pull away. '*Don't*,' I warn him, my chest heaving with fury.

He steps back as if electrocuted. 'Maddie, what the hell is *wrong* with you?' he asks, obviously alarmed. Because the gullible little worm has turned?

I stare at him, disbelief and humiliation burning inside me. 'How's your mother?' I ask, sure he will be able to read the contempt in my eyes.

He runs his fingers through his hair, stumbles to answer. 'I... didn't go. I rang her. There was an emergency.'

I whirl around and hurry along the corridor.

'Maddie, *wait*.' He doesn't give up, following me, taking hold of my arm again. Without my permission. Does he just take everything he wants? Because he thinks he's entitled? He does have a god complex, doesn't he? Just like his father. 'Please calm down,' he begs. 'You're upset. I get why you would be, but—'

'Upset?' I eye him with absolute incredulity. 'You're a liar, Cole. You've lied to me. You *keep* lying to me.'

'Could you just let me explain?' he asks, his gaze drifting past me to where it seems an audience has gathered to witness his lies. 'I should have let you know, but—'

'Don't come home, Cole,' I say flatly, and walk away.

TWENTY-NINE

ELLIE

Seeing her dad pull up on the driveway, Ellie went to the hall to check her mum was still upstairs in her bedroom, then hurried to the front door to release the latch and let him in. Her mum wouldn't be pleased, but if she didn't want to hear anything he had to say, Ellie herself bloody well did.

'What the hell's going on, Ellie?' her dad asked, his eyes sliding past her to the stairs as he stepped cautiously into the hall.

She gawked at him in astonishment. 'You have to ask?'

He closed his eyes and sighed wearily. 'She told you, then?'

Ellie folded her arms across her chest, majorly unimpressed that he had the nerve to look despairing. Also deathly pale, she noticed, and felt suddenly torn. *Uh-uh.* She quashed any sympathy she absolutely shouldn't have for him. Whatever was happening here was down to him. He'd made his decision. That decision being to cheat on her mum simply because he could. Why not? It was obviously on offer. Was that what Luke Wainwright had done? Taken what was on offer? She'd woken in his bed. She had no idea how she'd even got there, but she'd gone *home* with him. Why hadn't she realised? How could she have been so stupid?

She glanced warily at her dad. He wasn't anything like Luke Wainwright. He would never abuse a woman. Yet he'd abused her mum's trust. He was *lying* to her. Blatantly. 'That you were at the hospital when you told her you were going to Nan's, you mean?' she asked, squeezing back tears of angry frustration.

'I should have texted her.' Her dad kneaded his forehead, indicating that he was stressed. Like it wasn't him creating the stress. Ellie had her real-life psychology project coming up and her head was a complete mess. The twins would probably be screwed up for life, and he was slowly destroying her mum. Where did he get off feeling sorry for himself? 'I meant to,' he went on. 'I got a call. It was urgent and—'

'Oh, right. Of *course* it was,' Ellie snapped over him. 'I mean why else would you be rushing to the hospital to get up close and personal with another woman? *Again.*'

Her dad drew in a tight breath. 'There was a reason, Ellie. She—'

'Save it, Dad.' Ellie turned away. 'It's Mum you need to convince.'

She heard him blow out a frustrated sigh behind her. 'Where is she?' he asked.

'Here,' her mum said before she could answer.

Ellie glanced up to see her descending the stairs. She was clearly making a valiant effort to hold back her tears, undoubtedly for the sake of her children, who apparently her dad seemed not to give a shit about. When had that happened? How could Ellie have had such blind faith in him just because he was her dad?

'Maddie...' His expression at least one of contrition, he stepped towards her as she reached the hall. 'Look, I know you're in no mood to listen, but will you please hear me out?'

Her mum ran her eyes over him, her expression impassive. Her eyes, though, were filled with hurt and disillusionment. 'In here,' she said flatly, leading the way to the kitchen.

'I'll go and check on the twins,' Ellie offered. As they were in their bedroom playing an interactive game with their headsets on, they were probably oblivious to their dad coming home early for once. She guessed her mum would want them to stay that way. Giving her dad an unimpressed glance, she headed for the stairs. He looked crushed at that. Ellie didn't care. Except she did. She wanted to hate him, but she couldn't. There was still a part of her that hoped he would make this all go away and be the dad she'd thought he was. She hated that bitch who was the cause of all this with a vengeance.

Her heart dropped as she climbed the stairs to find the boys sitting on the top step.

'Why's Dad come home early?' Jayden asked, a troubled V creasing his forehead.

Lucas's face was etched with worry. 'Why has Mummy been crying?' he whispered.

'They've had a little argument, that's all.' She went to join them, squishing in the middle of them and wrapping her arms around them. 'You know, like you two sometimes do with kids at school?'

'Will they make friends again?' Jayden asked apprehensively.

Ellie searched his eyes, wide, honest eyes, filled with the innocence of childhood, and had no idea how to answer.

She didn't get a chance to try before she heard her dad's angry voice from the kitchen. 'It was nothing of the *sort*. For Christ's sake, Maddie, will you just *listen* to me? My relationship with Hannah is strictly professional.'

THIRTY

MADDIE

I look my husband over. His eyes are blazing with fury. I would laugh at the absurdity of him expecting me to believe his lies, but for the fact that I feel like weeping. That he's dared raise his voice to me is pushing me beyond any capacity I might have had for forgiveness.

'So you were just comforting her then? Because she was upset? *Again?*' I ask. My tone drips sarcasm but I'm careful to keep my voice low for the sake of our children. It hurts so much that he would come here and lie to me in front of them. He has called me, several times, but I couldn't make myself talk to him. I considered texting him, asking to meet on neutral territory, but then realised how absurd that was too, that I would have to call my own husband and make an appointment with him to discuss his infidelity.

'Yes,' he answers. 'No,' he backtracks, confused, clearly, as to what exactly he was doing with his arm around the woman he's having a strictly professional relationship with. 'I was trying to reassure her.'

'Ah.' I smile scornfully. Avert my gaze. I can't look at him.

'She *was* upset,' Cole goes on, his voice tinged with despair.

I glance back at him, unable to believe that this is the same man I once thought I knew, who I thought knew me, who kissed my tummy so tenderly after I'd had the twins and swore he loved me. There were days after the birth, weeks, where I was lost in a sea of bewildered emotion, overwhelmed, feeling inadequate, overawed with the responsibility of caring for two brand-new, fragile lives. He was there for me, picked me up and glued me back together. He held me. Loved me. Now he's breaking me.

'The *reason* she was upset,' he continues, an impatient edge now to his voice, 'is that apparently there's going to be an internal investigation.'

Around his father's death, I assume he means. I want to feel something for him, but my emotions are frozen solid inside me.

'She's worried it might go to the General Medical Council,' he goes on, 'the effect it might have on her career. She's grieving the loss of her mother and now she feels she can't take time out to go home for her funeral. Obviously she's feeling upset. She turned to me. What was I supposed to do?'

I study him. He looks gutted and guilty in turn and I'm not sure what he wants from me. Sympathy? I can't give him that. I say what I actually feel. 'I don't think I believe you, Cole.'

He closes his eyes. 'Why?' he asks.

'It's too much,' I reply tiredly. 'The comforting. The hand-holding in cosy bars. The lies.'

'What lies?' He frowns, as if he doesn't recall lying to me this very morning.

I say nothing, holding his gaze meaningfully instead. He draws in a breath and blows it out slowly.

'The late nights,' I continue, watching him carefully. 'The *messages*, Cole. I'm careful not to say how many messages I've received. Maybe I consider it some small victory that he might be in doubt about how much I actually know. 'The ones *you* thought I should just ignore.'

He emits a short, surprised laugh. 'Jesus, Maddie, you don't really think there's any truth in messages sent by some bloody crackpot?'

I don't respond. I could show him the message asking me if I *trust him* – which was sent by someone who, crackpot or not, quite obviously knows he's cheating on me – but I simply don't have the energy.

'You do, don't you?' He stares at me in astonishment. 'You think I'm cheating on you, deliberately deceiving you. You actually believe I killed my own father, don't you? What else do you think I'm capable of?' His tone grows angry as he looks at me accusingly. 'Killing *you*, for God's sake?'

You are *killing me*, I want to scream. 'Give me your phone,' I say instead.

Cole laughs disbelievingly. 'You want to check my phone?'

I hold out my hand.

As he continues to stare at me, something behind his eyes shifts, growing darker. 'I think I should leave,' he says, turning abruptly to yank open the kitchen door.

Deep, visceral anger swirls inside me. 'Fine,' I seethe. 'Go! I really don't need to see it. Because you've just confirmed everything I already know.'

Cole turns back. 'There's nothing on my phone I don't want you to see, Maddie,' he says, a telltale tic tugging at his cheek. 'The thing is, you've just confirmed that you don't believe a single word I say.'

'Then show it to her,' Ellie says behind him. 'If you want her to believe you, show it to her.'

'Ellie...' he turns to face her, 'could you please give us some space and—'

'Show her the fucking phone!' she yells, her face rigid with anger.

Cole kneads his forehead. 'I need to get by, please.'

'You're screwing her, you know you are!' Ellie seethes. 'Mum knows you are. Kelsey knows you are. *I* know you are.

You must be seriously sad to throw away your family for some skanky cow who's clearly trying to further her career.'

'Ellie, stop,' Cole says shakily. 'This is ridiculous. Complete rubbish.'

'Is it, Cole?' I ask. 'She had an affair with a consultant while she was doing her final-year neurosurgical training, didn't she? Was it you?' I'm not expecting an answer, but I ask anyway.

His reaction is swift and furious. 'Jesus Christ!' He slams the heel of his hand into the door frame, causing Ellie to jump. 'Will you stop!'

He rounds on me as I take a bewildered step back. 'I am *not* having an affair, for fuck's sake! Not with Hannah. Not with anyone. Why won't you just *listen*.'

'You're lying to me,' I yell back. 'Do you not realise how insulting that is?'

'I'm leaving.' He turns back to the door.

Ellie squares up to him. 'Not until you've shown Mum your phone.'

'Ellie, please... just let me get by.'

She doesn't budge.

'Look, I'm sorry,' he says throatily. 'I know you don't believe I'm not doing any of the things you and your mother imagine I am, but I don't want to argue any more. I think I should go before the boys get upset.'

'They're already upset!' Ellie rages, tears springing from her eyes. 'They hate you! *I* hate you.'

'Christ, Ellie.' Cole goes after her as she flies to the hall. 'Don't do this. Please don't cry.' He attempts to put his arms around her.

'Don't *touch* me.' She struggles, pushing him away.

'Leave her.' I manoeuvre past him, wrap my arms around her and draw her to me. 'You're right, you do need to go.' I lock my gaze icily on his. 'Now, please.'

Cole hesitates, glancing from me to Ellie, looking sick to his soul.

'And don't come back,' I add, and pull Ellie closer.

As the front door closes behind him, Ellie eases away from me and takes a tremulous breath. 'I'm not sure I want to know what you find on it,' she says – and hands me his phone.

THIRTY-ONE

I wasn't sure he would be at his mother's house. I assumed he would be with *her*. He's here, his car parked on the drive – in his father's spot, ironically. Does his mother know, I wonder, that her son appears to be a chip off the same block? I doubt it. Unlike his father, Cole has kept his misogynistic tendencies well hidden. How did this happen? When did my selfless, softly spoken man turn into a selfish, uncaring monster? I can't believe I wouldn't have seen it before now. That I wouldn't have known he was using his charm as a weapon to destroy women's lives, to destroy his children's lives in turn, even after all he suffered as a child himself.

I wonder whether to knock on the door, but I can't bring myself to. If his mother finds out that we've split up, she'll be devastated. She must be wondering why I'm not there for her, though, as I promised to be. As I so badly want to be. I thought she might finally have the relationship with her grandchildren she was denied by the vile man she was married to. Now it seems her son would deny her that too. Does he care about *anyone*?

There were reams of messages on his phone, all sent from

someone called Jack, with a cute puppy-dog profile, no doubt to allay suspicion should I notice messages flash up. Many initially were seemingly innocent: *I'll see you tomorrow* or *We need to meet*, some of which Cole had responded to: *Too busy* or *Talk on the phone*. Then came the threats. *You need to own what you did. Ignoring me isn't going to make this go away, Cole. Call me!* He hadn't responded to either of those, ghosting her, clearly. No wonder she was upset. I smile sardonically.

Face up to your responsibilities! another screamed. Again there was no reply from Cole. My assumption was that they'd spoken on the phone or in person, heatedly, from the tone of the messages. Then followed the one I'd seen: *You need to tell her. You have no choice. Do it, Cole. You know there'll be consequences if you don't.* And another. *Tell her. Do it tomorrow, or I will.* That one was a definite threat, enough I would imagine to cause Cole to break out in a cold sweat. Surprisingly, his reply seemed quite measured. But then he was always that. Calm in a crisis. In control. Or he had been. *We need to talk more*, he'd sent back. *Meet me tomorrow evening.*

OK. She'd responded in seconds. *When and where? XX* My chest burns with anger as I note the two kisses.

The hospital, Cole had suggested, clearly hoping to cover his tracks. And he had seen her, of course. That was the day his father died. Were they both too preoccupied, I wonder, to be paying due diligence to their task? In which case, I can only pray the GMC do find them negligent and for their lives to be ripped as excruciatingly painfully apart as mine has been.

The latest message, which pops in as I'm actually sitting here debating whether to speak to him, strikes fear down to the core of me. *Do not imagine you can continue to ignore me, Cole. I'm warning you, it will be you who suffers if you do. Your family will too.*

She's threatening my *children*? I gasp in astonished disbelief. Oh no. This twisted creature has seriously underestimated me if she imagines I wouldn't tear her apart before allowing her to do that. Fighting back my terror and my tears, I find his mother's landline number. I don't want to call him, but I need him to know that I'm aware what a complete bastard he is. I also need him to know that if he comes anywhere near me or my children without my explicit say-so, I can't promise to be as clinically calm and measured as he clearly is.

Bracing myself, I'm about to call when the front door opens and Cole steps out. I watch as he wipes a hand over his face and approaches his car, his walk no longer the brisk stride it normally is as he heads purposefully to the hospital to perform complicated lifesaving surgeries. He looks like a man defeated.

Nearing the car door, he pauses and glances in my direction, almost as if he can sense me, then turns to face me. From a distance, we hold eye contact for a second, and then he breathes visibly in, bracing himself too, I suspect, before walking towards my car.

I don't climb out. I have no wish to talk to him for any longer than I need to. Instead, I lower my window.

He doesn't speak. He looks as if he wants to, but I guess he's realised there's nothing he can say that I want to hear.

'I thought you might want your phone back.' I hold on to it, curious to see his response.

He glances at it, looking sick to his stomach. I notice as his gaze comes guiltily back to me that his face is paper white, the dark bruises under his eyes more pronounced than ever. He obviously hasn't slept, which makes two of us.

'How are the kids?' He finds his voice after a moment. It's ragged and hoarse, and I feel for him, fleetingly. He looks broken, but he's not half as broken as I am.

I look him over with a mix of incredulity and disdain. 'Do you really have to ask?'

He swallows and closes his eyes. Finally he shakes his head, as if realising his children might just be the slightest bit traumatised.

'They're devastated, obviously,' I answer sharply, making sure he understands the harm he's caused. Will continue to cause. 'They'll never get over this. You *know* they won't.' I eye him furiously. 'Why couldn't you have just admitted you were having an affair and saved them witnessing all of this? Do you not care about them at all?'

'Of course I *care*,' he responds angrily, astonishingly. 'I care about them more than my *life*. I would never...' He stops, presses his thumb and forefinger hard against his forehead. 'For the umpteenth time, I am *not* having an affair. Will you please try to believe me.' He looks unflinchingly back at me.

I want to laugh, loud and long. Were it not for the fact that I'm having to work to control an urge to climb out and slap his face, I might.

'I love *you*, Maddie,' he says earnestly. 'There's no one else. There never will be.'

I force myself not to react. I will *not* allow him to humiliate me further. I won't humiliate myself by crying in front of him. 'Your phone,' I remind him, nodding towards it.

As if on cue, it pings as he reaches for it, and we both freeze. Briefly, his fearful gaze meets mine, and then, as if realising that this could be the final nail in his coffin, he closes his eyes, looking like a man condemned, as he relinquishes his hold on it.

My stomach twists with indecision and ice-cold trepidation and I hesitate. Do I need to see yet another threat, not just to my marriage, but my sanity? Wouldn't simply letting him have the phone communicate far more than words ever could? That I no longer care? Part of me wants to be strong enough to do that, but another part knows I have to discover how deep his cruel deceit runs.

Cursing my trembling hands, I look at the screen, and my

world stops turning. 'So there's no affair?' I glance glacially back at him.

He answers with another defeated shake of his head.

'*Liar!*' Feeling as if he's just reached inside me and ripped my heart from my chest, I thrust the phone at him.

Cole looks as if someone's just punched him as he reads the two words that put the noose around his neck and kick away the steps: *I'm pregnant.*

THIRTY-TWO

'Will Daddy come home soon?' Lucas asks, looking beseechingly up at me as I study the painting he's done at school. This alone is breaking my heart. It's a typical six-year-old's picture, a house with his matchstick family lined up alongside it. His family, though, is minus one: his daddy, and his mummy has pear-shaped tears spilling from her eyes.

I swallow back a hard lump of emotion and crouch down to him. 'I'm not sure, sweetheart.' Smiling to try to reassure him, I reach to brush his unruly fringe from his forehead. 'He's staying with Nana. Remember I told you she's feeling a bit sad because your grandad was poorly and now he's gone to heaven?'

Lucas nods. 'Like we were when our hamster went to heaven?' he asks, looking worried and uncertain – and I hate Cole for doing this to them.

'That's right, sweetheart. That's why Daddy's keeping Nana company.' I give him a quick hug and then straighten up before the tears do spill from my eyes.

'He'll be playing with Hammy in the soft clouds,' Ellie says, glancing at me as she comes into the kitchen.

'So Hammy won't be lonely?' is Lucas's next question, and I feel another part of my heart fracture inside me.

'Exactly,' Ellie answers for me. 'Come on then, little man.' She extends her hand towards him. 'We're all set up.'

She's keeping them occupied with their interactive dance game, and I'm so grateful to her. Despite her own heartbreak, she's showing a level of maturity I didn't realise she was capable of. Mind you, she hasn't yet learned of the immaculate conception Hannah Lee's pregnancy must be. I dread to think how she will react to that. 'You're sure you'll be okay?' I ask her as they head for the kitchen door.

Ellie doesn't reply with one of her usual despairing retorts, telling me that she's not *aged two* or *incapable*. 'We'll be fine,' she says. 'Give Kelsey my love.'

'Thanks.' I smile. I'm actually not going to see Kelsey, and from the curious look Ellie gave me when I said I was, I suspect she knows I'm not, but she didn't pursue it.

Minutes later, with the disco ball rotating and the dance action about to get under way in the lounge, I slip out. Once in the car and on my way, I call Kelsey.

'Hey, you, how's things?' she asks gently.

'Not great,' I answer, and take a huge breath. 'Cole's gone.'

She's quiet for a moment. 'You mean he just left?' she asks, incredulous.

'I asked him to go,' I explain, my heart sinking icily to the pit of my stomach as reality starts to bite. 'I think he was going to leave anyway, but in the end, I told him to.'

'Oh, babe, I'm so sorry.' As Kelsey sympathises, the tears that were perilously close to the surface escape. 'Mind you, after the other night, I don't blame you,' she adds angrily. 'He was way out of order. I can't believe how aggressive he was.'

'It gets worse.' I emit a strangled laugh.

'Worse how?' Her voice is wary.

I take another deep breath. 'She's pregnant. Hannah Lee,

she's having his baby.' My voice quavers. 'There was a message on his phone.'

Clearly stunned, Kelsey doesn't respond for a moment. Then, 'The absolute *bastard,*' she gasps. 'I'm so sorry, Mads. You must be heartbroken. What will you do?'

I wipe my tears away, attempt to pull myself together. 'I'm not sure yet. I'm playing it by ear at the moment. I don't want him back, though, not now. And I don't want him to have contact with the children. At least until he admits what he's done.'

'He's not still denying it, surely?' Kelsey asks, astounded.

'Don't they always,' I reply wearily.

'Bastard,' she repeats. 'Not only does he totally humiliate you, he then insults your intelligence by perpetuating his lies? Where does he get off doing that? God.' She pauses to draw breath. Then, 'Put his stuff outside,' she suggests. 'Preferably in the middle of the road. If you don't, he's bound to use it as an excuse to get back in.'

'I'm not about to let him in,' I assure her.

'I'm not saying you would, but the kids?' Kelsey lets it hang – and I get it.

The first thing he did this morning was ask how the children were, trying to guilt me, I suspect. He doesn't seem to realise how much he's hurt them. In my heart, I don't believe he would use them to gain access to me or the house, but then my heart has clearly been ruling my head, hasn't it? Considering all he's done, he might be capable of anything.

'Oh, and get the locks changed. I would,' she adds.

I blow out a shuddery breath. 'I will. I was going to do that anyway.'

'Do you want me to come over?' she asks kindly.

'No, thanks for offering, Kels. I'm just out grabbing a few things from the supermarket and then I'm going to spend some time watching a film with the boys.' I'm lying, but it's a small lie,

I consider, next to Cole's humongous heartbreaking lies. I love Kelsey and I would like nothing better than for her to come over – I really need a shoulder. Tonight, though, once I get back, I do need to spend some time with the boys, Ellie too. Also, I don't want Kelsey to know where I'm going. She would probably try to dissuade me, but I have to know where it is Cole goes rather than come home to his family. I've no idea why. I'm punishing myself. Kelsey wouldn't be slow to tell me that.

After establishing he's at the hospital, which I assumed he would be, I find his car and then park discreetly in the X-ray car park, where I'll be sure to see him driving towards the exit. I've already decided I won't go into the hospital. I don't want to punish myself quite that much. I don't have to wait long before he leaves, hours earlier than he would have come home. Realising that all we had together – the memories we made, the laughter we shared, the tears we cried over the loss of our babies – meant nothing, my heart weighs impossibly heavier as I wait for him to drive away.

As he goes by, I start my car and pull out after him. I'm not sure why I'm doing this – if I've been reduced to having to spy on my husband then there's no hope for us anyway. In which case, do I really want to see the evidence with my own eyes? Realising how deceitful he's been, though – is still being – I may well need all the information I can gather, in order to protect my children.

Staying well behind him, I'm able to keep track of him despite my mind wandering, imagining where she might live. I picture a plush apartment, maybe in the city centre. I can almost see him, circling her with his arms as they stand on the balcony, looking out over the twinkling skyline, his breath hot on her neck, her face tilting towards him.

I'm surprised when he heads towards the suburbs. I don't know why I would be. It's possible she's renting a house. Maybe she's buying. Maybe Cole is buying a house with her. Nausea churns my stomach as I imagine the scenarios. Him squeezing her hand as she pushes out his baby. Cradling his newborn, promising he would kill to keep him or her safe, just as he did Ellie, then Jayden and Lucas. Does he realise, I wonder, that *I* would kill to keep my children safe? But he didn't *know* she was pregnant, I remind myself. He didn't look pleased when I informed him of the message I'd read on his phone. He was hardly going to, though, was he, in front of me, the wife he's discarding?

With my focus on his tail lights and my mind all over the place, I'm not paying attention to where he's going until I begin to recognise the landmarks. A cold shiver of apprehension crawls over me as he turns a corner into a road I know well.

My heart palpitates wildly as he slows outside a familiar house, stops and turns off his engine. His car door and her front door open simultaneously. He hesitates, and then walks towards her. I'm frozen with shock as I watch Kelsey run to meet him. Nausea roiling inside me as she throws her arms around him, I stifle the moan that comes from my soul and reverse sharply. My husband and my best friend...

THIRTY-THREE
COLE

'Are you fucking *insane*?' Cole grappled to unhook her arms from his neck as she attempted to drag him into her house.

Dropping her arms to her sides, Kelsey looked nonplussed for a second; then, to his amazement, she smiled with delight. 'You've left her,' she said.

Jesus. Cole followed her as she twirled around and headed through her front door. 'You've destroyed my *marriage*.' He stared at her in bewildered incomprehension as she closed the door and turned to face him, still smiling.

'Really?' Losing the smile, she tipped her head to one side. 'I'd say what *you* did was responsible for that, wouldn't you?'

'I didn't *do* anything.' The hard knot of fear he'd carried around since that night tightened inside him.

'Oh, come on, Cole.' She emitted something between a sneer and a laugh. 'Do you really believe that? More to the point, do you think anyone else is going to believe it?'

Her expression now one of contemptuous amusement, she folded her arms under her breasts, in so doing showing off her cleavage to maximum advantage. 'See anything you like?' she purred, clearly noting where his gaze was.

Cole met her eyes. He'd once thought their myriad of browns and gold intriguing. Now they looked like those of a she-wolf mercilessly stalking its prey. His mind went to Maddie, and his guilt ramped up tenfold. He was lying to her, *destroying* her, and it was crucifying him.

Bile rising like rancid acid in his throat, he scrutinised the woman who it seemed would stop at nothing until she'd devoured him. 'You're attractive, Kelsey,' he said, his voice thick with suppressed fury, 'on the surface. What happened, I wonder, that made you so ugly on the inside?'

She emitted a small gasp, her expression now somewhere between shocked and wounded. And then it hardened. 'Men,' she replied icily. 'Specifically you.'

'For Christ's *sake*.' Pressing his fingers hard against his temples, Cole spoke pleadingly. 'What do you want from me, Kelsey? Why are you doing this?'

'Just for you to love me,' she said, actual tears welling in her eyes. 'You did once.'

When? Cole looked at her in astonishment. He'd never said he loved her. The sex had been good, but other than that, their short-lived relationship had been a disaster. He'd seen warning signs when she'd sulked the entire evening because he was late after attending an emergency. When she'd gone apoplectic because he got an emergency call while they were in bed together, he'd realised it was never going to work. He'd been bloody relieved when she'd ended it before he did.

'And then *she* comes along, blinking her big green cat's eyes at you, digging her claws into you,' she went on sourly. 'Then, whoops-a-daisy, she gets pregnant. You know as well as I do that you would never have married her if it wasn't for Ellie. I mean, she's quite pretty, if you like the feral look, but she hasn't got much going for her in the boob or brain department, has she? She doesn't have a clue about you and me.'

'That's *enough*.' Cole moved in an instant, catching hold of her arms, gripping them hard. 'There *is* no you and me. It's all a complete fantasy, and you know it.'

'Oh dear. Is the good doctor getting a teensy bit angry?' Kelsey fluttered her eyelashes coquettishly.

'I'm leaving.' Cole loosened his grip. 'You're delusional, Kelsey. You need help.'

Kelsey ignored that. 'You were angry when we fucked.' She stepped towards him, snaking an arm around his neck. 'It was hot.' She leaned towards him, her lips straying towards his. 'Or were you too drunk to remember? Hmm?'

'Kelsey, you need to stop. *This* needs to stop. Here. Now,' Cole warned her.

'Do you have angry sex with Maddie?' she went on regardless. 'Does she let you play out your fantasies with her?' she asked, her tone goading, her free hand working its way down his torso. 'Or is it just me you lose your inhibitions with? Do you do it with the lights on, Cole? With her?'

As the tip of her tongue brushed his lips, Cole felt something primal explode inside him. 'I said that's *enough*!'

THIRTY-FOUR

MADDIE

I feel as if the air has been sucked from my lungs as I watch them through the opaque glass in the door, their bodies coming together, him taking the lead, pushing her aggressively against the wall. Is that what he likes? What he needs to spice up his sex life, which he obviously finds lacking? Sadomasochism, deriving his pleasure from inflicting pain on women? On *me*? He's torturing me, enjoying my uncertainty, the hold he has over me, because I've borne his children. Because I *loved* him.

Go! screams my pulverised heart. But I can't. Morbidly fascinated, I watch her thread an arm around his neck, pressing her mouth to his, and icy coldness spreads through to the core of me. Up until this very moment, there was the tiniest smidgen of hope inside me that I was wrong. Wrong to make assumptions, to judge Cole. I *was* wrong. Wrong to trust that he was everything he appeared to be, a kind, caring family man. A respected surgeon who deplored the kind of man who would disrespect women, destroy them simply because he could. I thought he loved me. He doesn't love me. Has he ever? I swallow back the sharp shard of glass lodged in my throat.

I should go over there, rap on the door, bang on the glass –

smash the glass – and confront them. Do I really want to? Do I want him to witness my utter humiliation? As much as I try to tell myself the humiliation will be his, it won't be. It will be mine as I turn into the sad woman spurned. Catching a ragged breath in my chest, I swipe at the tears spilling hotly down my cheeks and pull away.

I'm driving blindly, intending to go home and be the glue that holds my fractured family together, when all-consuming anger erupts inside me, and I step on the brake. It doesn't matter what impression my so-called husband has of me. The realisation hits me painfully. He obviously thinks nothing of me anyway. Feels nothing. Breathing in hard, I turn around in a cul-de-sac not far from her house. I'm not going to allow pride to rob me of the satisfaction of seeing his face when he realises I know just how despicable a bastard he is.

Arriving back in her road, I park in an empty space a few cars behind Cole's and try to slow the frenetic beating of my heart. How long will they be? I wonder, nausea rising like thick bile in my throat. I imagine that if they couldn't make it as far as the stairs, it will be no more than sex for gratification's sake, primal thrusting right there against the hall wall.

The climax is going to be bit of a damp squib, isn't it, when I arrive to piss on their parade?

THIRTY-FIVE

KELSEY

'You're bored with her, admit it,' Kelsey murmured close to his ear. 'It's okay. I wouldn't blame you. Sex with her is bound to be predictable after all these years.'

Shit! Easing back, she saw the dark thunder in his eyes and wondered if she might have gone too far.

'Do *not* mention my wife's name *ever* again,' Cole seethed. Clutching hold of her wrist, he wrenched her arm upwards and forced her back against the wall. 'Just don't, Kelsey,' he warned her, pushing his face close to hers. 'If you do, I'll kill you, I swear.'

Kelsey felt her heart jolt. His gaze was intense, definitely murderous, an implicit warning therein. 'All *right*. I'm sorry,' she said, attempting to placate him. 'I didn't mean to disrespect her. I like her. I just wanted you to realise that—'

'*Ever*.' He tightened his grip.

Seeing his unflinching fury, she nodded and lowered her eyes. She'd wanted to rile him. She'd wanted to rouse emotion in him, for him to realise that what they'd had together, could have together – explosive sex, a mutual meeting of bodies and minds – was worth so much more than a marriage that must have gone stale years ago.

'I'm sorry,' she repeated, moving to find his mouth with hers, breathing onto his cheek as he turned his head to avoid her kiss. Desperate to rescue the situation, she tried another tack, allowing her free hand to stray to his most vulnerable parts, which might hopefully distract him from his dark mood.

Cole reacted by digging his fingers hard into her wrist. 'Is this what you want?' he asked, eyeballing her furiously. 'Rough sex. To give in to your most basic carnal desires any time, anywhere. Is that it, Kelsey?'

Her breath caught in her chest. 'I just want what *you* want,' she murmured, her need for him spiking as she noted the conflict of emotions playing across his eyes. It was there, pure, animal lust. She was sure he would give in to it.

'I *want* my family back,' he grated. 'Thanks to you, that's highly unlikely, isn't it?'

'I... don't know,' she answered, feeling hugely turned on yet terrified at the same time.

'I guess I might as well take what's on offer instead.' Smiling scornfully, he pushed himself closer, reached for her top with his free hand, tearing it downwards along with the wispy lace bra she was wearing.

Bastard, Kelsey thought, as he locked his mouth hard over hers, shoving his tongue into her mouth. A low moan escaped her as he moved his hand lower, hitching up the short skirt she was wearing, pushing her underwear roughly aside and forcing her legs apart. Kelsey felt her pelvic muscles contract, her will to resist evaporating as his fingers explored with easy expertise. She was wet already at the thought of what he might have in mind. Anger-fuelled sex was guaranteed to be orgasmic; painful possibly, but highly satisfying. And then she would definitely have him right where she wanted him. In her bed. In her life. He was hers.

She'd told him not to bother coming back on that long-ago night when he'd answered a bloody call on his phone at the crucial moment while they'd been having what she considered pretty spectacular sex, but she hadn't expected him not to. She'd loved him then. She'd always loved him. She knew he felt the same. He would have pursued her had Maddie not snatched him right from under her nose. Once she had him, she'd dug her talons deep into him, getting pregnant before he'd had time to catch his breath. Smart move. Kelsey couldn't blame her. What woman wouldn't? A soon-to-be consultant neurologist with a good pay cheque, Cole was a catch. Encapsulating the dark and broody trope women found so irresistible, he was dangerously good-looking. Dangerous. He didn't want safe little Maddie. He never had. He was with her because of the children, Kelsey was sure. It was *her* he wanted. With his body pushed hard against hers, she could feel how much.

Another moan of ecstasy climbing her throat, she closed her eyes. 'Fuck me. You know you want to,' she whispered, perilously near the peak of arousal. But Cole pulled abruptly away.

'Not that much, Kelsey, trust me,' he said, yanking the front door open.

Stunned to the core as he walked out, Kelsey scrambled to make herself decent and flew after him. '*Bastard*,' she yelled.

Cole didn't so much as flinch. Pressing his key fob, he climbed into his car without even a backward glance.

How dare he? Massaging the welts already forming on her wrist, Kelsey thought fast, snatching up her phone from the hall table and snapping his car with a clear view of his number plate as he drove off. Did he not realise what was at stake? He'd accused her of destroying his marriage. It hadn't taken much, had it? Precious Maddie had no actual proof he was cheating, yet she was ready to put his belongings out on the street. And *he* was grieving the loss of her. He would have a hell of a lot more to grieve over if he pissed Kelsey about. Did he not realise she could ruin everything for him? No one would believe his version of events, but they would believe hers. Especially now.

Stepping back, she slammed the door shut, then photographed her wrist. The bruises on her forearms were forming nicely too. She took a photo of those. Then, seething inside, she braced herself and smashed the hard edge of her phone against her mouth. She didn't have to fake the tears that sprang from her eyes, trickling down her cheek to mingle with the salty taste of her own blood on her lips. It made a damning image.

Going to her messages, she noted he hadn't even bothered to reply to her last one, telling him she was carrying his child. Anger and hurt churned inside her. He wanted Maddie, a woman who didn't want him, who didn't need him. She had a mother she could turn to, where Kelsey had no one. Her parents had been dancing on the edge of destruction since the day she was born, living a chaotic drug- and booze-filled life, until Kelsey and her brother had been taken away from them. As a grown-up she'd watched other people get families while she herself had ended up with a string of selfish, weak men – all because Maddie had taken Cole. She'd tried to move on after he'd become involved with her – so fast, as it happened, Kelsey had almost had whiplash. She hadn't been able to. But *he* had, because she'd allowed him to. She shouldn't have. He was *hers* first.

Quickly she typed out another message. *You'll be sorry.*

THIRTY-SIX

MADDIE

Having seen Cole storm from her house, his face livid, I'm doubly stunned to see *her* step out in a state of unflattering semi-undress and hurl a not very affectionate expletive after him. Lovers' tiff? I wonder. Was he too rough? Too uncaring? Did he tell her it was over, maybe? A flutter of hope rises inside me. I squash it flat. I don't want him back, assuming that might even be what *he* wants. His cheating might have been forgivable, but not this, with her. His lies would never have been. Fury and adrenaline driving me, I thrust my car door open and walk towards her house. I falter on the pavement, debating the wisdom of what I'm about to do. I have to, though. I have to see her face to face, look into her deceitful eyes as I impart my opinion of her.

Determinedly I march to her front door, steel myself and knock hard. She doesn't come immediately, and I wonder whether she's going to answer. After a moment, I hear her footsteps as she strides towards it, reaching for the latch and flinging the door open.

The expectant look slides from her face. I note the fleeting fury in her eyes before it gives way to shock and then obvious fear. Clearly it wasn't me she was expecting.

'Maddie.' She lets out a small gasp, her hand fluttering to her mouth.

Her lip's bleeding, I notice. 'Did he get a little too rough?' I enquire, eyeing her icily.

Her look hardens. Making some attempt to rearrange her top to cover her extremely exposed cleavage, she straightens her shoulders. 'If you've come here for some melodramatic confrontation, you're going to be disappointed.' She notches her chin up. 'I'm not prepared to argue with you on the doorstep.'

Not bothering to hide my contempt, I simply continue to study her. Her gaze falters, but she doesn't back down, lifting her chin higher instead, as if she has any dignity left.

'I'm not here to argue with you, Kelsey,' I assure her, my voice amazingly calm, considering. I hesitate another second, long enough to make her squirm, I hope, and then, smiling languidly, draw back my hand and deliver a stinging blow to her face.

'Stay away,' I hiss as she visibly reels. Then, satisfied, but not nearly enough, I spin around and stalk off.

'*Bitch*,' she screams after me. 'He doesn't *want* you. He wants to be with *me*! He was mine before you got your claws into him. You know he was.'

I stop, turn slowly back. 'Really? And if he doesn't want you, what will you do, Kelsey? Make him suffer? Make me suffer? My *children*?' I hold her gaze, trusting she can see that her vile threats have strayed into very dangerous territory. 'If I were you, I'd back off,' I warn her. 'Because you really have no idea what I'm capable of.'

THIRTY-SEVEN

As I stuff Cole's clothes into black bin liners, I mull over what Kelsey said. If he doesn't want to be with me, I can't hold on to him. My pride certainly won't allow me to beg him. Nor would I want to be with a man who doesn't want me. Still, though, there's the tiniest part of me that wishes there was a way he could make me believe he does.

I'm so distracted, I don't hear Ellie come into the bedroom. 'Is he staying with her?' she asks behind me, causing me to start.

'I don't think so, sweetheart.' I turn to face her. I've told her only as much as I need to, that it's Kelsey he's involved with. I had to. I don't want her going anywhere near her. God only knows what the woman might tell her. She's obviously distraught, her face filled with such tangible hurt and confusion I feel my heart bleed. 'He'll be at his mother's, I imagine.'

But I already know he isn't there. Concerned about Lizzie, I called her, apologising for not visiting her, making excuses about work. She assured me she was coping. Her sister was staying with her, she said, helping her organise the funeral. She obviously realised there was something I wasn't telling her, though, possibly because Cole's behaviour has been so odd. Not wanting to add to her worries when she asked if everything was all right between us, I was about to assure her we were fine when she caught me completely off guard, asking me whether Cole was cheating on me. 'Some woman rang him while he was here,' she added. 'He took the call upstairs but I overheard some of it. He sounded very distressed, but he wouldn't talk about it. I couldn't help but be suspicious.'

Because of her own experiences, obviously. Knowing she would have to learn the truth eventually, I told her I thought he was, my voice defeated.

Lizzie was quiet for a long moment. Then, 'He's nothing like his father, Maddie,' she said intuitively. 'Please don't do anything impulsive until you know the whole story.'

Now, looking at his bereft daughter as we stand surrounded by the broken remnants of our lives, I'm thinking that he's worse than his father. I recall one of the malicious messages – from Kelsey, clearly. *You're sleeping with the enemy*. How right was that? The fact that he told me he loved me, that he told Ellie he loved her more than his life, makes his actions all the more despicable. Anger hardening inside me, I stuff the last of his work shirts into a bag and carry it to the door.

'Are those his things?' Ellie asks.

I note her taut body language, how young and vulnerable she looks, and I want to fold her to me and keep her safe from all of this. But I can't. Cole knows I can't. He knows she will suffer, that the boys will, and I hate him most of all for that. 'I can't have him coming here right now, Ellie,' I try to explain. 'I don't want him coming back for his things either, not yet.'

She answers with a small nod. 'I'll give you a hand,' she says, walking across to pick up a second bag.

I'm reluctant to let her. I don't want her involved in any of this, yet how can she not be? 'I'm sure he'll be in touch with you.' I attempt some small reassurance.

'I don't want to see him, Mum,' she replies adamantly.

'Maybe not right away,' I say, understanding how betrayed she must feel, 'but in time.'

'No, Mum. Not *ever*.' As she looks at me, I see the bewildered tears in her eyes and wonder if there will ever be a way Cole can mend their relationship. 'How could he do this?' she asks. 'How could *she*?'

A graphic image of my husband and my best friend having lust-fuelled sex crashes into my mind and nausea swirls inside me. Swallowing hard, I try to quash it. 'She's obviously in love with him,' I murmur.

'She's a complete bitch,' Ellie seethes, hoisting up the bag.

Wishing I'd waited until the children weren't around before doing this, I follow her down the stairs. 'I'll put them out, Ellie,' I tell her. 'You go and check on the boys and then run yourself a nice warm bath.'

'I don't want to run a bath unless it's to drown *her* in,' Ellie replies caustically. 'And the boys are sleeping, finally. I think I must have read every story from the 365 *Bedtime Stories* book.'

'Thanks, Ellie.' I give her an appreciative smile.

'No problem.' She shrugs. 'I thought it might make up for their dad not reading to them. Not that he did much of that lately.'

Sighing inwardly as I note the way she referred to Cole as 'their' dad, I take a fortifying breath, open the door and place my husband's clothes on the doorstep.

Ellie dumps her bag without ceremony. 'What about his PC and the stuff in the garage?' she asks, coming back in.

'I'll put them out tomorrow, text him before I do,' I tell her. 'I wouldn't want them getting stolen.'

'I'd love them to get stolen,' she huffs. 'And I hope you're putting his treadmill out screw by screw.'

I almost smile. I can't help thinking I would get immense satisfaction from seeing Cole's face if I did.

'How about I bag up the last of the clothes and you pour us

a glass of wine?' I suggest. She's not quite eighteen, but I'd rather she stay in and drink with me than go out and get off her head on God knows what. Anger surges through me as I remember her recent drinking escapade, why she was drinking and who she turned to in her moment of need. She's right, Kelsey is a bitch. A scheming, nasty-at-the-core, manipulative cow.

I fill the last bag quickly, then scrub the tears from my face and take it down to dump alongside the others, careless of the fact that it's beginning to rain. Closing the door, I drop the latch and slide the bolt. That should send him a clear message. He's not welcome here. He won't get in even if he begs. Not that I expect him to now that he's got what he needs in life, a twisted whore to fulfil his every fantasy, which I clearly didn't. Suddenly the image of Kelsey's petrified face submerged in a tubful of water seems extremely appealing.

Attempting to quash that image too, because the vitriol I'm feeling right now scares me, I join Ellie in the kitchen, where I pick up the wine she's poured me and tip it back – and promptly choke on it.

'Bit of a rubbish drinker, aren't you, Mum?' Ellie sighs and comes round to pat my back. She's smiling, though, I notice, and congratulate myself on at least making my broken-hearted daughter do that. 'You'll have to work on it if you're going to claim diminished responsibility when you strangle her.'

As she climbs back on her stool, I push my glass towards her. 'Pour me another.'

She smirks and obliges. 'You need to get a good solicitor,' she says. 'But avoid Wainwright & Co.'

I eye her warily, wondering how she would have any knowledge of solicitors. 'Why?'

Her eyes flick to mine. 'I had a date with a guy.' She shrugs vaguely. 'Wainwright's his father. I'm not sure whether he's a barrister or a solicitor but either way his son's a wanker.' She takes a drink of her wine. 'I think we must attract them.'

'No, Ellie,' I say firmly. 'This is nothing to do with who *we* are. We're not to blame for other people's inadequacies. And there are lots of good guys out there.'

'What, like Dad, you mean?' she mutters cynically.

I say nothing. There's nothing I can say, is there?

'I could come with you if you like,' she goes on, changing the subject. 'I could take some time out. I've almost finished my...' She stops, swapping cautious glances with me as we hear a key in the lock, followed by a knock on the door.

'Are you going to answer it?' she whispers, sliding from her stool.

I shake my head, then flinch, nerves tightening my stomach as Cole calls through the door, 'Maddie, could you let me in, please?'

'Don't, Mum,' Ellie says as I glance that way.

I've no intention of letting him in. If he'd admitted what he was doing, regretted it bitterly and begged my forgiveness, then maybe I would have listened to what he had to say, but not now.

'It's not what you think,' he tries. 'Maddie, please open the door. Please talk to me,' he asks, his voice catching.

I glance at Ellie. She shakes her head hard.

'For God's sake, Maddie.' He's shouting now. 'Don't *do* this. It's exactly what she wants. She's *lying*. Manipulating both of us, don't you see? She...' He trails off. I can almost feel his frustration. 'Open up?' he pleads. 'Give me a chance to explain.'

Before I can stop her, Ellie flies to the hall, unlocking the door and swinging it wide. 'She doesn't want to hear your explanations,' she fumes. 'None of us do. Fuck off.'

'Ellie.' I join her, thread an arm firmly around her. This isn't her battle to fight. I don't want this. For his daughter to hate him. 'Cole, you need to go.' Forcing myself to ignore his haggard appearance, the dark shadows under his eyes, in his eyes, I lock my gaze on his.

He looks from me to Ellie, then away. I see the swallow slide down his throat as he presses his thumb and forefinger hard against his eyes. He draws in a deep breath, looks back at me – and then past me.

Quickly I twist to follow his gaze, and my stomach turns over as I see the twins standing hand-in-hand halfway down the stairs. The wide-eyed fear on their faces is like an icicle straight through my heart.

'Can I at least say goodnight to them?' Cole asks throatily.

I look back at him, see the tears he's struggling to hold at bay, and almost waver. I can't. I won't survive any more of his lies. And I have to. 'Go away, Cole,' I whisper, my chest almost exploding with emotion as I step back and close the door.

THIRTY-EIGHT

COLE

After dropping the bags in the boot of his car, Cole climbed in, glanced at the house, where the lights at the front had gone out, then rested his head back and let the tears fall. He guessed it didn't matter since there was no one to see them. He had no idea where he would go. He couldn't face his mother. When he'd called round to check on her, she'd told him she'd spoken to Maddie. She hadn't said any more. She hadn't needed to; the mixture of pity and disappointment in her eyes had been enough to convey her opinion of him.

He'd got the message when she'd walked across to the kitchen table to sit down with her sister. They were finalising the funeral arrangements, she'd said. It didn't bother him that he wouldn't be involved. If he was asked to give a eulogy, he had no fond memories to share. It bothered him that his mother seemed to be distancing herself from him, though. He'd let her down. Let everyone down. There was no way to explain it to her, any more than there was a way to explain it to Maddie, to Ellie. He swallowed back a jagged knot in his throat as he thought of his daughter. There'd been nothing but bitter disillusionment in her eyes. He had no idea how he would ever convince her he wasn't the person she'd thought he was.

How had it got to this? His marriage over. Most likely his career if Kelsey circulated those damning photos on top of a possible investigation regarding his father. He'd tried not to think about what had happened on the night he had only fractured memories of. Even in his own mind, it was too preposterous to be believable. What chance then that anyone else would believe it? None. He had known it. Better to forget it, he'd thought, hoping it would go away. But it hadn't. It wouldn't. Because she wasn't going to let it.

Dragging an arm across his eyes, he made some attempt to compose himself, then started the car and pulled away, heading for the hospital, where he knew he could find a bed somewhere, though the chances of him sleeping were nil. His chest constricted as the knowledge sank in that he would never sleep in his own bed again with the woman he loved completely.

An incoming message distracted him from his thoughts, then refocused them on the woman he was beginning to feel nothing but loathing for. *I won't use it*, she'd sent. *Not unless you force me to.*

He pulled over, his blood pumping so fast he felt his head swim.

Snatching up his phone, he messaged her back. *Do you think I actually care? I've lost everything.*

You have me, she replied after a moment.

He shook his head, incredulous, and jabbed an angry reply. *Do you have any concept of the damage you've caused? My marriage is over. I'm alienated from my kids.*

He drew his hands over his face, relieved on some level when she didn't reply. With no idea where this was going to end, he shouldn't be entering into dialogue with her of any sort.

He'd gone another couple of miles when she did respond. *She can't do that. The complete bitch.*

Cole felt his gut twist as another message arrived almost immediately, one that left him petrified. *I love you. I'm here for you. I'll speak to her. I'll make her see that she can't stop you seeing them. We'll get through this. Together. XX*

Panic rose fast inside him, threatening to choke him. She was clearly unhinged. Dangerously so. It was becoming obvious she would stop at nothing to get what she wanted. If she didn't, she might even go to the authorities, as she was clearly hinting she would. Sweat wetting his forehead, Cole clutched the steering wheel hard. He had to stop her. Somehow he had to find a way.

THIRTY-NINE

MADDIE

Unfurling myself from the ball I'd curled myself into as I waited for the long night to give way to day, I roll onto my back and stare listlessly at the ceiling. I hoped that if I slept, I would wake up to find the nightmare was over. I didn't sleep. The space in the bed where my husband should be is still empty. My throat closes, tears sliding silently from my eyes. Is he with her? I picture him there in the house I've been in so many times, where so many times over coffee I confided in her, feeding her information, I now realise. She hates me, doesn't she? All the while she was posing as my friend, she was silently seething inside, imagining I'd taken her man, that I was living the life she should have had. It isn't true. She and Cole were over. She finished it. Cole said he was relieved, that she was too full-on. Possessive. He realised it was never going to work when she said he rated his job over her because he'd left her bed to attend an emergency. Have I turned into that woman, expecting him to choose between me and his work, something that makes him fundamentally who he is?

No. I heave myself from the bed, refusing to blame myself for his disgusting behaviour. Didn't I tell Ellie she should never do that? Clearly he went to Kelsey because there *was* something lacking in his sex life. I swallow back the pain where my heart should be. It's his sordid little problem, not mine. He obviously gave in to whatever turns him on. I can't make myself believe he loves her. She's clearly still in love with him, though.

Sweeping back my hair, which is as much a mess as the rest of me, I brace myself and pick up my phone. With sick trepidation, I wake it up to find a ream of texts from Cole, most begging me to talk to him. The final one sends a shiver of apprehension through me: *You need to be wary of Kelsey. Please don't talk to her before speaking to me.*

Does he know I already have. Is she making threats? I note he's left voicemails. I smile cynically, wiping away another tear, as I listen to him telling me yet again that things are not what they appear to be. He's obviously not an original thinker.

I steel myself to listen to the next. 'Maddie, I have lied to you, and I am so, *so* sorry,' he says, his voice hoarse and filled with heart-wrenching remorse. 'I lied because I couldn't face telling you the truth. If you'd just talk to me, I'll explain. Try to. Please call or text me. I need to know you're okay. That the kids are.'

I shake my head, staggered. He needs to know the family he's decimated is okay? Quickly I text him back. *Are you serious? The kids are not okay. I'm not. Your excuses are pathetic. Please don't call or text again. I need some space.*

Fighting back tears, I pull on my dressing gown. I need to go and see to the priorities in my life, my children, which have obviously never been his. Ellie's downstairs with the twins. I can hear her chatting and clattering around in the kitchen, probably preparing their breakfast. She's trying to play mother to everyone. She needs to know she has one, and that I'm still standing.

I've reached the foot of the stairs when the landline rings. I stay where I am and let the answerphone pick up. 'It's me,' Cole says with a dejected sigh. 'I'm guessing you don't want to see me – I don't blame you – but can I at least see the children? They are my kids too.'

What? I'm across the hall in an instant, snatching the phone up. 'What the *hell* are you doing, Cole?' I demand, seething. 'Bombarding me with calls? Acting as if it's *you* who's the injured party.'

'I'm not,' he denies quickly. 'I didn't mean to. I... Jesus, I just need to talk to you. I *have* to. Please—'

'You're fucking someone else,' I hiss, my eyes skidding to the kitchen door, which remains closed, thankfully. 'You're destroying our marriage without a second thought about what this is doing to the children. And now you're telling me you want to see them, as if you *care* about them.'

'*Christ*, will you please just listen to me, Maddie. I am not doing what you think—'

'No, Cole, *you* listen,' I growl over him. '*You're* the guilty party here, and I'm not prepared to expose the children to any more of this toxic rubbish until you at least admit what you're doing. You've seen so little of them lately, the twins probably won't miss you for long anyway. As for Ellie, you're an intelligent man, supposed to be. Do you really think the best way to convince her you give a damn is by lying through your teeth?'

He goes quiet. Then, 'I guess that pretty much sums it up, doesn't it?' he says.

I draw in a tight breath. 'Don't call here again, Cole. We'll talk through our solicitors.' I hang up and try to compose myself.

I have to speak to the boys, I realise, somehow begin to explain that their daddy and I are separating. How can I do that, though, without reassuring them he still loves them and that they will still see him? I can't run him down in their eyes. That will only traumatise them further. I know I will have to allow him access, but not now, not yet. It's not just because I'm crushed by what he's done. The truth is, he's acting so differently to the man I've always known him to be, he's scaring me.

I'm girding myself to go into the kitchen when my phone beeps in my pocket. Cole, I guess, harassing me with yet another text. Agitatedly, I retrieve it – and freeze. It's not from Cole. It's from her. Goosebumps crawl over my skin as I read it. *You really are a selfish cow, aren't you? If you think you can punish him by cutting off contact with his children, you'd better think again.*

He's told her already? But that must mean... he's *with* her.

FORTY

COLE

'Okay?' Cole glanced at Hannah as they assessed a patient suffering vision and breathing problems who'd become dizzy and disorientated shortly after arriving.

Hannah nodded and smiled, and Cole appreciated it. She'd provided information about his father's operation to the hospital board. She'd apparently vouched for him, saying that he'd stepped in appropriately when sweat had obscured her vision. He himself had said that Hannah had been efficient and professional and that the rupture had been unavoidable. For now, it looked as if it wouldn't go to external investigation. He supposed that, along with the fact that Hannah didn't appear to have lost faith in him, was something to hold on to while his world was falling apart. Without his career as well as his family, he would have nothing worth living for – and he didn't dare dwell on that, or on the fact that Kelsey seemed to have taken to physically stalking him, seeking him out whenever the opportunity presented itself. She was currently hovering around A&E, no doubt looking for him.

Focusing his mind where it should be, he turned to the patient, a sixty-five-year-old woman with no other known health issues. 'I see you had a car accident recently,' he said, checking her file. 'How long ago was that exactly?'

The woman frowned, as if she might be having difficulty recalling. 'About a week,' she said vaguely.

'And you banged your head?' Cole asked.

She nodded and sighed. 'It was my fault,' she said. 'My dog slipped his...' she paused, as if searching for the right words, 'restraining harness. He was jumping all over the back seat and I'm afraid I was distracted.'

'I can see why you would have been.' He smiled reassuringly, but his guess was she was suffering some memory loss, too. All of which indicated she might have been walking around with an intracranial haemorrhage. 'So, given the symptoms you describe, I think we might need to do a little further investigation. Are you okay with that?'

'Yes, thank you, Doctor,' the woman replied, though she was clearly worried.

'Hannah?' Cole glanced at her. 'Are you in agreement?'

Hannah nodded efficiently. 'I'll organise a CT scan,' she said. 'Plus an MRI?'

'Great.' Cole turned back to the patient. 'We think you might have a small bleed on the brain,' he said gently, 'but try not to worry, you're in good hands. We're going to organise a scan, which is basically a diagnostic imaging procedure that uses X-rays to have a look inside your head. Depending on what that shows, we'll then send you for some more detailed imaging, which will give us a better idea of what's going on. Once we have all the images back, we'll have another chat about what to do going forward. Does that sound okay?'

'Will it hurt?' the woman asked tremulously.

'Not at all.' Cole glanced again at Hannah, his smile still in place, but he was having to work to hide his irritation as Kelsey actually called across to him, asking if she could have a word once he was finished. 'I'll leave you with Dr Lee and talk to you again shortly,' he said.

He felt his jaw clench as he turned to meet Kelsey's unwavering gaze. She wasn't going to let up, was she? What was it she wanted from him? Actual blood?

Steeling himself, he walked to the door, swinging by her without making eye contact and heading for the corridor, where he kept going, his stride brisk. She had to almost run to keep up with him, but he didn't slow until he found a relatively quiet spot in the hospital grounds, where he turned, kneading his forehead hard until she caught up with him. 'What the fuck are you playing at?' he growled furiously.

The smile she was wearing sliding from her face, she eyed him stonily for a second, then, 'Shouldn't it be me asking you what you're playing at, Cole?'

Emitting a snort of derision, he shook his head. 'You actually do think this is a game, don't you? What's your goal, Kelsey?' he asked. 'You've ruined my life. Maddie's life. My children's lives. Isn't that enough?'

Her expression hardened. 'You ruined *my* life, Cole,' she retaliated, her hazel eyes seething with resentment. 'Did you really think you could get away with what you did? Just walk away, no consequences, is that it?'

Cole's heart rate slowed. 'What did I do?' he asked, scrutinising her carefully. What *was* her endgame? he wondered. What new lies was she going to spew out? What fabrications to ensure she did actually destroy him?

'You know very well what you did.' She eyed him angrily.

'No, Kelsey,' he said, his chest tightening, 'I don't.'

'*Liar!* You coerced me into having sex with you.'

Jesus Christ. Cole felt the ground drop from beneath him.

'You *drugged* me.' Tears sprang to her eyes.

'Kelsey, stop,' he said shakily. Aware of Alex walking by with another member of staff on the path just yards from them, he stepped towards her, taking hold of her arm and trying to steer her away.

She snatched her arm back. 'You raped me, Cole,' she hissed. 'How could you have done that? *Why* would you? You didn't need to. I *love* you. I've always loved you.'

As she stared at him, tears streaming down her face, Cole tried to do the most basic thing in life and just breathe. This was complete insanity. He felt as if he'd woken up in a parallel universe where everything was back-to-front, upside down, utterly distorted.

'You said you loved me.' The madness just kept coming. 'You apologised and said you *loved* me. And you lay with me and held me and you kept apologising – and in the morning you were gone. You left without a word. *Why?*'

Cole backed away, stumbling as he did. Righted himself. Kept going.

'I waited for you to call,' she shouted after him. 'You never did. That's why I'm sending messages, because I'm upset. You said you wanted to be with *me*, not her. I'm having your baby!' She pressed a hand to her stomach. 'You can deny it all you like, but the proof is right here.'

FORTY-ONE

MADDIE

Wary of what she might do after her last message intimating I was punishing Cole by cutting contact with his children, I decided to keep the twins home, where I could make sure they were safe. But then I realised they needed normality around them now more than ever. I need to convey to them that Cole will still be part of their life, just less often. I feel a pang of guilt when I recall my cruel comment about his seeing so little of them they wouldn't miss him. Up until recently, when he was with them, he was with them totally, tactile and loving. With Ellie, too. I have to let him see them, of course I do, but he will have to accept it will be on my terms. Does he imagine for one minute that I would let Kelsey anywhere near them? Near Ellie, who she pretended to be a friend to while clearly wheedling information from her?

Breathing in hard to hold back the tears, I squeeze the boys' hands as I walk them to their classroom. My heart aching, I crouch and pull them into a firm hug before they go in. 'Be good,' I tell them. 'Love you both to bits.'

'Love you too, Mummy,' Lucas says, a troubled frown creasing his small brow as he studies me. His striking blue eyes

– a mirror image of his father's – are filled with such concern, it almost breaks me. These are Cole's children. How can he be as callous as he appears to be? It makes no sense. There are parts of himself he has kept hidden, things he can't talk about, his childhood traumas. Those, though, only make him a stronger father, determined to show his love for his children, or so I thought. Perhaps those wounds run deeper than I imagined. There is clearly a side to him I've never glimpsed.

'Will Daddy be home to take us swimming on Saturday?' Jayden asks, his eyes as troubled as his brother's.

'I'm not sure, sweetheart.' My throat catches as I lie. 'Daddy and I have to have a little chat about when he will be seeing you.' My heart almost folds up inside me as I recall the last Saturday swimming session; how Kelsey looked after Lucas, masquerading as my friend. She was laying the poison even then, trying to convince me Cole was seeing Hannah Lee. She was obviously manipulating me, trying to get me to throw him out, leaving the coast clear for her.

Jayden nods, though not very enthusiastically, and I straighten up, ushering them towards their classroom as their teacher walks to the door to greet them.

She takes hold of their hands, giving me a sympathetic smile. 'Don't worry, we'll make sure to look after them,' she reassures me. I've spoken to her about the situation at home, explaining why they might be upset. I told her about the threatening messages too. I felt I had to. I have to be confident the boys will be safe here.

'Thank you.' I give her an appreciative smile in return, then hurry off as my emotions threaten to get the better of me.

I never imagined I would find myself sitting in a cubicle in the infants' toilets sobbing my heart out. Unable to hold the tears back any longer, I cry until my ribs feel so bruised I can't breathe. Eventually I reach for a wad of loo roll to dab my face, then start as my phone beeps. Hands trembling, I check it. The message is filled with the same vitriol as the others, but this time more considered than shot out in seething haste. As I read it, the dark grey cloud that's been pressing down on me all morning grows suffocatingly heavy. *Since you've decided to be so unreasonable regarding Cole's access to his children, you should know we've consulted a solicitor. I've taken your husband. Now I'll take your children as well.*

FORTY-TWO

With Kelsey's messages becoming increasingly aggressive, I'm growing scared. Worried about Ellie being home alone, I considered ringing in sick, but I was supposed to be covering at the children's hospital and didn't want to let them down. In the end, I called Ellie, warning her to bolt the door behind her once she got back from university, and made myself come in. I'm monitoring a toddler with breathing problems, paying close attention to her facial expressions and movements to establish how she's feeling, when my phone buzzes in my pocket. Reaching for it, I quickly switch it from vibrate to silent. I'm determined not to allow the poison that's seeped into my life affect my work. These children need my full attention. And I need this. I try hard to make their stay in hospital as minimally daunting as it can be. I love what I do. My life is unravelling so fast my head is spinning, but I won't let them take my job away from me, my sanity. I won't give them that any more than I will hand over my own children to a woman who's quite obviously mentally unbalanced. I recall the spiteful text she sent saying that *they* were seeking legal advice. Is Cole really going that route already? With her?

Dismissing it from my mind for now, I concentrate on my patient, keeping a close watch on the little girl, who even through her discomfort manages a small smile when I tuck her Peek-A-Boo teddy bear up with her. That's my reward for doing what I do. That smile, the light in her eyes. Chatting softly to her, I wait until another nurse comes to collect her for her X-ray, then, swallowing back another bout of tears that comes out of nowhere, take my break.

Finding myself alone in the staff room, I pull out my phone, then hesitate. For my sanity's sake I desperately don't want to check for messages, but I have to. I have to know what's going on in Kelsey's warped mind in order to protect my children. Cold foreboding settles inside me as I consider that she actually might resort to more than threats to get what she wants. She obviously wants Cole. But it's more than that, isn't it? This vicious campaign is not just about taking my husband. She wants my life. How far will she go to get it?

My blood pumping with both anger and fear, I force myself to look at the phone, hoping above hope that Cole might have contacted me, sent a text or left a voicemail that might somehow convince me he's not party to this vile harassment. There's nothing. He's letting her do his fighting for him. In my wildest dreams I would never have imagined him a coward, but that's what he is, clearly. He's hiding behind her. I picture them together, him hurt by my supposed cruel treatment of him, her oozing sympathy, indignant for him, urging him to fight me legally, and nausea roils inside me.

With sick trepidation, I open the message and my heart stalls. *Why are you doing this?* it starts, as if it's me who's tearing *her* life apart. *Your games won't work, Madelyn. He doesn't want to be with you. He wants to be with ME.*

Pure unadulterated rage rips through me. *You can fucking well have him!* I send back. *But you can't have my children.* My whole body trembles as I type. *I will die before I let that happen.*

There's a pause. Then her response arrives, and my hands shake as I read it.

You just might.

FORTY-THREE

Desperate for my children not to pick up on my devastation, I make a massive attempt to be upbeat once we're home, chatting away nineteen to the dozen to the twins about their day at school, offering them whatever they want for tea as a special treat. They plump for KFC, and I order two sharing buckets with Pepsi Max, which delights them.

'Is Daddy going to share it with us?' Lucas asks. I note the uncertainty in his eyes, realise how insecure the boys must feel – Ellie too, for all her feistiness – and wish there was a way to make their world safe again.

Ellie glances at me and then to Lucas. 'He's staying with his mum,' she reminds him gently. 'Remember? I expect he'll have some dinner there.'

'Can we talk to him on his phone?' Jayden asks. He's studying me intently, and I'm struggling to know what to say that won't rock his world further.

'Soon, I expect,' I answer vaguely, and force a smile. Inside, though, my heart breaks for them. I'll have to let Cole speak to them, but there's no way that conversation's going to take place without me within listening distance. 'How about we all snuggle up in the lounge when the food arrives and watch a film?' I suggest, changing the subject in the hope of distracting them.

The boys brighten a little at that. '*Super Mario Bros.*,' Lucas says determinedly, already halfway to the lounge.

'*Sonic the Hedgehog*.' Jayden obviously has other ideas and scoots after him.

'How about *Despicable Me 4?*' Ellie suggests, giving me a tolerant eye roll as she follows them – and though I'm worried for her, sure that the emotion she's clearly bottling up will eventually explode, right now I thank God for her maturity.

Once the KFC is delivered, we all settle down with Ellie's choice of film. The story resonates with me, being about a family under threat who find their safe place is no longer home. Tears welling up again, I fight them back and snuggle my boys closer. Emotionally I will survive – I have to for my children – but I have no idea how I'll get by financially. The thought that I might lose my home, the only home the boys have ever known, fills me with rage. I will fight Cole and this creature he values over his family with everything I have. My own dear mum taught me that when your back is to the wall, you either fight or give in. Grieving the loss of my father though she was, she didn't buckle when she realised her financial situation was precarious. She fought to build up her business, to keep the roof over our heads. I won't buckle either. I will kill before I let any harm come to my children.

When Ellie offers to read the boys their bedtime story, I clear up the leftovers. As my gaze falls on my phone on the coffee table, I hesitate and then pick it up. Despite my determination not to check it for vile messages this evening, with a sense of impending doom looming I feel compelled to. My breath stalled in my chest, I go to the app and exhale a sigh of relief. There are no new messages, no more threats I have to worry myself sick over tonight.

'I've made us some hot chocolate,' I say to Ellie, heading back to the lounge after taking the rubbish out. I grind to a halt, my stomach turning over as I realise she has picked up my phone. She looks from it to me, her expression thunderstruck, and I curse myself for leaving it lying around. I've never bothered with password protection; I've never felt the need to hide my phone activity from Cole. I never considered there would be any activities in his life he would want to hide from me.

'She's insane,' Ellie murmurs in shocked disbelief. 'How *dare* she send this sort of shit?' Visibly seething, she looks back at the phone and then pulls her own from her jeans pocket. 'I'm going to ring Dad.

'No, Ellie.' I dump the mugs I was carrying on the table and hurry across to her. 'Don't do that. I don't want you dragged into the middle of all this.'

She looks at me in astonishment. 'I *am* in the middle of this. He's my dad. You're my mother, and that fucking psycho bitch he's shacked up with threatened to *kill* you.'

'She didn't,' I mumble, trying to play it down, a lurch of fear inside me nevertheless as I acknowledge that Ellie is right.

'Yes, she *did*.' She eyes me incredulously. 'It's right here, Mum. She's dangerous, for God's sake. Certifiable. Does *he* know she's doing this?' She scans my face, her own a mixture of outrage and fear. 'I'm calling the police.'

'Ellie, no.' I reach to stop her as she goes to her keypad. 'I am going to speak to the police – tomorrow, not tonight while the boys are here. I probably should have done it straight away, but I hoped your father might call.' I did, but I don't know what I hoped he might say that would make this any less horrifying.

Looking marginally reassured, Ellie gauges me carefully. 'And has he?' she asks.

I shake my head, hopelessness settling more heavily inside me.

'You need to do something, Mum. There's no way she

should be allowed to get away with this. No way she should be anywhere near the boys either. She's bloody evil.'

'I am going to do something about it, trust me. I've already looked up a solicitor. I suppose I was hoping your father might have realised how unbalanced she is,' I admit. 'I can't have him back here,' I add quickly, 'but I hoped he might be able to make her stop.'

Ellie studies me, a mixture of emotions playing out on her face: worry and disillusionment, above all, palpable anger. 'He needs to,' she mutters, drawing in a breath and almost pushing past me. 'Because if he doesn't, *I* bloody well will.'

I watch her storm into the hall, a new kind of fear twisting inside me as I worry about what she might do.

FORTY-FOUR

Though I crave sleep, dark and dreamless, where the horror can't reach me, it doesn't come. I've been up twice, imagining I heard floorboards creaking, triple-checking the front and back doors were locked. Making sure the boys were tucked safely up in bed, that Ellie was. She's right, of course. This woman is evil, and definitely unbalanced. She needs to be made to stop. *I* need to make her stop. I have to keep my boys safe. Take the weight of responsibility from Ellie's shoulders. She's just seventeen years old, visibly affected by all of this, distressed and angry. So angry. Her whole world has been turned upside down by her own father, who I can't make myself believe is part of this hateful campaign. Yet nor can I believe that he doesn't know what's happening and what this deranged creature might be capable of.

Watching the clock click over, I don't realise I've finally drifted off until I'm woken with a choking jerk by a peal of wedding bells. I was dreaming about a wedding. The wedding was mine. I flinch inwardly as the details come starkly back to me. I was standing outside the church, looking into the eyes of my new husband, striking blue eyes, caring and kind, and filled with love for me. Then something behind his eyes shifted, and I was standing in front of a man I didn't know any more. Incongruous with his smile, the sharp blue eyes drilling into mine were as cold as a glacier.

It was symbolic, prophetic. I'm sure it was. Terror strikes right through to the core of me as I hear my phone ding, and I jolt to sitting. Desperately I try to brush the cobwebs of my dream from my mind, and scramble out of bed. The phone dings again as I stumble across to the dressing table. I can't breathe. Can't think straight. I stare at the phone as if it might bite me, then, my heart banging a frenetic rat-a-tat in my chest, I reach for it. Fear crackles through me like ice as I open the first message. *Cole's solicitor is taking our case to the family court. He's confident you'll be found guilty of parental alienation. I'd watch your back if I were you.*

Nausea roils inside me, rising so fast I have no hope of holding it back, and I only just make it to the bathroom, where I bring up the sparse contents of my stomach. Shakily I reach to turn on the cold tap and rinse my mouth, then go back to read whatever other vicious hatred she's spewed.

My hands tremble as I read the next message. *By the way, claiming that Cole's a bad father, neglectful or abusive won't work. He loves his kids, you know he does. It's YOU he doesn't love. In fact, he told me he's grown to hate you.*

Cold dread crawls through me, and I want to sit down and weep. In this moment, if not for my children, I feel I would have nothing to live for. Feeling numb inside, I go back to bed and curl up tightly under the duvet, watching the dawn break and the grey day grow greyer. My chest heaves as I fight back impotent tears lest my children overhear. I never said he'd been abusive – he never has. He has come close, though. As I lie there crying like a child instead of getting up and finding a way to crush this before it impacts irreparably on my children, I recall with vivid clarity how, so adamant in his denials, he lost his temper, slamming his hand so hard into the door frame right next to Ellie he caused her to jump. I can't let this go on. I *won't*.

Hopelessness and fear give way to fury, and I scramble back out of bed and grab the phone. *He has a temper*, I reply to her last pathetic message. *Maybe YOU should watch YOUR back*.

Making up my mind to change my number, I slam the phone back on the dressing table and head towards the bathroom to shower and pull myself together. I'll have to check that Ellie can take some time out of uni, but I will go to my mother's. I can't be on my own with this, feeling so isolated and alone. I'll need to ring Mum, tell her what's happening, which will break her heart. She loves Cole. She won't blame me, though, as it seems Cole is determined to do. I still can't believe he's doing all of this. It's as if he's had a personality transplant.

Checking the damn phone when it pings another message, I can't believe the response she's shot back either: *He's going to kill you*.

FORTY-FIVE

ALEX

'Christ, you look like death warmed up,' Alex commented, looking Cole over as he arrived for their team meeting to review the day's allocated surgeries. The man was a mess, clearly exhausted and not fit to carry out complicated surgeries. Alex had covered for him regarding his father's procedure. Given Cole's relationship with his dad, he hadn't been surprised he wasn't on his game, but he hadn't been for some time. Maddie was clearly worried about him. Alex had sensed it when she'd 'swung by' to pick up his jacket – an excuse for being here, he had guessed. She'd clearly been checking up on Cole, wanting to know what his movements were the previous evening. That had been awkward. Cole hadn't been here, where he'd said he was. Nor had Alex texted him asking him to drop by regarding the treatment of the kid with the spinal tumour.

After the argument he'd witnessed between Cole and Kelsey in the hospital grounds, he didn't really need to wonder why Maddie was worried. He hadn't heard all of it, but what he had heard was damning. He was torn between pity and anger as he recalled what Kelsey had shouted. *I waited for you to call, Cole. You never did. That's why I'm sending messages, because*

I'm upset. You said you wanted to be with me, *not her. I'm having your baby!*

It seemed that Cole had dented his impeccable image. He was clearly cheating on Maddie. That didn't sit well with Alex. His dilemma was how to tell Maddie what he knew. Cole might care so little for her he would lie through his teeth to her, but Alex wasn't prepared to do the same.

'You don't seem very with it,' he said, glancing again at Cole, who was attempting to make coffee, and quietly cursing as the machine refused to oblige.

'What?' Cole twisted to look at him, then cursed again as he knocked the milk carton over.

'Definitely not with it,' Alex observed, walking across to assist.

'Thanks.' Cole sighed wearily as Alex grabbed some paper towel to mop up the mess. 'Sorry. I didn't get much sleep last night.'

'Obviously. Something keep you awake?' Alex glanced curiously at him.

Cole shook his head. 'I'm not feeling great, to be honest. I think I might be coming down with something.'

'In which case, you shouldn't be here,' Alex pointed out. He was trying to be amenable, but he was feeling dangerously close to telling the man exactly what he thought of him. As in, asking him how many more people's lives he was intending to fuck up. Had he any concept of the impact this would have on his kids, on Ellie? Of course he bloody well did.

'No, I know.' Cole smiled apologetically. 'I thought it was just a twenty-four-hour thing, but I can't seem to shake it off.'

'Go.' Alex nodded him towards the door. 'Hannah can cover most of the routine surgeries, and if there are any emergencies, we can get some short-term cover. 'You shouldn't be here, putting patients' lives at risk. You above all people should know that.'

Cole looked confused. Clearly he was wondering why Alex appeared to be less than friendly with him. Alex hadn't treated Maddie well himself when they'd gone out together years back. He'd been young, reckless, a complete idiot. Cole wasn't an idiot; he had no excuse for treating her so badly. If he continued to do so, Alex would have no choice but to do something about it.

FORTY-SIX

MADDIE

Ellie clearly notices I'm distracted, my mind on that last petrifying message. 'You look terrible,' she observes as she comes into the kitchen

'Thank you.' I glance at her from where I'm trying to encourage the twins to eat their cereal. 'Looks like we're a matching pair.' I sigh sympathetically and give her a smile. She looks as tired as I feel.

'Didn't sleep much.' Ellie rolls her shoulders and yawns widely.

'Lucas didn't either,' Jayden says through a mouthful of Cheerios. 'He wet the bed.'

Lucas's gaze hits the table. 'Didn't.'

'Did,' Jayden retorts.

'Jayden, enough,' I warn him. The twins' love for each other is fierce, but they can fight and disagree with equal ferocity. I'm aware it's all about development of individuality, necessary and inevitable, but I do worry that Lucas, being the more sensitive of the two, might suffer for it, especially now. 'Accidents happen, as you very well know.'

As Jayden drops his gaze, looking suitably chastised, I

glance again at Ellie, who looks at Lucas, concerned. 'Don't worry about it, mate,' she says, going across to give his hair a ruffle and drop a kiss on the top of his head. 'Even I have accidents sometimes.'

Lucas looks sheepish as she hitches herself onto the stool next to him.

'He had a bad dream,' Jayden says, craning his neck around Lucas to look at her.

'Did you, Lukie?' Ellie frowns sympathetically.

'Uh-huh.' Lucas nods. 'I lost my football in the park and Daddy went to find it, but he didn't come back and I didn't know what to do.'

My heart wrenches for my boy as his gaze skitters back to the table. Ellie swaps glances with me, her expression both furious and upset for him, and then threads an arm around his shoulders. 'You'll see him soon, sweetheart,' she promises, her voice tight.

'And we'll go swimming, won't we, Ellie?' Jayden says, also sliding his arm around his brother – and I'm so grateful that they have each other.

'Hopefully.' Ellie gives Lucas a squeeze. 'I should get off,' she says, climbing off her stool. 'I'll see you guys later. Be good.'

'Are you not going to have some breakfast?' I ask, worrying now about her. All three of the children are clearly affected by Cole's appallingly selfish behaviour. Whether or not I told him to leave, he'd already abandoned them, hadn't he? In his heart, he must have done.

'Not hungry,' she replies. 'Are you going to make the call we discussed?' she adds, giving me a meaningful look.

'I am,' I assure her, going across to give her a hug.

Ellie hugs me back hard. Then, 'Gotta go,' she says, her voice catching as she pulls away.

I watch her head quickly for the hall, an ache in the pit of my stomach as I realise that my girl is suddenly being forced to be far too mature for her years. What kind of impact will all of this have on her? How will she ever get over it and form proper relationships?

'Ellie.' I follow her. 'I will make the call,' I promise.

She looks at me as if she's not quite convinced, but she nods eventually, and then steps towards me to throw her arms back around me. 'You're way prettier than that bitch,' she murmurs into my shoulder. 'I wish she'd do the world a favour and die.'

'Ellie...' A ripple of apprehension runs through me as she drops her arms and spins around, tugging the front door open and hurrying through it. There's so much anger stuffed inside her. Recalling the night she was so distraught she ended up drinking until she made herself ill, I'm scared for her and what she might do.

Going back to the kitchen, I chivvy the boys on, telling them to quickly brush their teeth, then check my phone as they gallop up the stairs. There are no further messages, thank goodness. I fully intend to report Kelsey to the police. I have no choice. I can't let her do this to me, to my children.

Minutes later, we're heading out of the front door, Jayden and Lucas squabbling over slimy frogs. I suspect that one or more of the frogs might have found their way into their school bags, but decide to let it go. They're upbeat for the moment; I don't want to take that away from them. 'Lucas, this side,' I instruct him as they embark on a new argument about who's sitting where. I guess it's because we're halfway through the alphabet game, spotting letters of the alphabet on the journey, and they think the person sitting driver's side has an unfair advantage.

I can't help but smile as Lucas, now looking extremely disgruntled, troops back around to the rear passenger side. 'You can swap seats on the way home,' I tell him, opening the door for him.

He looks up, a small smile twitching his mouth, and then his face lights up and he practically beams. 'Daddy!' he exclaims, charging past me – and my blood freezes.

With Jayden a second behind him, I whirl around to see Cole at the end of the drive, crouching down ready to catch them as they throw themselves at him.

'Hey, guys. How're you doing?' he asks, his voice thick with emotion as he hugs them tightly to him.

Jayden pulls away. 'Where've you been?' he says, a scowl knitting his brow.

'I, er...' Cole falters, clearly struggling for a way to lie to his child. 'I have to stay with Nana for a while,' he says.

He isn't there, of course, and he must be aware that I know he isn't. I've spoken to Lizzie again, who's appalled and devastated by his behaviour. She's coping, she told me, would rather cope without him than have him lie to her, to me. She's clearly a much stronger woman than I imagined her to be. But then I suppose she'd always had to be strong, if quietly so, for her son, who it seems is repaying her by being completely uncaring of the pain he's causing her.

'She's a bit upset right now, so I have to be there for her,' Cole goes on shamelessly.

Lucas continues to stare uncertainly at him. 'Our mummy's upset, too,' he says in a small voice. 'She's been crying, hasn't she, Jayden?'

Jayden answers with a firm nod.

Cole swallows. 'I know she's upset. That's why I've come to see her,' he says with an attempt at a smile. 'Can we talk, Maddie?' He straightens up, his gaze agonised as it meets mine.

I'm too dumbfounded by his brazenness to speak. Too scared by the fact that he could so easily sneak up on me, so easily win the boys over.

Lucas slips his small hand into Cole's and looks up at him, and then to me, as if willing me to fix whatever he clearly senses is broken between us.

'Please?' Cole adds.

I glance at Jayden, who's also gazing at me with such hope in his eyes, it tears me apart. 'I have to take them to school,' I manage past the tight lump in my throat.

'Is it okay if I wait?' Cole asks, unfairly. What am I supposed to say to that in front of the children? I realise I have to relent. I can't let him wait in the house, though. Coming back to find him there will kill me. Is that why he's here? I think of that last petrifying message, and cold fear seeps through to the bones of me.

'I won't be long,' I answer, trying to read what's in his eyes, eyes in which I once thought I could interpret his every emotion. I can't. I have no idea any more what my husband is thinking.

Nodding, he brings the boys back to the car. As I watch him helping them in, checking they're buckled in safely, I feel I've slipped into another dimension where everything is normal in my life, where I don't think my husband, the man whose children I bore, the man I swore to love till death us do part, is planning to do me harm.

Once the boys are settled and the car doors closed, he looks across to me. 'It's wrong, Maddie,' he says, his gaze filled with the same sadness and sincerity I saw when he told me he loved me, that he wouldn't know how to be without me, and it almost breaks me completely. 'Everything you think you know about Kelsey and me is wrong,' he adds – and my heart hardens in an instant.

'Keys,' I demand, holding my hand out. He looks at me in confusion. 'Your house keys,' I clarify, making sure to keep eye contact.

He retrieves his keys from his pocket, breathing in tightly, then drops them into my palm.

They're attached to his car key fob, I realise, and debate whether to start separating them. I decide not to. I simply don't have the heart for dramatics on the front drive. Instead, I walk to the road, point the key fob at his car parked diagonally opposite and unlock it. 'You can wait there,' I tell him.

He looks at me in bewilderment. 'Can I ask why?' he says.

I might be amused if I wasn't so bewildered myself – and utterly terrified of the man I once thought I knew through and through. Eyeing him steadily, I reach for my phone, flick quickly through it for the last message sent by the sick, twisted individual he's chosen over me, and hold it towards him.

The blood drains visibly from his face as he reads it. 'Please tell me you're not taking this seriously?' he murmurs, snapping his gaze back to me.

I say nothing. Instead, I hold his eyes determinedly for a second longer, and then turn and walk to my driver's door. My breath is trapped in my chest, my heart and legs like lead, but my head is high, affording me at least a little dignity as I climb in and drive away.

FORTY-SEVEN

COLE

'*Fuck!*' Sucking in a frustrated breath when there was still no response to the message he'd sent Kelsey, Cole slammed his hand hard against the steering wheel. She was stalking his *wife*, sending threats deliberately intended to terrify her. He couldn't let this go on. He had to do something. But what? By going to the police he would unleash a retaliation that could see him in prison, where he would have no way to protect the people he loved more than his life. How had this all happened? At first, he'd tried to ignore her, hoping it would all just go away. It wasn't going to. After her astonishing claim that she was pregnant with his child, he'd guessed she'd had an insane game plan from the outset. First she would destroy Maddie's belief in him. Then she would hold what she'd said he'd done as a threat over him, resorting to blackmail if she had to. Ugly, desperate blackmail. If she went to the police, as the photograph she'd sent hinted she would, his life would be over. Did she want that? He felt as if his own sanity was slipping away from him as he realised he was actually entertaining suicidal thoughts. It was the only way he could think of to bring this torture to an end, and it would at least ensure his family were well provided for.

How could he do that, though, to his kids, to Maddie? He breathed in hard. He *had* to make her stop. His mind made up, he was reaching to start the car when he remembered he'd handed his keys over to Maddie, who clearly didn't want him to have access to the house, to her or to the children. She was scared. Of him. His chest tightened, cold hollowness settling inside him, as he realised he'd probably already lost her. In which case, it really didn't matter what he did, did it? Anger – an emotion he'd worked so damned hard to control – unfurling dangerously inside him, he shoved his door open and climbed out. He was about to start walking when he saw Maddie's car returning. She didn't look in his direction as she swung onto the driveway. His gut churning with a combination of nerves and nausea, he waited for her to park and head for the front door, then crossed the road towards the house. Expecting to find the door closed when he reached it, he was surprised to see it open. 'Maddie?' he called, going tentatively into the hall.

'In here,' she called from the kitchen.

He steeled himself and headed that way. Looking her over, he felt his heart tear apart inside him as he noted the determination tinged with tangible fear in her eyes and knew it had gone too far for him to convince her he would rather die, right here, right now, than allow any harm to come to her. He *had* allowed harm to come to her, hadn't he? And in her mind, he'd done it knowingly.

'What are you doing here, Cole?' she asked, her expression a kaleidoscope of emotion: bewilderment, hurt, uncertainty. 'What do you want from me? Are you trying to strip away my last shred of self-esteem? Is that it? To take my children away from me?'

'No,' he denied quickly. 'Why would I? Christ, Maddie, you're their whole world. I would never do anything that would hurt you or them. You must know that.' He gazed at her imploringly, willing her to believe him.

'That's not how it looks from where I'm standing,' she said.

As Cole noted the tear sliding down her cheek, he felt like crying with her. He wanted to go to her. To hold her. To try somehow to explain. How? He had no explanations, none that sounded plausible. He couldn't bear to tell her what would inevitably sound like another lie. Yet he had to if he had any hope of making her believe that none of the evil in those messages had come from him.

'I'm sorry,' he said, then faltered, realising how inadequate his apology sounded. He tried again, groping for the right words, any words. 'What happened between us happened once.'

'I think you should go,' Maddie said coldly.

'Maddie, please...' Dropping his gaze, he willed himself to do what he had to. 'It happened without my consent.' He'd said it, finally, and he felt like the weakest specimen of manhood that ever walked the earth.

When she didn't respond, he looked up to see her staring at him in bemused astonishment. 'You really expect me to believe that?' she said.

'It's the truth.' Cole's voice caught in his throat.

She emitted a scornful laugh. 'So you're telling me you were *forced* to have sex with her?' Her voice was incredulous. '*How?*'

He squeezed his eyes closed. 'I was drugged.' He shrugged, and paused, guessing it would take a second for her to glean the implication.

'So you don't remember fucking her then?' she replied eventually, derisively – as he'd expected she might. Even to his own ears, it sounded pathetic. It was.

He ran his fingers through his hair. 'I have some recollection,' he said quietly. 'Snapshots, that's all. I'm not sure how much actually happened.' What more could he tell her? His memories were fractured, coming and going like elusive wisps of smoke on the air. His stomach turned over as what he did recall hit him again with blinding clarity. Her hands sliding languidly over his torso. The room revolving nauseatingly as she'd climbed on top of him, her hungry wolf's eyes burning unwaveringly into his as she'd straddled him. *Jesus.* There was no escaping it. He was there, in her bedroom.

'Right.' Maddie breathed in tightly. 'Would you like to expand?' she asked. 'Because I'm struggling here, Cole. *Really* struggling.'

Had he imagined she wouldn't be? *He* was struggling. With the fact that it had happened, that he'd allowed it to. To admit that he had. Most of all he was struggling with that.

'Did you go to a hotel with her?' she demanded. 'To her house?'

'No.' Cole snapped his gaze back to her. Looked away again. 'Yes. Her house. I... don't remember much. I—'

'For God's sake, just *tell* me,' Maddie yelled impatiently.

He swallowed back the sour taste in his throat. 'I was in the bar near the hospital,' he began. 'I needed some time out after—'

'Oh, the infamous *bar*,' she snapped sarcastically over him. 'Don't tell me, let me guess. She was upset, so you held her hand?'

Cole sighed. It sounded like complete bullshit. How could he expect her to believe it? Any of it? 'I'd lost a patient,' he went on. He'd lost patients before. It was inevitable. This one, though, was different. The man had put so much faith in him, believing his operation would be successful, that he would see his family again. 'It shouldn't have happened,' he said, working to keep his emotion in check. 'The procedure to remove his tumour went well. The damned infection wasn't my fault, I knew that, but... He had two children, a girl and a boy around the twins' age, and I... I needed time, to process.'

'So you went to the bar,' she said flatly.

He nodded defeatedly. 'I'd just delivered the news to his family, and I... I was upset for them, imagining what it would be like for his children.' He paused, glanced at the ceiling, blinked hard to hold back the tears he was too ashamed to cry. 'I ordered a brandy and Coke,' he continued, forcing himself to look at her. He owed her that much at least. 'She was there.'

'Kelsey,' Maddie responded bitterly.

Cole nodded and took a deep breath. 'We started talking. Somehow the conversation got around to the few times we'd gone out together. *Good times*, as she referred to them. She started flirting. I knew she was. I should have stopped it, but...'

'You encouraged it?' Maddie stared at him in astonishment.

He nodded again, feeling more ashamed by the second. What was he going to say? He hadn't? That would be a lie. He'd thought it was harmless banter. He'd been a complete idiot.

'And?' Maddie waited.

Cole had no idea what to say. What reassurance he could offer her. Whatever his own involvement in what had happened, he *had* encouraged Kelsey. At least, he hadn't *dis*couraged her. How could he hope to convince Maddie he hadn't wanted it to happen?

'Things started to get hazy after that,' he said quietly. 'I felt light-headed, unsteady. I thought maybe I'd caught something. When I stood up to leave, I reeled. I remember that, crashing into the bar, glasses smashing.'

'But you'd had nothing more to drink?' she asked, studying him hard.

He shook his head. 'Nothing.'

'And she helped you?'

'She said I was in no state to drive. She was right, obviously. I tried to tell her I would call a taxi. I couldn't even articulate the words, let alone make the call.'

'And?' she pressed him.

Cole's gaze drifted down again. He couldn't look at her, not now. 'She said she would drive me. I remember her putting her arm around me as I stumbled on my way to the door. I recall her helping me into her car, me smacking my head on the door rim as I tried to climb in. After that, nothing much.'

'Just snapshots,' Maddie said, after another long, loaded silence.

He shrugged again helplessly. 'Hazy images.'

'And you don't remember whether you actually had sex with her?' she asked, as she was bound to.

Cole stumbled over his answer. 'I... She was on top of me. I... don't know.'

'Yet she's pregnant,' Maddie stated calmly.

He had no idea how to answer. 'She claims to be, yes,' he said eventually.

Maddie considered. 'So do you think she spiked you?'

Cole wiped away the sweat wetting his forehead. 'It would have been easy enough for her to get hold of Rohypnol,' he suggested, feeling now deeply ashamed, and very aware of how a victim of sexual assault might feel having to reveal all of this in a soulless police interview room. 'I'm guessing there was probably something else in there.'

She conceded the point with a short nod. 'And yesterday? You were at her house,' she pointed out. 'She ran to greet you. I saw you. I also saw you through the glass in the door. I hadn't realised there was quite so much suppressed anger inside you, Cole.'

Jesus. He closed his eyes, every last vestige of hope slipping away from him. 'I went to ask her to stop. She wouldn't listen. She...' Realising how implausibly inadequate any attempt at explanation would be, he stopped.

'Coerced you?' Maddie suggested with a mixture of cynicism and heartbreaking disappointment.

Cole didn't answer. How could he?

'I don't believe you,' she said, after another agonising pause.

He had guessed she wouldn't. Still it hit him like a punch to his stomach. 'Which is why I didn't tell you,' he said, his voice choked. 'I don't blame you. It all sounds pretty ludicrous, doesn't it? Can I ask you something, though, Maddie?'

She didn't reply.

He asked anyway. 'Don't you think my supposedly hating you enough to want to kill you is pretty ludicrous too?' He paused, hoping to God she would believe him on this if nothing else. 'Whatever Kelsey might tell you, it's all lies, I swear. She's living a fantasy, suffering from some sort of delusional disorder, something... I don't know. I do know I'm not in a relationship with her. I would never want to be in a relationship with anyone but you.'

FORTY-EIGHT

ELLIE

Guessing the conversation was over when her mum said she needed some space, Ellie stayed where she was at the top of the stairs, feeling bewildered and furious in turn. When her dad came through from the kitchen, she was shocked by his appearance. He looked humiliated and ashamed, having bared his soul in there. Just as Ellie had felt after being assaulted by that bastard Luke Wainwright. She'd felt degraded, too bloody stupid to tell anyone what had happened to her. Was what her dad had said true? She watched as he paused in the hall, breathing in hard and wiping a hand across his eyes. His shoulders were slumped, his body language defeated. It was the truth, Ellie could feel it. She guessed the sticking point for her mum was that bitch claiming she was pregnant. She couldn't blame her for that.

She watched him walk to the front door, her heart hitching in her chest. Once he'd stepped out, she went quietly downstairs. She didn't want her mum to know she hadn't gone to uni, her intention to pay that evil cow Kelsey a visit instead. Nor did she want her to know that she'd heard them talking. Not until she'd had a chance to speak to her dad anyway.

Slipping out of the front door, she raced down the driveway. He was in his car, about to pull away, so she hurried to the kerb and flagged him down.

He stopped as soon as he saw her, opening his window as she approached. She could see the guardedness in his eyes, and she guessed he was wondering whether she might have overheard anything. 'I forgot my essay.' She shrugged and gave him a smile.

'Ah.' Her dad managed a small smile back.

It didn't do anything to change the fact that he looked like death. Judging by the dark shadows under his eyes, he hadn't slept in days, and she was sure he'd lost weight. 'I'm sorry, Ellie,' he said, dragging a hand over the back of his neck. 'It's an inadequate word, I know, but it's all I have. I never meant for any of this to—'

'I believe you.' She blurted it out, because she could see he was tearing himself apart, and it was tearing her apart too. 'Can we talk?' She nodded towards the passenger side as he looked at her with a mixture of surprise and confusion.

'Yes, of course.' Shaking his head as if trying to process what she'd just said, he reached to open the passenger door.

Ellie glanced back at the house as she went around the car. She would talk to her mum, but she wanted first to let her dad know that he had someone on his side, that she understood. Why she would. Should she tell him about Luke on top of all the other shit he was dealing with? She debated and decided she would play it by ear, although she thought it might make him feel less alone.

'Probably a good idea to drive away from the house,' she said, reaching for her seat belt.

'Any preferences?' he asked. 'Do you want to go for a coffee?'

'How about the park?' she suggested. 'We could walk around, or maybe just sit in the car for a while?'

Minutes later, they pulled up in the car park. 'So, walk or sit?' he asked, killing the engine.

'Sit.' Ellie glanced at him. 'It's more private.'

He nodded, and then fell silent. 'I take it you heard?' he asked after a moment.

Ellie saw the flicker of embarrassment cross his face and felt for him. 'I was on the stairs,' she admitted.

Her dad fixed his gaze forwards. Ellie guessed he would be feeling foolish and weak, and empathised completely. She took a breath, wondering where to start. Then decided to just ask what she needed to. 'You know when you told Mum about the drugs and said that there was something else in there, did you mean Viagra?' she asked.

'*Jesus*.' Her dad emitted a short, uncomfortable laugh.

'I'm seventeen, Dad,' she reminded him. 'A big girl now. I do know about this stuff.'

He nodded pensively. 'I guess you do,' he said, glancing briefly at her and then away again. 'Yes,' he said awkwardly.

Ellie considered. 'So did you do a test? Before the Rohypnol was out of your system, I mean. You would have the facilities at the hospital, wouldn't you?'

Her dad hesitated. 'No,' he answered eventually. 'I didn't.'

Ellie glanced at him. She didn't think it was possible for anyone to look more guilty. 'Why?' she asked, but she already knew the answer.

'Because I didn't want my colleagues to know,' he answered simply.

She got that completely. 'I understand,' she assured him. 'I didn't want anyone to know either.' She fiddled with her charm bracelet, felt her dad's gaze swivel towards her.

'Know what, Ellie?' he asked cautiously.

Her heart beating manically against her chest, she gathered her courage. 'It happened to me, too,' she whispered.

She heard her dad's sharp intake of breath. Didn't dare look at him. 'Ellie, are you telling me what I think you are?' he asked, his voice strained.

She nodded and risked a glance at him. His face was deathly pale, his eyes bewildered – and she wished she could reel the words back in. She hadn't thought it through. He was her dad. She didn't want to make him feel bad. She didn't want to be on her own with it any longer, though – it was a secret that was burning a hole inside her. She couldn't eat. Couldn't sleep. Cried silently at night so no one could hear her. She needed him to know why she'd been so angry seeing the way he'd been treating her mum, lying to her, hurting her – deliberately, she'd thought. Most of all, she needed to know he would still love her.

He gave her a moment. Then, 'Ellie? You can talk to me, you know,' he said softly.

Nodding, she forced herself on. 'My drink was spiked,' she murmured. 'At least I think it was.'

Her dad fell silent for an excruciatingly long moment. Ellie was sure she could hear her heart booming. Eventually he spoke. 'Did he rape you?' he asked quietly.

Feeling suddenly claustrophobic in the confines of the car, she reached to open her window.

'I know it's difficult for you, but you can tell me,' he urged her gently.

Ellie glanced back at him. The look in his eyes was agonised, as if he could feel her every emotion. She knew that he could. 'He said I was begging for it. I wasn't,' she added quickly, swiping at the tears that squeezed from her eyes. 'I didn't have any choice. I wasn't conscious.'

Her dad's jaw tensed. 'Bastard,' he grated, clenching the steering wheel hard. 'Sorry. Sorry, Ellie. I...' Turning towards her, he hesitated, scanning her eyes cautiously, then reached to thread an arm around her and draw her to him. The tears came in earnest then, tears she hadn't dared cry openly before spilling from her eyes to slide wetly down her cheeks.

'Was it someone you knew?' he asked tightly.

Ellie nodded into his shoulder. 'He's a guy from uni,' she managed, easing back a little to look up at him. 'Luke Wainwright. He's older than me. I thought he was all right, you know. That he liked me.' She searched his eyes confusedly. 'His father's a big-shot barrister in Brum. Luke's doing a law degree and... I don't know. I suppose I thought I was safe with him. Then I thought what happened was my fault, that I'd sent out the wrong signals – you know, that the clothes I was wearing were too revealing.'

'This was *not* your fault, Ellie.' Her dad locked his gaze hard on hers. 'You didn't give your consent, which definitely makes it rape. You know that, right?'

She nodded. 'I might have said yes, though,' she admitted. 'If he hadn't been so rough in the taxi. If I hadn't passed out.'

Her dad tugged in another tight breath. 'Would that have been because you wanted to, though?' he asked carefully. 'Or because you would have felt pressurised to?'

'I'm not sure.' She glanced miserably up at him.

'He took away your choice, Ellie. The decision was yours to make,' he reminded her quietly. Easing her back to him, he stroked her hair and pressed a soft kiss to her head, as if she were still his little girl, somehow making her feel whole again, less broken. 'Should I go to the police?' she asked tentatively.

He took a moment. 'Have you spoken to your mum about this?' he asked.

'No.' She shook her head. 'She's had so much going on.'

'I know,' he said, his voice choked. 'I think you should talk to her, though. She'll want to be there for you, I think you know that. As for going to the police, I think you should, but that also has to be your choice. Do you feel you should?'

'I suppose,' she answered, looking back at him. 'Don't you think you should go to the police too, though? What that woman did to you was wrong, Dad. What she's doing to Mum is wrong.'

FORTY-NINE

Ellie could hear her mum upstairs when she let herself back in through the front door. She headed for the kitchen, nerves churning inside her as she wondered how her mum would react to what she'd just shared with her dad. She would undoubtedly be upset and angry for her. But possibly also because she hadn't felt able to tell her.

She grabbed a quick glass of water and was about to go up to talk to her when she noticed her mum's phone on the kitchen island. Glancing up to the ceiling, she realised her mum was taking a shower, possibly getting ready for work. Her heart thudding, she hesitated for a second, then grabbed the phone. She'd seen the reply the psycho bitch had sent when her mum had said she would die before letting her near her children. *You just might*, she'd said, which was clearly a threat. Recalling what her dad had said, something about him supposedly hating her mum enough to want to kill her being ludicrous, it sounded to Ellie as if the mad cow had taken things a step further.

Quickly she woke the phone up, then sighed in frustration as she realised it was suddenly passcode-protected – no doubt because her mum didn't want her looking at it, which indicated there had been more correspondence. She tried her own birthday, which was the passcode her dad used. Nothing. She tried the twins' date of birth. That didn't work either. It could be anything. The last thing she expected it to be was her dad's date of birth, but *bingo* – the home screen appeared and she was in. Reading the last message received, fear crackled through her veins like ice: *He's going to kill you.*

Fury mounting inside her, she flicked back through the messages, and a jolt of pure rage shot through her. *Cole's solicitor is taking our case to the family court. He's confident you'll be found guilty of parental alienation. I'd watch your back if I were you,* she read. There was more, all of it crap: *By the way, claiming that Cole's a bad father, neglectful or abusive won't work. He loves his kids, you know he does, It's YOU he doesn't love. In fact, he told me he's grown to hate you.*

Reading the last sentence, she gasped incredulously. Was the woman on something? This was as mental as it was possible to get. Ellie had no idea what she was trying to do... Yes, she did. She was obviously trying to goad her mum into reacting. If she did, things would undoubtedly escalate and anything might happen. The twins could end up being considered at risk. Ellie felt sick to her soul at that thought. This woman needed stopping. Her mum needed to take this shit to the police. If she didn't, Ellie would. She pulled out her own phone and took photos of the messages, then jumped as her mum walked in.

She looked from Ellie to the phone she still had in her hand. 'I obviously didn't think of an original enough PIN,' she said, smiling weakly.

'It wasn't one I immediately thought of.' Ellie gave her a guilty smile back. Then looked at her seriously. 'You have to report her to the police, Mum.'

'I know.' Her mum emitted a shaky sigh. 'But it's complicated, Ellie. There might be a backlash for your father. I can't tell you everything, and I know I shouldn't care, but...'

She did care. Ellie could see the indecision in her eyes, the tears that were close to the surface, and felt a tiny spark of hope that her parents' relationship wasn't broken beyond repair. They'd always been friends. They argued – who didn't – but they always agreed about the important stuff. They were a unit. And that woman – if she was even human – was *not* going to destroy them. Ellie wouldn't let her. 'I know, Mum,' she said. 'What Dad told you.'

Her mum looked at her quizzically.

'I came back from uni. I heard it all, and...' She hesitated. 'I followed Dad out. I talked to him. I think he'll go to the police, so... You have to report her, Mum. She has to be made to stop.'

Still her mum looked reluctant.

Ellie hardened her resolve. 'If you don't, then I will. You can't just ignore it. Think of the twins. She's obviously sick. Who knows what she might be capable of.'

Her mum squeezed her eyes closed and drew in a deep breath, then finally she nodded.

FIFTY

MADDIE

I glance again at the wall clock in the reception area of the police station, counting down the minutes until I might possibly place Cole in the most humiliating situation of his life. A man who suffered such humiliation throughout his childhood and must be wondering what he ever did to deserve the awful abuse he's suffering now. *If* all he told me is true. She's pregnant, I remind myself. *Is she, though?* A little voice in my head nags. She might be lying, a pathological liar with some sort of delusional disorder, as Cole said, though wouldn't I have seen signs before? I'm reminded then that she went to great lengths to befriend me, seeking me out at the hospital when Cole and I were first dating. Was that simply a way to get close to Cole when she realised her mistake in letting him go? If she is pregnant, the child might not be his, is highly unlikely to be his, in fact – *if* he's telling the truth. Cole would have no way of proving it without a pre-natal paternity test, and I can't see her agreeing to that. I go over and over the possible scenarios until I feel I'm going out of my mind. I want to believe Cole, with my whole heart and soul, but I am *so* scared. One of them is lying, and I have no way of knowing who.

Finding myself backsliding, I glance at Ellie, who's sitting with her hands tucked under her thighs, one foot tapping rapidly on the floor, indicating how nervous and upset she is, and I realise I have to go through with this. I have to show the police the messages. They're threatening and abusive. Terrifying. Ellie's right. She has to be made to stop. The police have the power to do that, at least I hope they do, whereas I would have to resort to confronting her. Face to face with her, I have no idea what I might be capable of.

My mind goes again to Cole and the unimaginably cruel, criminal thing he claimed she'd done to him. He seemed so genuinely ashamed, where – if it were true – he shouldn't be. So deeply traumatised. Still, I wonder if his story is just that, a sob story because he's realised he actually doesn't want to be with her. As I glance again at Ellie, she turns and offers me a small smile, but her eyes are filled with such angst and uncertainty, it frightens me. If Cole is lying, he's putting her through hell too, and I could never forgive him for that.

'Are you sure you're not missing anything crucial at university?' I ask her, wishing she would go in for the rest of the day. She needs some kind of normality around her. I suspect, though, that she's determined to stay superglued to my side until I've done this.

'Just a lecture.' She shrugs. 'I can always crib Claire's notes. It's not a problem. I wouldn't be able to concentrate anyway. I can't believe I was so taken in by that scheming cow. She's seriously messed up, Mum. There's no way she's going to stop until she's ruined all our lives. It's no wonder Dad didn't know how to tell...' She stops, her gaze going past me as a door opens to my side.

I turn to see a slightly dishevelled-looking man with a four o'clock shadow heading towards us. 'Mrs Chase,' he says, offering me his hand. 'Detective Inspector Steve Ingram. Sorry to have kept you waiting. There's been a major incident, I'm afraid, so we're a bit thin on the ground. What can I do for you?'

'Oh, is this not a good time then?' I ask, feeling immediately flustered.

'Crime doesn't choose a convenient time, unfortunately.' He smiles tiredly. 'The desk sergeant tells me you've been receiving death threats. Would you like to let me have some details regarding the nature of these threats so we can assess the risk?'

'They're death threats,' Ellie replies flatly. 'Pretty high-risk, I'd say, wouldn't you?'

He glances in her direction, eyebrows raised. 'And are these direct threats?' he asks.

'I'd say sending Mum texts telling her someone is going to kill her is pretty direct,' Ellie retorts, not looking overly impressed. 'She's called our landline number too. We know who it is and you need to make her stop.'

His forehead creasing into a frown, he looks between us. 'And does the sender say who she thinks is going to carry out this threat?'

'My husband,' I provide, now wondering if we really are wasting his time. Is what she's doing even a criminal offence? 'We're separated,' I add.

'Ah.' He nods, as if he's already drawn his conclusion. 'And the sender – a woman, I'm gathering – what relationship is she to your husband, Mrs Chase?'

I take a fortifying breath. 'An ex-girlfriend, Kelsey Roberts. She's been purporting to be my friend for years. I believe she's actually been stalking my husband. She's intimating that the two of them are involved, but he's adamant they're not.' I stop and exchange a glance with Ellie, whose taut body language relaxes a little as she realises I'm at least prepared to consider that Cole's version of events is the truth.

'I see.' DI Ingram nods noncommittally again. I'm almost expecting him to tell me to fill in a form and then go away and keep a track of the messages or something. He doesn't. 'Shall we go somewhere a little more private?' he suggests, and relief surges through me, quickly followed by a new kind of fear as I wonder where all this will lead. If Cole is trying to manipulate events, somehow hoping to make out that I'm the unstable one and that I'm trying to alienate him from his children, aren't they likely to believe him, a respected surgeon? And wouldn't my 'unreasonableness' add to his case in the family court? I couldn't bear it if they sided with him, meaning my children might be forced to spend time with him and this monster.

Once in an interview room, DI Ingram studies the messages on my phone, his eyebrows alternately raised in surprise and furrowed in consternation. 'Well I can see why you would be worried. These would definitely fall under the criminal offence of harassment,' he says, looking back at me. 'And you don't think your husband has resumed his relationship with her?'

'He says not,' I answer.

'Yet from the content of the messages, it appears that they are involved.' I note a degree of scepticism in his voice and it sits uncomfortably. He probably thinks I'm as gullible as I feel. Or else squirming with jealousy.

'They're not,' Ellie intervenes firmly. 'I spoke to my dad and I believe him. He'll probably be coming to see you about what that mad cow has done to him as well. She's deluded. She's convinced herself she's in a relationship with him. You have to do something. She's dangerous. You can see that.' She nods at my phone.

He gives her a tolerant smile and looks back at it. 'The messages do appear to be threatening.' He sighs, his frown reappearing. 'You mentioned that you and your husband are separated, Mrs Chase?'

'I didn't believe he wasn't in a relationship with her at first,' I admit. 'I asked him to leave.'

He eyes me thoughtfully. 'But you do now?'

'I'm not sure.' I sigh in confusion. 'I've read messages on his phone that seem to confirm she's harassing him too, though. If he is telling the truth, then I'm concerned for him. Right now, I'm concerned about the effect this is having on my children. The effect it will continue to have on them if it goes on. I have six-year-old twin boys. They're traumatised by the impact this is having on me and their sister, even though we're obviously trying to pretend everything is fine. There has to be a way to stop her.'

'I have a six-year-old boy myself. Kids are shrewd.' DI Ingram smiles fondly. 'I don't suppose you managed to grab a screenshot of the correspondence between the sender and your husband, did you?' He looks hopeful.

Ellie produces her phone. 'Mum didn't, but I did,' she says, selecting her photo app and passing the phone to him. 'Mum had Dad's phone. She has a habit of leaving them lying around.' She glances at me and I guess she's taken a shot surreptitiously.

'Like I say, shrewd.' Ingram eyes her approvingly and proceeds to read through the screenshots, obviously noting the one announcing that Kelsey is pregnant. As I watch his eyebrows rise and fall, conveying his doubt that my husband is a victim, his surprise that I would even consider he might be, I wish I could just get up and walk away. But I can't. My children are in the middle of this madness. Whatever it takes, I will end it, for their sakes.

'What does your husband do, Mrs Chase?' he asks curiously.

'He's a neurosurgeon at the general hospital,' I tell him. He looks impressed, as I knew he would. 'She works there too. She's a nurse.'

He appears to debate, then, 'Okay.' He places the phone down, wipes a hand over his face and leans back in his chair. 'As this does seem like the beginnings of a campaign of harassment, in the normal run of things we might pay this woman a visit. Unfortunately, however, we have no evidence that the messages are from her. My guess is that she's probably sending them from public Wi-Fi addresses and she's obviously anonymising her internet traffic. We'll get our analysts to take a look – as long as you don't mind your data being downloaded?'

'No, I have nothing to hide,' I assure him, almost wishing I did.

'Good.' He collects up my phone. 'Meanwhile, I would advise you not to engage with the sender; definitely don't message back. If you could ensure you keep good records of further messages sent, that would be helpful.'

Relief on some level surges through me. Although *the beginnings of a campaign of harassment* seems like a vast understatement.

'I'd also like to have a chat with your husband. Do you have an address for where he's staying?' he asks.

My heart drops. I have no idea where Cole is. Deep sadness settles inside me as I imagine him to be lonely. But then I pull myself up sharp. I need a harder shell if I'm to get myself and my children through this intact. 'He was going to stay at his mother's, but... I'm not sure where he is, to be honest. Possibly at a hotel near the hospital.'

He nods and stands, indicating that our meeting is over. 'Perhaps we'll stop by this Kelsey's address,' he says, with another one of his short smiles. 'Just in case.'

'He's not there,' Ellie says, her tone adamant. 'She bloody well abused him. There's no way he'll be there.'

Ingram looks at her through narrowed eyes. 'Abused?' he repeats interestedly. 'How?'

She hastily drops her gaze. 'You'll have to ask him,' she mumbles. 'He wouldn't share anything about me I might be uncomfortable with, so I'm not saying any more.'

'Ellie?' Alarm shoots through me as I note the tears spilling suddenly down her cheeks. 'What is it, sweetheart?' I wrap my arm around her.

'Nothing.' She shakes her head hard, wipes her hand across her face, then looks back at Ingram. 'If you talk to him, will you tell him that I've made up my mind I will.'

He looks nonplussed at that. 'I'm not sure I understand.'

'Dad will understand,' she says. 'Can you please just tell him what I said.'

FIFTY-ONE

Once we're in the car, I turn to Ellie. She keeps her eyes firmly on her phone. 'Ellie, is there something worrying you?' I ask.

She doesn't answer, and seems to shrink into herself. And now I'm sure.

I knew in my bones that there was something troubling her before Cole turned her world upside down. She was so moody and withdrawn. 'Ellie,' I reach to brush her hair away from her face, 'what is it, sweetheart? Please talk to me.'

She closes her eyes. 'I didn't know how to tell you,' she murmurs.

My heart falters. 'Tell me what?' I ask, ice-cold dread seeping through to the core of me as it occurs to me that she empathised deeply with Cole, steadfast in her belief in him since she spoke with him in his car. Why would that be? 'Why are you so sure your dad was telling the truth?' I ask carefully.

She fiddles with her charm bracelet, reluctant to look at me.

'I'm here for you, darling,' I assure her. 'You know that, don't you?'

'I know.' Ellie nods. 'I do know, Mum. I didn't not want to talk to you. It's just... What Dad said, about the Rohypnol...'

She looks up at me finally. 'I knew how he felt. How hard it was for him to tell you,' she goes on falteringly, 'because...'

She's been through it too. My heart stops stone-cold dead. I knew. Something. She was different, subdued, suffering in silence, and I didn't press her because I was too preoccupied with my own problems. 'The absolute *bastard.*' The words spill from my mouth before I can stop them.

'I knew you'd be upset,' she blurts tearfully. 'I should have said something, but I didn't know how to. I thought it was my fault because of the way I was dressed. How I behaved. I still don't know how it even happened. It's just that with what Dad said, I had to let him know I knew how he felt. I shouldn't have done that without speaking to you. I'm sorry, Mum.'

Oh dear God. I slide an arm quickly around her and hug her hard to me. 'You don't need to apologise, sweetheart. It doesn't matter who you told first. I understand. I'm glad you felt able to talk to your father,' I assure her, my heart twisting as I realise how much she obviously still trusts him, where I can't. 'It matters that you appear to be blaming yourself for something that absolutely *isn't* your fault. Don't do that to yourself, Ellie. Not *ever*, do you hear?'

She nods into my shoulder.

'Don't doubt yourself, sweetheart, and never apologise for who you are,' I go on forcefully. 'You should be proud of yourself. I'm proud of you. Your father is. Despite all that's happening between us, I know he loves you fiercely. In my heart, I know that to be true.' The words pour out, and I don't know whether I'm saying the right or the wrong thing, but I need her to know she is worth loving. 'You're a beautiful person, unique and special and strong. Strong enough to care about other people, even after all you've gone through. Please never feel you can't talk to me, no matter what's going on in my life. There is nothing, *nothing*,' I emphasise, 'that could make me love you any less than I do, and that's completely.'

She emits a muffled sob, and I hold her tightly.

I press a soft kiss to her hair as her sobs slow to a shudder. 'What did your dad say?' I ask cautiously.

She eases away, wipes a hand under her nose. 'He was angry, hurting for me,' she says. 'I could see it in his eyes. And I could sense he understood. He told me once, when we used to go out running, you know, that I should trust my gut feeling. He said if your instinct is telling you something, then it's probably right. And it was, Mum. I could feel he was telling the truth. That's why I believe him.'

She looks at me with such conviction in her eyes, I can't help but be swayed. What Cole told me did sound ludicrous. He was right about what he said afterwards, though. His supposedly plotting to kill me was so ludicrous it was off the scale.

'He told me it wasn't my fault. That it happened without my consent,' Ellie goes on passionately. 'He was right. If I'd been aware of what was happening, I might have said yes, but Dad made me realise that my choice was taken away. He asked me whether I might have said yes because I felt pressurised. He was right about that, too. He made sense, made me feel better. He wasn't lying, Mum.'

As she searches my eyes, willing me to believe her, believe in him, I nod and offer her a small smile.

She smiles tremulously back. 'He said I should talk to you, but you had so much going on. I was waiting for the right time.'

'As if there's ever a right time.' I sigh ruefully. 'If you ever need to talk, Ellie, just say so, okay? You will always have my attention if you need it, I swear.'

She nods, looking a little more reassured. 'He said I should go to the police when I asked him. He said it was my choice, though. That's why I told that detective to tell Dad I will.'

'So you were hoping it would give him courage?' I gather her meaning.

Again she nods. 'He didn't believe it, did he, that detective guy? That Dad wasn't having an affair?'

'I'm not sure,' I answer honestly. If Cole's story sounds far-fetched to me, isn't it bound to to the police?

'He's being victimised.' Ellie breathes deeply. 'We have to help him, Mum. We can't let that cow do this to him. To us. Someone has to stop her. If the police won't, then I'll find a way to.' Her face is filled with angry determination. 'I swear to God I will.'

FIFTY-TWO

COLE

After assessing an urgent admission, his dishevelled appearance no doubt giving the woman an abysmal impression, Cole went to the single-patient room he'd slept in to try to make himself presentable. Once there, feeling jaded to his bones, he sat heavily on the bed and rested his head in his hands. What was he going to do? Maddie didn't believe him. How could he have hoped she would? He felt utterly powerless. Pathetic, allowing himself to be used the way he had, allowing his family to find out the way they had, and – despite having spent his formative years with a man who'd lived to humiliate him – more demeaned than he'd ever felt in his life. The only chink of light in the unremitting darkness was Ellie. His daughter believed him. The daughter he hadn't been there for when she'd needed him.

A toxic mix of anger and shame writhing inside him, his mind went to the piece of scum who'd raped her. He'd thought about nothing else since she'd told him. It was eating him alive. Would she report him? She would need courage to do that. She was looking to her father to give her that courage. Cole knew that no matter how much more humiliation he suffered at the hands of a woman who seemed to want to strip him of everything, he would have to lead by example. He didn't much care about what happened to him any more, but he cared about his kids with every fibre of his being. He couldn't allow Ellie's sense of self-worth to be slowly eroded because she didn't believe in herself.

Dragging his hands over his face, he got to his feet, tugged off his white coat and began unbuttoning his shirt. He needed a clean one. Him walking around looking as if he didn't care about his personal appearance wasn't going to inspire much faith in his patients. He was halfway out of the shirt when the door opened and Alex looked in. 'I wondered where you'd got to,' he said. 'You were needed in resus. Hannah's on it, though, so...' He stopped, a quizzical look on his face. 'Have you been sleeping in here?'

'Temporarily.' Cole sighed, pulled the shirt off and reached for the clean one he'd retrieved from one of the bin liners Maddie had stuffed his clothes in. 'I'm going to book into a hotel later.'

'Ah.' Alex stepped into the room. 'You're in the doghouse, I take it?'

Cole smiled despondently. 'Makes it sound as if I might be let back in. I doubt that's going to happen any time soon.'

'That bad, hey?' Alex frowned pensively. 'Look, tell me to mind my own business if you like, but this doesn't have anything to do with Kelsey Roberts, does it?'

Cole's gut constricted. 'No. Why?' He glanced at him as if he didn't have a clue what he was talking about.

Alex tipped his head curiously to one side. 'I couldn't help noticing you two having a rather heated conversation in the hospital grounds,' he said.

Cole looked away. 'It was just a difference of opinion, that's all,' he lied, and hoped to Christ Alex didn't pursue it.

'A pretty major one, if you don't mind me hazarding?' Alex suggested.

Cole's mind raced. How much had he heard?

'You're obviously having some marital problems,' Alex went on, clearly fishing for information.

'It's just a blip.' Cole kept his attention focused on fastening his buttons. 'All marriages have them.'

'I see.' Alex paused. 'And would this blip have anything to do with the fact that you've apparently fathered a child with another woman? Just out of curiosity.'

Jesus. Cole's gaze shot sharply back to him. 'It was bullshit,' he said shakily. 'All of it. I don't know how much you heard, but—'

'Sort it out, Cole.' Alex cut him short, obviously unimpressed. 'Do the right thing by the woman you promised to love and cherish for life, or else get *out* of her life.' Dragging eyes full of icy disdain over him, he spun around and stalked away before Cole could formulate an answer.

Watching him leave, Cole felt his heart plummet. He had to talk to him. There was no way he wanted Alex repeating this to anyone else. Panic spiralling inside him, he grabbed his white coat and followed him into the corridor, then ground to a halt as he collided with Hannah.

'Sorry,' she mumbled, looking flustered.

'It's fine. My fault.' Cole glanced past her to where he could see Alex disappearing through the doors.

'Can I have a quick word?' Hannah stopped him as he made to step around her. 'It's quite urgent.'

Cole glanced back to her, apprehension tightening inside him as he noted the wariness in her eyes. 'Is there a problem?' he asked, praying there wasn't.

'I had my letter from the hospital board,' she said, and Cole felt his heart drop to a whole new level. 'It says the enquiry into your father's death is going to external investigation. I just wondered whether you'd had yours?'

Christ, no. Cole's throat dried. It just got worse, didn't it? His life was being destroyed inch by painful inch. He was losing his family, his friends. Losing his grip on everything. All because of one woman's dangerous obsession with him. Surely she'd be satisfied now.

FIFTY-THREE

ALEX

Fuming inside, Alex headed back to Neurology. He hoped he didn't see Cole again until he'd gained some control over his emotions. The way he was feeling now, he wasn't sure he wouldn't take a swing at him. What was the bloke thinking, treating Maddie with such blatant disrespect? Had he imagined Alex was the only one who'd overheard his *difference of opinion* with Kelsey? Someone else was bound to have; the guy from Radiology who'd been walking alongside him for a start. He'd had his earphone in, apparently on a call, so he hadn't taken much notice, but once the drums started beating in this place, gossip travelled like wildfire. Maddie was bound to find out what Cole was up to sooner or later, assuming she hadn't already. Kelsey was claiming to be carrying his *baby*. Did he not think that would have consequences? Did he not care?

Obviously not. Alex couldn't quite believe it, but Cole appeared not to give a damn about how many lives he was ruining, least of all Maddie's. He'd completely destroyed any faith Alex had had in him. Alex had looked up to him, been a friend to him, there when he needed him. Maddie had too, supporting him through his training when his old man was making life intolerable for him. She'd obviously been slightly besotted with Cole even before she and Alex had split up, and Cole had clearly fancied her. He was good at hiding his emotions – damn good – but it was apparent from the shine Alex saw in his eyes every time he spoke to her. When he'd found out that Alex and Maddie had finished, he'd wasted no time asking her out.

Eventually realising that Alex still cared for her, that he bitterly regretted what he'd done in a monumentally stupid, booze-filled moment of madness, Cole had asked him if he was okay with it. What was Alex going to say? He'd cut his losses. Figuring she would be with a better man than he could ever be, someone who was appalled by his father's misogynistic treatment of women and would therefore treat her with the respect she deserved where Alex had failed, he'd swallowed his pride and stood aside. He'd given Cole his blessing. Been best man at his wedding. It had crucified him watching the woman he loved marrying the man he'd looked on as a brother. They'd married fast, as it happened.

Maddie had looked radiant. Several months pregnant, she was clearly happy as she walked down the aisle to marry the man of her dreams, a good-looking bastard who garnered appreciative glances from female staff and patients alike. That killer smile of Cole's had women swooning, swapping glances and theatrically fanning their faces as he walked by, but it was the fact that he was so caring that melted hearts. Genuinely caring, Alex had thought. That was what had stopped him asking Maddie the question he'd wanted to. Should have done. But for the fact that he'd realised Cole was in love with her, would have done. He just couldn't do that to him. He had no choice now, though, but to do something about what was happening. And what then? Hope that Maddie would realise he was there for her when her marriage fell apart, which surely it would – unless Maddie loved Cole enough to close her eyes to what he was doing.

Alex couldn't allow her to do that. She was worth so much more. He would have to find a way to convince her that Cole wasn't the man she thought he was, that Alex had thought he was, someone who, because of all he'd endured, would never knowingly hurt another living soul. Alex had felt for him in the operating theatre when, in the split second Cole had frozen, he'd looked as if all his ghosts had come back to haunt him. Yes, his old man would likely have not made it anyway, but Alex had covered for him, as he'd thought Cole would for him. He couldn't any more. Cole shouldn't be allowed to get away with what he was doing. Clearly he had no morals or conscience and cared little for the emotional impact he was having on Maddie, the consequences for Kelsey or for the patients who needed him to be focused.

Alex couldn't just stand by and watch. His conscience simply wouldn't allow him to ignore his responsibilities, as Cole seemed to think he had a right to.

FIFTY-FOUR

MADDIE

Pulling up outside the university, I wait while Ellie finishes her text and then grabs her stuff. 'Are you sure you're going to be okay?' I ask her as she climbs out of the car.

Peering back through the open passenger window, she nods and musters up a smile. 'Claire has a free afternoon, so we're just going to mooch around town and then go back to ours and watch some rubbish TV. What about you?' she asks with a worried frown, and I'm reminded again of what a big heart she has. She cares about people. She can also read people, which, in truth, is why I'm giving Cole's story credence where I initially dismissed it as another cruel pack of lies. She'll make an excellent psychologist one day, provided she's not completely distracted from her studies by the horrendous thing that's happened to her.

'I'll be fine,' I tell her, giving her a reassuring smile back. 'I'm only covering for a few hours. I'll go and grab us something special for dinner before I pick the twins up. How does that sound?'

'Like a promise. I'll text you what topping we want,' Ellie says, dropping not-so-subtle pizza hints. 'See you later.'

I watch her go, giving me a wave as she does, and breathe a sigh of relief that she looks a little happier than she did earlier. She needs to take her mind off things and just do what teenagers do. And I have to find a way to bring an end to what's happening at home for the sake of my children as well as my sanity. I've lied to Ellie about the shift, out of necessity. I don't have any reason to go to the hospital other than to see Cole. I have to speak to him about what Ellie told me, and I don't want to do that over the phone. Anger rears furiously inside me as I imagine what that bastard did to her. If I knew who he was, I would find him and I'm absolutely *sure* I wouldn't be responsible for my actions.

Setting off, I take a breath and try to calm myself. It's impossible. My nerves are taut, my mind pinging thoughts back and forth. I just don't know what to believe. I do know I can't live in fear any more, feeling as if I need to be constantly looking over my shoulder. I won't.

My plan, such as it is, is to tell Cole I've reported the messages to the police and gauge his reaction. Once I've done that and then established whether he's absolutely aware of what Ellie has been through, I will try to talk to him more about his own situation, persuade him to be totally honest with me, for her sake, and tell me whether everything his daughter believes to be true actually is. Does he realise, I wonder, that she's looking for him to show her the way forward? That she still believes in him? *Please don't shatter her faith in you, Cole,* I beg silently. *Don't lie to her, not about this.*

Has he really consulted a solicitor? Or is that just more madness from the mouth of a woman who clearly needs urgent psychiatric help? What more is she capable of? I wonder. A cold shiver runs through me as I recall the lies she's told, the merciless manipulation of me and my child – and Ellie *is* still a child, grown-up in so many ways, but young and vulnerable too.

Kelsey has played on that mercilessly, using her as a pawn in her sick game.

I recall what she said to me when Ellie had gone to her house, shouting over me that Ellie had seen something that had made her think Cole was having an affair. The caution and sympathy in her voice as she pretended concern for her, for me; for the boys, hugging them lovingly and bringing them... My heart jarring suddenly and violently as the unthinkable occurs to me, I gasp out a breath. *No*. She wouldn't ever hurt the boys... would she?

FIFTY-FIVE

COLE

Cole was beginning to wonder if he was losing his mind as well as everything else in his life. He wasn't just not functioning properly, he didn't seem to be able to function at all. He should have made time to talk to Hannah, assure her of his support. Instead of which, feeling besieged whichever way he turned, he'd told her he had something pressing to attend to and would catch up with her later. He couldn't face it. The events of that day already played like a horror movie on a loop through his mind. He could still see his father rising from the operating table, his skull wide open, his eyes flint-edged and filled with contempt, his lips moving: *Didn't I say you were too weak to make a good surgeon? Perhaps you can see now where allowing your emotions to rule your head gets you.*

Maybe his father had been right. He had allowed his emotions to get the better of him. He'd sworn an oath to abstain from all intentional wrongdoing and harm, but now he had blood on his hands. How had he arrived at this point in his life? His thoughts swung to that night he couldn't remember, which had kicked off a chain of events that had caused his world to come crashing down. Remorse washed through him as he recalled his reaction after finding Kelsey at his house, trying to get Maddie to leave him. He wasn't sure what had sparked such violence in him. Why he seemed unable to do what he'd always done and not give in to his anger – a dangerous, destructive emotion. He should never have gone to Kelsey's house the other day, where he had as good as assaulted her. Shame swept through him as he tried to imagine how much Maddie had seen. Why the hell had he done it? He didn't really need to search for the answer. It was because Kelsey had made him feel just like his father had. Impotent all over again. Like he was someone to be treated with nothing but disdain. Like nothing. As if his feelings were irrelevant. He'd hated his father, but he hated himself more – for allowing him to control him. He hated Kelsey too. He'd wanted to hurt her, to humiliate her. He badly wanted to hurt the bastard who'd dared lay a finger on his daughter.

Feeling no better for the shower he'd taken, he bought a sandwich from the hospital café, sat down and looked at it, then pushed it away. In need of the caffeine, he swigged back his coffee, then pulled out his phone and googled barristers named Wainwright. It didn't take him long to find the address of a likely candidate on the barristers' register. Having a father with such a prestigious CV was no doubt why his shit of a son thought he could get away with what he'd done. He probably *would* get away with it, he thought, fury building inside him. Maybe he should pay the barrister a visit. It would be informative to see what kind of man had made his son what he was.

Finishing off his coffee, he left the café to go and find Hannah. He needed to talk to her, try to reassure her that the odds had been stacked against his father coming through the operation, that the aneurysm would have haemorrhaged anyway, but he had to own his actions. He had frozen at a critical moment, casting doubt on her skills as a surgeon. All he could do was tell the truth. The external investigation would review the treatment received by the patient with a view to improving future care. Cole hoped it would end there.

Going into the department, where he noted Alex's decidedly hostile gaze as he glanced in his direction, he asked around for Hannah. Finding she'd just left for her break, he headed back towards the café. He'd obviously missed her. His step faltered as he saw Kelsey coming towards him along the corridor. With her gaze on her phone, her thumbs tapping away at it, she didn't notice him until she'd almost walked into him. Her eyes shot wide when she saw him. 'Messaging someone?' he asked interestedly.

'I really don't think that's any of your business, Cole, do you?' she retorted.

She was unbelievable. Cole shook his head scornfully. 'I think it actually *is*, don't you?' he asked, trying very hard to remain calm as there were people about.

She ignored that. 'Excuse me,' she said, nodding past him.

Cole stayed where he was. 'You need to stop, Kelsey,' he warned her, his gaze locked hard on hers.

She looked away, a smile curving her mouth as she made to walk away. He caught her arm, squeezing it none too gently as he leaned to whisper in her ear.

'If you don't, I'll fucking well make sure you do. Got it?'

FIFTY-SIX

ALEX

Alex watched with a mixture of disdain and growing anger as Kelsey tore her arm from Cole's grasp. When Cole turned around to watch her hurry away from him, Alex stepped back into the side corridor he'd just emerged from. Having decided to keep tabs on Cole with a view to obtaining whatever evidence he could to persuade Maddie just how deep her husband's deceit ran, he hadn't expected to be provided with it quite so soon, though he hadn't been quick enough to get a clear photo of the intimate conversation he'd just witnessed.

Seeing Kelsey walk past, her face like thunder and agitatedly tapping at her phone, he gave it a second and then stepped back into the corridor behind her. Cole was continuing in the opposite direction, he noted, dragging a hand over the back of his neck as he went. Was he realising that illicit sex wasn't quite such a thrill after all? He would be pissed off, Alex imagined, realising his marriage as well as his career might be on the line. Upset, too, undoubtedly. If it wasn't Maddie he was treating so deplorably, Alex might have been able to forgive him his moment of madness and be there for him. Knowing it was Maddie, though, he simply couldn't.

Debating, he went after Kelsey. She was supposed to be Maddie's friend. He didn't like to think badly of the woman – affairs happened – but fucking her best friend's husband behind her back while smiling to her face took betrayal to a whole new level.

As he followed her along the corridor, heading towards the general surgery department, she glanced back at him, almost as if she could sense his eyes boring into her. Hitching her bag higher on her shoulder, she quickened her pace. What would she do if he confronted her with what he knew? Make a scene, probably. The performance he'd witnessed in the hospital grounds hadn't been solely to give Cole grief. She'd been upset, yes, but Alex reckoned she'd wanted to draw attention. She wanted it out in the open in order to force Cole's hand. She wanted Cole. The thing was, Alex was pretty sure Maddie wouldn't give him up easily.

When she paused at the doors leading to the ward, Alex hung back, pulling out his own phone and pretending to talk into it while he waited for her finish her messaging. What was she writing? A book?

As he saw her reading over what she'd typed and pressing send, he hurried towards her and reached to push the door open for her.

'Thank you,' she said.

'No problem.' He smiled, following her through into the ward reception area. 'I'm just checking on a patient.'

'Oh, right.' Her expression was cautious as her gaze travelled over him. She would know he worked with Cole, so he guessed she would be wary.

'I was wondering...' He paused, waiting while she pushed her phone into the pocket of the bag hanging over her shoulder. 'Feel free to say no,' he went on as, arching one perfectly groomed eyebrow, she looked curiously back at him, 'but I wondered if you fancied going for a drink sometime? Or a coffee maybe?'

She folded her arms, her look now one of boredom. 'No,' she said bluntly, and twirled around.

Suit yourself. Your loss. Alex shrugged and followed her to the doors into the ward. He felt sweat prickle his forehead as he reached past her to do the gentlemanly thing again, enabling him to slide the phone from the pocket of her bag.

Once back in the corridor, he checked the home screen. Seeing it was still lit, he scrolled to keep it that way as he diverted into the nearest patient toilet. Who was it she was so frenetically texting? Recalling Maddie's reaction to the text she'd received when she'd come in on the pretext of picking up Cole's jacket, his intuition told him he knew. Maddie had been wary as she'd checked her phone. More than that, he'd sensed she'd been scared.

FIFTY-SEVEN

MADDIE

Seeing a vacant spot close to the hospital, I park quickly and hurry to the entrance. I've made up my mind to seek Kelsey out before talking to Cole. With fear gnawing at me that her demented threats might become more than verbal, I have to find a way to warn her off. Make her realise I would kill before allowing any harm to come to my children, as any mother would. *If* she's pregnant, maybe one day she will realise that.

The advantage of being an agency nurse is that I'm known here, meaning I can wander around without attracting too much attention. Nausea and nerves churn inside me as I make my way to the general surgery ward. Finding she's on her break, I head for the neurosurgical department, praying that Cole will be there. I have to talk to him. If all he said is the absolute truth, then she really is more dangerous than I've allowed myself to imagine.

As I walk along the corridor, I see Tara coming towards me. 'Hey, Mads, how're you doing?' she asks, smiling widely.

'Good.' I force a smile back. 'You?'

'Overworked, underpaid. Usual story,' she replies with a

good-natured roll of her eyes. 'Are you working here today or have you come to see Cole?'

'I thought I'd surprise him.' I somehow manage to keep the smile fixed on my face. 'See if he's got time for a quick coffee. You haven't seen him around, have you?'

'I did earlier,' Tara says. 'There haven't been any emergency admissions, so I guess he's either in surgery or floating around somewhere. Have you checked his schedule with Neuro?'

'Just about to. Oh, how's the little one?' I remember to ask. Tara's baby is just six months old. After her partner did a runner, she decided to go it alone. I have no idea how she does it and manages to stay so upbeat.

'Oh, he's doing grand,' she assures me, smiling fondly. 'A handful, as my mam never fails to inform me when I pick the little fella up. But I won't bore you with all that now and keep you from your gorgeous hubs. Doesn't have a brother by any chance, does he? One who's willing to take on a slightly knackered but gorgeous single parent?'

I emit a half-hearted laugh. 'No. Sorry.'

'Damn.' Tara sighs theatrically. 'You can't blame a girl for trying.' Her smile back in place, she gives me a hug. 'We'll have a catch-up soon. See you later.'

As she hurries back towards A&E, I swallow back a lump of emotion. Tara's incorrigible; she makes eyes at all the good-looking men who come into the place, doctors and patients alike. The fact is, though, I know she genuinely likes Cole as a person. Everyone does. Without exception, people think he's kind and caring. That's what makes what he's done to me, to his family, so incredibly unbelievable. *Has* he done anything, though? My thoughts swing back and forth. He must have encouraged her, mustn't he? Given her some sort of green light. He was drinking in the bar with her, after all. Wouldn't she have made assumptions that... My thoughts screech to a halt as I realise what I'm doing. I'm applying double standards and I'm appalled at myself.

Jabbing at the access button once I reach Neurology, I give my name, saying I've come to see Cole.

'Oh, okay,' someone says and buzzes me through.

It's Hannah Lee, I realise, as she hovers by the desk looking uncertainly towards me. 'Hi.' I give her a brief smile. 'Is Cole around, do you know?'

'I'm not sure,' she says, smiling timidly back. 'I spoke to him a while ago, but I haven't seen him since.'

'And he's not in surgery?' I check.

She shakes her head. 'There are no further procedures on the list. You could ask Alex,' she adds, nodding behind her as she moves to walk past me. 'He's in the department somewhere, I think.'

'Okay. Thanks.' Perturbed, I watch her hurry to the door. 'Hannah,' I stop her, 'is everything all right? You seem a bit distracted.' It's possibly because of my reaction when I found her in the relatives' room with Cole, but she seems to be avoiding making eye contact with me.

'I have an appointment,' she says, looking nervous as she turns back. She hesitates for a beat, then, 'I'm sorry,' she blurts.

Sorry? Why? Apprehension twists inside me as I recall what Cole said to Ellie. *She'd just heard that her mother had died.* Wasn't she supposed to be going home for the funeral? But then Cole said that with the investigation looming, she thought she wouldn't be able to take time out to go. Was the whole thing just another convoluted web of lies? Nothing but a sob story to get Ellie on side? He was in the bar with her. Drinking with Kelsey in that same bar. He doesn't *drink.* 'What is it you're sorry for?' I ask warily.

Again she hesitates, and I want to shake the information from her. 'My appointment is with the hospital board,' she says eventually.

Relief surges through me, swiftly followed by a new kind of fear. 'What will you tell them?' I ask, desperate to know, not wanting to. 'I heard you talking to Alex, telling him you thought Cole froze. Did he?'

She looks back at me, nodding reluctantly – and my heart falters. *Did* he kill him? 'But only for a millisecond,' she says quickly.

I wait, every nerve in my body tensing.

'It was my fault,' she goes on. 'It was a complicated procedure and I panicked. I know that in all probability the patient... his father... wouldn't have made it anyway, but it was my fault, not Cole's.' She lifts her chin as if owning the blame. 'He's a good surgeon. A good man. I've wanted to be a neurosurgeon since I started medical school. I've worked hard, but it's difficult for a female surgeon in a male-dominated industry, you know? It's like a boys' club sometimes. You're totally dependent on your trainer, and Cole was there for me. I wouldn't have made it this far without him.' She smiles tentatively again as I stare at her, dumbfounded. 'I trusted him with my life in a way,' she adds. 'He didn't let me down. I owe it to him to be there for him now.'

As what she's saying sinks in, my emotions collide. Everyone seems to trust my husband but me. I want to believe him, desperately. But can I? I have to talk to Kelsey. Confront her face to face. I can't avoid it any longer.

My mind racing, I'm making my way back to the general surgical ward when my phone pings. Shakily, I pause and check it to find another blood-freezing message that stops my heart dead, *You think you know what he's capable of, but you don't. Check his car.* Terror permeates every cell in my body.

FIFTY-EIGHT
COLE

Having learned that Hannah was currently being interviewed by the hospital board, nerves tightened Cole's stomach like a slip knot. They would also have contacted Alex, he realised, in whose estimation he appeared to be a complete bastard. What might he say? Would he tell them he was involved with a member of staff? That the relationship was volatile, aggressive, bound to be affecting his work? Sweat beaded his forehead as he recalled the argument with Kelsey, the accusations she'd hurled. Had Alex heard everything? Nausea churned inside him. If he was asked, he would have to be honest, bare his soul to the trust and tell them what was going on. They would want to speak to Kelsey, who would claim that he'd spiked *her* drink, that she was the victim. Who were they likely to believe? He would be suspended. God only knew what might follow. A police investigation? How would he cope with that? How would his family? Panic gripped him, rising so fast it threatened to choke him. He couldn't think straight. Couldn't breathe. As the walls of the corridor seemed to shift violently towards him, he headed swiftly for the exit.

Once he reached his car, he sat in it with the door open and tried to drag air into his lungs. It took him several minutes to get some kind of control over his emotions. When he reached for his phone, his hands were shaking. *Jesus Christ*, he was supposed to be a surgeon and he couldn't even focus on his phone. Managing the task after a moment, he selected Alex's number. Alex didn't pick up. He probably wanted nothing to do with him. Cole was gutted, but he wasn't surprised. Alex cared about Maddie. He might even see Maddie and him splitting up as an opportunity. He quashed the thought fast. He was angry, angry and mistrustful of a man who'd always been there for him, covering his back when he had no obligation to. He wouldn't be doing that now.

He needed to find Kelsey. She was the last person on earth he wanted to speak to, but he had no choice. He had to convince her to keep her mouth shut, beg her if he had to, do whatever it took.

He was in the main corridor when his phone buzzed. Hoping it might be a reply from Alex, he checked it and cursed himself when he realised it was a message from Ellie, asking if he was okay. She'd sent a previous message, a good two hours earlier, and he'd been so preoccupied with his own problems, he hadn't seen it.

Quickly, he responded. *Ish. You?*

Ellie texted back straight away. *Ish. Been shopping with Claire. I was going to go into uni but saw Wainwright in campus grounds. Sneered when he saw me. Was laughing with his mates. Can we talk later?*

Cole felt rage, white-hot, bubble up inside him. That piece of scum was wandering around the campus as if he didn't have a care in the world, joking with his mates about *his* daughter, what he'd done to her. It wasn't happening. No way was Cole about to let it. Unable to trust himself to speak to her right then, he texted her back. *Of course. Something I need to do now, but can I call you?*

Please. Her reply came back with a smiley emoji attached, and it cracked his heart wide open. She was playing it down, trying to buoy him up, even though she was clearly struggling.

About an hour, he texted. *Love you.* X

After calling Neuro and praying no emergencies came in that might have to be transferred to another neurosurgical unit, he headed again for the exit. An hour should be long enough to do what he had to. The university was only a short drive away.

Love you too. X Her reply came up on his hands-free as he drove, steadily, purposefully. He didn't want to get pulled over before he arrived.

Parking in the university car park, he headed for the School of Law, located on the far side of the campus. After striding through the foyer, checking his watch and trying to look as if he belonged there, he took the lift to the floor teaching undergraduate law. Judging by his father's CV and assuming his son would likely be aiming to join his team, Cole was thinking that was where he might be. If he wasn't, then he would find out where he lived. Whatever, he would find him.

He waited for a while – unchallenged, thankfully – then headed to a lecture room as the students spilled out. 'Excuse me.' He caught the attention of a guy and a young woman chatting together. 'I'm looking for Luke Wainwright. I was told downstairs he might be attending the lecture.'

The young man furrowed his brow questioningly.

'It's about his father,' Cole added, lying through his teeth.

'Oh, right.' Concern crossing his features, the guy looked him over, then glanced back towards the lecture hall. 'He's just on his way out,' he said.

Following his gaze, Cole wasn't sure who he meant until someone further back called, 'Hey, Luke, wait up.'

Cole waited until the man he gathered was the one he was looking for came ambling out. He was good-looking, he noted, as much as he could judge good looks in a man, the sort Ellie would go for. Also tall. As tall as him, and well built. Obviously he worked out. No matter.

He stepped forward as the man exited the doors. 'Luke Wainwright?' he asked, smiling amiably.

Wainwright frowned. 'Who's asking?' he said, clearly wary.

And so he should be. 'Cole. Cole Chase,' Cole introduced himself, getting some small satisfaction when the penny dropped and the look in the man's eyes switched to fear.

'Whatever she said is bullshit.' Wainwright made to move around him.

Cole sidestepped, stopping him. 'My daughter has a name,' he said, trying very hard to hold on to his temper. 'I assume it's her you're talking about?'

As the man's mate joined him, squaring up next to him, Cole kept his gaze fixed firmly on the human flotsam in front of him. 'Or are there other young women making accusations against you, Luke?' he asked. 'Might that explain why your memory's a little bit hazy?'

'She's lying,' Wainwright answered shakily.

'Luke?' Another guy joined him. 'Need any help?'

'No.' Wainwright swallowed. 'I'm good,' he said – wisely.

Cole's gaze didn't flinch. 'Ellie,' he reminded him. 'Do you remember what you did to her, Luke?' His tone was remarkably calm, considering.

Shaking his head, Wainwright emitted a weary sigh. 'I've told you, whatever she said, she's lying.'

Cole glanced down, kneaded his forehead hard with his thumb. Looked back up.

'I hooked up with her once and then I ditched her,' Wainwright went on with an insolent shrug. 'Sorry if I hurt her feelings and all that, but she was a bit needy, you know? Lovestruck, I guess. I mean, what's a bloke supposed to do?' He glanced at his mates, a smirk on his face.

It was that smirk that lit the fuse that caused Cole's temper to explode. In one second flat, he pulled his fist back and floored him.

As Wainwright went down, Cole was on him before he had time to blink. Clutching the front of his T-shirt, he yanked him towards him until they were eyeball to eyeball. 'You raped her, you bastard,' he seethed. 'And before you or your minions decide to call the police and then bring Daddy in to get you off any charges, perhaps you would like to consider what such an accusation becoming public might do to your career. I doubt my daughter was the first. Consider that too, *Luke*. If you want this ball to roll, I'm happy to go with it.'

He held Wainwright's gaze meaningfully for a second longer, then dropped him. 'Incidentally,' he said, straightening up, 'spread any rumours about my daughter or go within fifty miles of her, and I'll do more than bloody your nose. I'll break your fucking neck. Got it?'

He waited until the guy nodded before walking away.

FIFTY-NINE

MADDIE

As I hurry away from the hospital entrance towards my car, someone calls out behind me. 'Maddie, everything okay?' Alex, I realise. He obviously saw me all but running down the main corridor, desperate to get away from the hospital. From Cole. From the deranged woman we were both of us fools to have anything to do with.

'Yes. Late for an appointment,' I call back, pressing my key fob and climbing quickly in. He's still watching me, I notice as I glance through the windscreen. Clearly concerned, he waits until I start the engine and then turns to go back inside.

Sighing with relief – I can't talk to anyone right now – I start to pull out, then stamp on the brake, shove the door open and vomit what little food I've eaten. I give myself a moment, then close the door and rest my head against the headrest. What am I going to do? I heave in a breath, and another, a raucous sob shuddering through me as I try to think. I have no choice. I have to call the police. What does he have in his car? My mind conjuring up terrifying scenarios, I grab my bag from the passenger seat and dig out my phone. My heart stops as I realise there's another message. *I just spoke to Ellie. She called me a psycho bitch. She's going to end up in serious trouble if she's not careful.*

When did she speak to her. *How?* Hands trembling, I grope for my purse, pull out the card DI Ingram gave me and call the number.

After a moment, he picks up, thankfully. I don't think I would be capable of trying to explain the urgency of the situation to someone else. 'Detective Inspector Ingram,' he answers efficiently. 'How can I—'

'It's Maddie,' I blurt. 'Madelyn Chase. I've received more messages. I believe they're a direct threat and...' My voice cracks. 'I'm terrified. For myself. For my children. I don't know what to do.'

'Okay, slow down, Mrs Chase,' he urges me, his voice soothingly calm. 'Would you like to relay what the messages say?'

I read them out falteringly, my terror mounting. I simply can't make myself believe there's such evil in my husband. That he would risk his family, his career, for a woman who's blatantly wicked. Am I *so* wrong about him?

'Do you know your husband's whereabouts at present?' Ingram asks.

'No.' I try to compose myself and focus. 'He was here at the hospital earlier, I've checked, but I've seen no sign of him.'

'Right.' He pauses. 'Where are your children, Mrs Chase?' he asks, still calm, while my heart is banging so hard I'm sure it's about to burst through my ribcage.

'The twins are at school. Ellie's at university. Do you think I should collect the twins and—'

'No,' he says quickly. 'We'll send a car to the school. What I would like you to do is go back into the hospital and make sure you have people around you.'

Back inside? Nausea swirls afresh at the thought.

'Call your daughter, make sure she really is at the university and that she also has company,' he adds, a grave edge to his voice now that makes my blood run cold. 'We'll endeavour to locate your husband. Meanwhile–'

'But what if you don't?' I interrupt. 'I have to collect the children.'

'I'm sending a car, Mrs Chase,' he reminds me. 'I'll keep in touch. Could you forward me the messages you've received meanwhile? It might help.'

I nod and swallow. 'Yes, okay.'

If these threats turn out to be empty, all this will be for nothing, but I simply couldn't ignore them. My stomach roiling, guilt twisting inside me at what might happen to Cole if this is all baseless, I end the call and select Ellie's number. It seems to ring for an age before her voicemail picks up. 'Ellie, it's Mum,' I say quickly. 'Where are you? Please call me back as soon as you get this. It's important, sweetheart.'

After sending her a text as well, I climb out and head back to the main entrance. I'm almost there when the squeal of sirens behind me freezes my blood in my veins.

Receiving a text from Ellie simultaneously, I check it and my breath stalls. *I'm in the hospital. I was looking for Dad.*

My heart lurches violently. Oh God, no.

SIXTY

COLE

Cole hesitated outside the house. He could still feel his father's presence. He thought he'd escaped him, but that was never going to happen, was it? The man would probably gain great satisfaction from knowing he would haunt him for the rest of his life. Bracing himself for the reception he would probably get, he knocked and waited, rather than use the key his mother had let him have when he was supposed to be helping her through her grief. He'd only added to it. She'd even had to organise the funeral with only her sister's help. He doubted he could have been of much use, though. He certainly wouldn't want to be a pallbearer. He guessed his mother would know that.

After a while, he heard her come to the door. 'Who is it?' she called warily.

'It's me, Mum, Cole,' he said, and waited again, thinking she might not even want to see him.

His mother fiddled with the door, releasing the chain and then opening it. 'Good Lord.' Her eyes widened in alarm when she saw him. 'You look dreadful.'

Cole glanced down. 'I feel it,' he said, looking back at her. 'How are you?'

'I think it's safe to say I've been better,' she answered him honestly as she moved back to let him in.

Once in the hall, Cole had no idea what to say. There was nothing that could make right what had happened, the fact that he'd as good as abandoned her when she needed his support. 'Sorry,' he said awkwardly.

His mother breathed out a long sigh, then reached to wrap her arms around him.

Swallowing hard, Cole hugged her back. He felt like weeping, for her, for all that she'd lost, the years kowtowing to a bully. Her faith in him, the son she'd been so proud of and thought she could rely on. For himself, selfishly. The mess his marriage was in was down to him. If only he'd been man enough to open his mouth, he could have saved Maddie and his kids all the hurt, stopped things escalating until they were out of control, until he lost control. But he wasn't man enough, was he? It wouldn't have happened in the first place if he was.

'I'll make you some tea,' his mother said, easing away and turning to the kitchen. 'It won't fix anything, and I gather you have some monumental things that need fixing, but it might perk you up a bit.'

Cole couldn't help but smile. It would take a hell of a lot more than tea to do that. He generally steered clear of alcohol, but he'd never in his life felt more like getting drunk to the point of oblivion.

His mother chatted on about the funeral arrangements while she made the tea. 'It's Wednesday next week,' she said, glancing up at him.

Cole took a second, then nodded. As much as he didn't want to, he would go, but for her, not for his father.

'You won't have to deliver a eulogy or anything,' his mother went on, carrying two mugs across to the table. 'I've asked one of his colleagues at the Rotary Club to do that.'

Someone who would no doubt expound on his father's

virtues, of which there were few. He was a good surgeon, but beyond that his colleague would be scraping the barrel. Ironically, Cole's own virtues wouldn't be listed as many now.

'I've made it strong,' his mother said, handing him his tea. Then, 'Have you been involved in a fight?' she asked, worry creasing her forehead.

She'd obviously noted the blood on his shirt, his bruised knuckles. Cursing quietly for not thinking, Cole took the mug and then reached to squeeze her hand. 'The door won,' he joked. He didn't want to worry her more.

His mother sat down at the table. 'I have to ask you, Cole,' she looked him over carefully, 'did your father die because of something you did?'

Cole closed his eyes. He'd guessed she would ask eventually. He couldn't lie to her. 'I froze,' he admitted, his voice strained. 'The aneurysm was large. It had ruptured. His chances were negligible to nil, but... I froze. I have no idea why.'

His mother searched his eyes for a long moment. 'Because you were emotionally traumatised,' she said finally. 'Just as you've always been by him. You were good at compartmentalising your emotions, Cole. You couldn't have achieved all you have if you weren't. Clearly they got the better of you in that situation.'

She already knew. Cole searched her eyes in turn. He had no idea how to respond.

'Frankly, I'm only surprised that hasn't happened before now,' she went on. Obviously she didn't know how close he'd come to losing it that day in the garden. 'Your father wasn't a nice man. A good surgeon,' she conceded, reiterating his thoughts, 'but as a man, he was an abhorrent bully and a coward.'

'Did you love him?' he asked, his throat catching.

His mother thought about it. 'When I first met him, I suppose, though it was more that I was awestruck, I think. If you're wondering whether I cared for him, then the answer is yes. Of course I cared.'

Cole dropped his gaze. He couldn't look at her right then.

'I would care for a sick animal too,' she added. 'My heart's not made of stone like his was.' She reached for his injured hand, brushing a thumb lightly over his bruises. 'I didn't love him, though. I haven't for a very long time. He killed the last scrap of love I might have had for him the day he killed your brother.'

Jesus. As Cole's mind went to the boy he'd hidden from his father with, cowered in the dark with, shared sun-filled days in the park with, argued with and shared his secrets and dreams with, he couldn't hold back the tears.

'Don't let what happened do this to you, Cole,' his mother said softly. 'Maddie loves you. She needs you. Your children do. Whatever's gone wrong between you, you have to make it right.'

Cole squeezed the bridge of his nose. Would that he could. It was too late.

'You have to make her believe you're sorry. That you love her. If you do, truly, you will convince her. Find a way, Cole,' his mother urged him. 'A woman who loves you has a large capacity for forgiveness, but it's not infinite. If you've made a mistake, you have to be honest with her. You have to end whatever fling or fancy it is you're having, even if it means hurting someone. Better one life is destroyed than the lives of your entire family.'

And therein lay the problem. A life had been destroyed. And he couldn't undo it.

SIXTY-ONE

After a brief visit to the cemetery to visit his brother's grave and give himself some space to think, Cole headed back to the hospital. He tried Maddie's phone several times as he drove. She wasn't picking up. She'd had time to think about what he'd told her and obviously didn't believe him. Could he blame her? Of course there was always the possibility that she did think there was some truth in it and found the whole thing so sordid and distasteful she didn't want to be anywhere near him. Did he really think that of her, though? No, he didn't. She would be appalled by what had happened to him, not by him.

He should have been honest from the outset. He missed her, ached for her, the closeness they'd once had together, with every bone in his body. He was wondering whether he should go and meet her when she picked the twins up in the hope that she would talk to him however she felt. After speaking to his mother, he'd made up his mind he would go to the police. He had to send Ellie a clear message that he was prepared to bare his soul whatever the consequences. He was about to turn around and head to the school when he thought better of it. Maddie was wary last time he'd ambushed her, and he didn't want to do anything that might destabilise Lucas and Jayden more than they already had been.

His priority now was to call Ellie back, as he'd promised he would. He only hoped she hadn't got wind of what he'd done to the bastard who'd raped her, which she might well have if someone had posted something on social media. He would rather that information came directly from him. It would come out anyway, undoubtedly. He would just have to deal with those consequences too.

He tried her number again once he'd parked the car, and again as he walked towards the hospital. Noting the presence of several police vehicles as he neared the main entrance, his heart jarred. Had what he'd done to Wainwright come out already? But there was too much of a police presence for them to be here for him, surely? Christ, he hoped there hadn't been a major incident while he was away. Breaking into a run, he pushed through the reception doors, only to be stopped by a police officer. 'Sorry, sir, we need to clear the area. If you could—'

'I'm a surgeon here,' Cole interrupted, dodging around the man as he saw Ellie hurrying through the doors from the main corridor.

Calling out to her, he raced towards her, his chest constricting. She was as white as a sheet and shaking. 'What is it, Ellie? What's happened?' He caught hold of her shoulders, his blood running cold as his mind shot to Maddie and the twins.

'Nothing,' she said quickly. 'I came to see you. I was looking for you, but...' She stopped, her eyes – frightened child's eyes – growing wide with alarm as she looked past him. Cole glanced over his shoulder, and his stomach lurched as he saw the officer he'd skirted around and another man, who looked like a plain-clothes officer, heading purposefully towards him.

'Cole Chase?' The suited guy showed him his warrant card. 'Detective Inspector Steve Ingram, and this is PC Saj Basu.

Following a tip-off, we have reasonable grounds to believe that you are in possession of drugs and/or an offensive weapon.'

'*What?*' Cole stared at him in shocked disbelief.

'Possession of an offensive weapon in a public place is an offence under Section 1 of the Prevention of Crime Act 1953,' the man went on. 'I'm therefore informing you that we intend to carry out a vehicle search.'

What in Christ's name were they talking about? Cole felt his heart rate escalate. 'I'm a doctor,' he said, squinting confusedly at him. 'I have had occasion to carry drugs in my car, but I'm not now. And I'm certainly not carrying an offensive weapon.'

'Failure to give consent will result in you being detained for twenty-four hours for questioning without formal arrest,' the man continued stonily. 'It would be helpful if you could show us where your vehicle is parked, sir.'

Cole noted the steely look in his eyes and his blood almost stopped pumping. Seeing the uniformed officer placing a hand on the cuffs he was carrying, his chest tightened. Refusing, he realised, wasn't an option.

'Sir?' the detective urged him, nodding towards the entrance.

Tugging in a breath, Cole glanced at Ellie. 'Call your mum,' he said. 'Don't move until she gets here.'

Looking back at the detective, he sucked in another breath and headed towards the doors, the two officers flanking him. He could sense eyes swivelling in his direction as he walked, suspicion burning into him. He felt like a condemned man. But what was it he was supposed to be guilty of? This was bigger than him punching Wainwright, he was sure of that.

'Dad,' Ellie called frantically behind him. '*Dad!*'

Cole's step faltered. His heart almost stopped beating when the detective took hold of his arm, physically encouraging him on. Wrenching his head around, he glanced back to see Alex approaching Ellie. Relief crashed through him. 'Look after her, Alex. Will you do that for me?' he yelled, desperate to keep his daughter safe.

Alex didn't hesitate, nodding sharply, despite their fractured friendship.

Cole kept walking. What was happening here? Where was Maddie? The twins? It was close to pick-up time. His gut turned over as his mind raced through every worst-case scenario. 'Are my family safe?' he asked the detective, who seemed determined to keep him in the dark about why he was being escorted from his place of work, accused of carrying drugs. An offensive weapon, for Christ's sake. This was a nightmare. It had to be.

Once in the car park, he indicated his car, then suffered the indignity of being searched in front of onlookers while being asked for his name and address, date of birth and self-defined ethnicity, as if they hadn't already established who he was.

After being handed his jacket back, which had also been thoroughly searched, he waited while the uniformed officer, assisted by another officer who'd joined him, went through the interior of the car, inspecting the glove compartment, even pulling the sun visors down and checking those – looking for anything taped to them, he assumed.

Ingram nodded as one of the officers shook his head, indicating they'd found nothing, then walked towards him.

'What the hell is this all about?' Cole asked, frustration rising rapidly inside him.

The detective avoided answering. 'Could you open the boot, please, Mr Chase?' he asked instead, his smile as brittle as ice.

Cole's glance was contemptuous. He couldn't help it. The boot was unlocked. All the man had to do was lift it. Sighing heavily, he walked around to it and opened it, and his heart stopped dead. 'It isn't mine,' he said, his throat drying as he stared down at enough ampoules of ketamine to kill a horse.

SIXTY-TWO

Cole felt the blood drain from his body as he looked up to see Maddie standing just yards away. She looked so vulnerable, so petrified, he felt something break inside him. He had no idea what to say. What reassurance could he offer her? How could he hope to convince her he hadn't been willingly complicit in any of the madness that had descended on them?

He kept eye contact with her, his heart dropping to the pit of his stomach as Ingram started to caution him. 'Cole Chase, we are legally obliged to inform you that we are arresting you on suspicion of carrying Class B drugs...'

Cole kept looking at Maddie. 'They're not mine,' he said, his voice a hoarse whisper.

'You do not have to say anything, but it may harm your defence if you fail to mention when questioned something which you later rely on in court,' Ingram went on, every sentence like a nail in his coffin. 'Anything you do say may be given in evidence. Do you understand, Mr Chase?'

'Yes,' Cole answered quietly. Dropping his gaze as an officer produced handcuffs and moved behind him to take hold of his arms, he gulped back the cold fear like an icicle in his chest.

How had this happened? he wondered dazedly. Feeling sick to the depths of his soul, he couldn't meet Maddie's gaze as he was led away. Couldn't look into the eyes of the woman whose love for him had never faltered, even when he hadn't been there for her. If he looked and saw what he was bound to see, he'd be lost, utterly.

'Cole!' Maddie called wretchedly as they walked towards a waiting police car.

He wrenched his head around to glance back at her. 'I'm not responsible for this, Maddie,' he said, his voice desperate. 'Do you believe me?'

She didn't answer, but continued to study him, her expression now a mixture of bewilderment, hurt and uncertainty. 'Maddie!' Panic twisting violently inside him, Cole shouted the words as they urged him on. 'Do you believe me?'

Still she didn't answer. Feeling as if a prison door had just slammed shut on him, he resisted for a heartbeat as the officer to his side tugged at his arm, and then turned away.

'Cole!' Maddie called behind him. 'I'm *trying*,' she cried, a sob catching her throat.

His emotion threatening to spill over, Cole swallowed hard. He didn't deserve her support. She had every right to walk away, but he simply wouldn't know how to be without her. Wouldn't want to be. Hoping against hope that they would find some evidence of who'd done this, he prayed hard that she wouldn't give up on him, that she would realise how much he loved her.

Assisted into the back of the police car, avoiding cracking his head this time thanks to a strategically placed hand, he felt very much as he had the evening his life had become a living nightmare: detached from his body, and more lonely than he'd ever been in his life. As they drove, he asked about a phone call. Ingram told him he'd be offered one in due course.

. . .

Once he'd gone through the galling experience of being processed at the station, the custody officer informing him of his rights and explaining how long they could hold him before applying for permission to hold him longer without charge, he was taken to a soulless interview room, where he waited for what seemed like an eternity.

Eventually Ingram appeared and asked him whether he would like them to provide legal representation. Cole declined the offer of a duty solicitor. He could change his mind later, he was told. He hoped to Christ he didn't need a criminal solicitor, but he had contacts at the tennis club. He would ask Maddie to make the call for him, assuming she would want to, that she would even speak to him.

Ingram proceeded to caution him again, explaining how often he could take breaks. Cole's heart pounded so hard it was all he could do to acknowledge what he was being told with a nod. The detective introduced another officer, a DS Conner, then informed Cole that the interview would be recorded, 'to protect the police and yourself from any claims you've been made to say things you did not wish to, or things that were untrue,' he finished with a smile that was anything but reassuring.

'So, Cole.' Ingram laced his fingers together and placed his hands on the table in front of him. 'Finally, just a reminder that anything you say is voluntary. If you do not wish to say anything at all, then you may exercise this right. If you do decide to talk to us, everything you say will be played to the court if you choose to plead not guilty to the charge and it goes to a trial. Do you understand?'

This was really happening, wasn't it? Cole wiped away the perspiration beading his forehead. 'Yes, I understand,' he answered, his chest tight.

'Right. Good.' Ingram shuffled his various papers. A

delaying tactic, Cole wondered, to make him feel more nervous than he already was? It was working.

'So how are you feeling?' the detective asked, with another one of his loaded smiles.

Cole almost laughed at that. 'Not great,' he said.

'You look tired.' Ingram furrowed his brow, appearing concerned.

'I work long hours,' Cole answered.

'Been losing sleep too, I bet,' Ingram said, now scrutinising him carefully. 'We've been looking at your phone. There are some interesting message exchanges.'

Cole said nothing. He really needed this to get to where it was going.

'Tell me about the drugs, Cole.' Ingram picked up his pen and tapped it on the table. 'While I can accept that you might have cause to carry a small quantity of ketamine, the stash we found in your car really does require explanation, don't you think? Particularly after the message your wife received.'

'What message?' Cole's heart missed a beat.

'A warning,' Ingram expanded. 'Hinting at what you were capable of. Telling her to check your car. You can see why we would be concerned.'

Jesus Christ. Cole reeled inwardly. Did she believe he would actually harm her? Clearly she must. She'd reported it. He swiped a hand over his face, a new wave of panic unfurling inside him. 'The ketamine's not mine,' he repeated. 'I didn't put it there.'

'I see.' Ingram placed his pen down, folded his arms and sat back in his chair. 'And do you have any idea who might have put it there?' he asked. 'Someone who would have access to your car keys, presumably? A member of your family, perhaps?'

Cole kneaded his forehead. It was going to sound incredible whichever way he said it, but what else could he do but tell it as it was? 'A colleague,' he answered, wiping again at the sweat tickling his forehead.

'A colleague with a grudge?' Ingram enquired, his eyebrows arched curiously.

Cole took a second. 'The woman I'm supposed to be having an affair with,' he replied uncomfortably. 'She's been harassing me, harassing my wife. She's obviously trying to incriminate me for some reason.'

'I see.' Ingram frowned. 'And if you could hazard a guess, what reason do you think that might be?' He leaned further back, tipping his head to one side, while the other detective looked as if he was actually enjoying watching Cole squirm.

'I'm not having an affair with her,' Cole tried to explain. 'She's delusional. She's managed to convince herself we are in a relationship. We're not,' he stated categorically.

'Your interchange of messages would suggest otherwise,' Ingram pointed out. 'Didn't she claim she was pregnant?' He turned to his sidekick for confirmation.

The man looked at his paperwork and nodded. 'That's right, sir.'

DI Ingram looked back at Cole. 'Yours?' he asked him.

Cole closed his eyes. 'I... don't know.'

'I see,' Ingram said again, his expression bland.

'I was with her for one night,' Cole went on awkwardly. 'It was a mistake.'

'It usually is... after the event,' the detective commented drolly. 'And? How did it make you feel, Mr Chase, the harassment that presumably began after this "mistake"? Angry? Bewildered?'

'Both of the above,' Cole concurred throatily. 'Plus...' he looked up, eyeing the man levelly, 'ashamed.'

Ingram looked him over questioningly. 'Why was that, Cole?' he asked.

Cole glanced down again, squeezed the bridge of his nose

hard between his thumb and forefinger. Then, taking a breath, he dispensed with whatever pride he had left and looked directly at Ingram. 'Isn't that how victims of sexual crimes usually feel?'

Ingram's eyes shot wide. Clearly he hadn't expected that.

Cole sucked in another breath. They would never believe him, not in a million years, but he had to do this. 'I was drugged,' he said, wiping again at his face.

Ingram stared at him, incredulous. 'Drugged?'

'Drugged,' Cole repeated. 'Rohypnol, and something else, obviously,' he confirmed, an avalanche of conflicting emotion hitting him all at once. He attempted to block it, to curtail his rage and his shame. He couldn't. He was feeling it. All of it. Every confidence-crushing emotion any victim would live through, some finding it impossible to live with. He wasn't sure he could.

Ingram said nothing for an excruciatingly long moment. Cole noted his pen tapping rapidly on the table again. The other guy had stopped doodling on his notepad and was now scribbling furiously. God only knew what. That Cole needed a psych evaluation probably.

Eventually Ingram coughed awkwardly. 'And?' he urged. 'The interaction between you didn't end there, clearly.'

Cole shook his head, didn't dare look at him for fear he would see the scepticism in the man's eyes. 'She accused me of spiking her drink, of raping her. She lied. She hinted she would go to the police, possibly the hospital board, the papers. I didn't know what to do. I didn't believe she was pregnant, but...' He stopped, hopelessness washing through him as he realised how weak and ridiculous he sounded.

'I see,' the detective said again, nodding slowly. 'And at what point did you decide to murder her, Mr Chase?'

SIXTY-THREE

Earlier that day

She is beautiful, I have to concede. On the outside. Inside, she's as ugly as sin. She doesn't look very pleased to have been set the task of carrying out an inventory of the storage room, which I assume she feels is beneath her. Standing silently behind her, I watch her huffily opening drawers, muttering to herself as she ferrets through medical supplies. Slamming one of the drawers shut, she turns around and starts when she sees me. 'Oh, it's you,' she murmurs, a hand fluttering to her chest. And then she has the actual temerity to smile.

'It would appear to be.' I don't smile back, but stare stonily at her instead. 'I'm glad I caught you on your own.' I watch interestedly as her eyes, a myriad of browns, from amber to umber, which I'd once found intriguing, kind even, grow nervous, flicking past me to the door. She holds no intrigue any more. She's transparent. A jealous, evil woman who cares for no one but herself. To have blithely torn a family apart, traumatising small children without conscience, she's far from kind, despite her vocation.

Clearly realising she isn't going to get through the door without getting through me first, her complexion pales. 'Look, before you say anything, I'm sorry.' She holds up her hands in a show of contrition. 'I didn't plan for any of this to happen.'

I don't answer. Does she really imagine I'm here to talk to her, to listen to her false apologies, her insane justification for what she's done? Judging by the apprehension I see now in her eyes, I think not.

'I should get back,' she says, her gaze darting again to the door. 'People will be wondering where I've got to.'

I see the swallow slide down her slender throat and realise she's scared. It gives me some small satisfaction that she feels a fraction of the fear she's instilled in others. 'You're not sorry.' I continue to stare at her. 'I don't think you actually know the meaning of the word. You're a liar, aren't you? Delusional and dangerous. You've ruined lives.'

'*I've* ruined lives?' Her eyes widen with indignation. 'Excuse me, but it's *you* who's—'

'*My* life!' I seethe, a toxic mix of hatred and hurt writhing inside me.

She snaps her gaze away from me, her eyes, now terrified, those of a cornered animal, skittering around looking for a means to escape the windowless room she's trapped in. With me. No doubt she's wondering what her fate will be.

'Could you let me past, please?' she asks tremulously. 'I have to get back. I'll be missed.'

'Really?' I laugh sardonically. 'About as much as a lung infection. People will be able to *breathe* with you out of the way. Rebuild what you've broken.'

'Let me past.' She takes a determined step forward. Then shrinks back as I do the same.

'I can't really do that, can I?' I point out. 'Not when you're likely to tell tales.'

'I *won't*,' she says quickly. 'I won't say a word, I promise.'

'Your promises are worthless, though, aren't they? "A liar will not be believed, even when he speaks the truth." I learned that at school,' I tell her, my gaze unfaltering as I take the syringe I've prepared especially from my pocket. 'It's attributed to Aesop,' I add, not that I imagine that information will be much use to her now.

'Please don't,' she murmurs, her face draining of all colour as her gaze swivels to the sharp point of the needle. Looking back at me, she notches her chin up, as if summoning her courage. 'You can't hope to get away with it.'

I shrug. 'I don't much care. You reap what you sow. You've destroyed people. Now it's your turn.'

Sensing she's about to scream, I'm on her in an instant, clamping one hand hard over her venomous mouth and shoving her backwards against the wall. 'Don't struggle,' I urge her, my face close to hers, my eyes holding hers as I slide the needle into the side of her pretty neck. 'You'll only make it more stressful.'

Her eyes, pleading for a heartbeat, fill with horror as the liquid flows through her veins. Instinctively she tries to fight, her fingers groping ineffectually at my hand, a muffled *mmmmph* escaping her mouth as she attempts to articulate.

I clamp my hand tighter, watch in fascination as her pupils dilate, magnifying her terror a thousand times. I'm mesmerised by the kaleidoscope of colour I see in her eyes, almost like the changing of the seasons from autumn to winter, as her mind disconnects from her surroundings and they begin to glaze over. Will the brief hallucinogenic effects of the drug be a blessing? I wonder, as she slips from this life into whatever awaits her. I hope so, despite all she's done.

'*Shh*,' I whisper, as the fight leaves her and her body goes limp. I curse silently when, even with my best attempts to help her, she smashes a cheekbone on one of the drawers she left carelessly open. I can't help but feel for her as I stand over her, watching the blood ooze from the deep gash in her face. Still, at least she won't have to mourn the loss of her fragile beauty. I console myself with that thought as the orbs that were a window to her black soul grow empty and she draws her last breath.

SIXTY-FOUR

MADDIE

Now

'Mum, where are you? I just saw Dad being taken away by the police. Why? What's he done, Mum? Please call me back. I'm scared.' As I listen to the tearful message Ellie's left on my phone, my stomach knots. She will be frantic with worry. After all she's gone through, is still going through, the last thing she needs is to witness that. *Dammit.* I jab at my phone in frustration and then, cursing the poor signal in the hospital reception area, head quickly for the corridor, where the signal is usually stronger. I daren't go outside for fear of not being allowed back in. There are police everywhere, swarming all over the hospital and the grounds. Sick trepidation tightens inside me. I don't want to be here, I want to put as much space as possible between myself and this place, but with no clue where my daughter is, there's no way I can leave.

As I push through the doors to the corridor, I almost collide with Tara coming back to A&E. 'Maddie, my God, are you all right?' Her face floods with concern as she looks me over. 'I saw

Cole going off in that police car. You must be out of your mind with worry.'

'I am.' The knot in my stomach ties itself tighter as I imagine what they found in his car. They obviously believed he was planning to kill me. My chest constricts painfully, a hard lump in my throat I can't seem to swallow as I acknowledge that he might have been.

'Well I don't know what he's supposed to have done, but I do know he wouldn't have done the bloody awful thing people are assuming he has,' Tara goes on, sounding indignant for him. 'We're talking about Cole, for goodness' sake, a man who's dedicated his whole life to—'

'What thing?' I stop her, my heart catapulting against my ribcage as my mind catches up with what she's saying.

'Oh no.' Tara's face drops. 'Haven't you heard?'

'Heard what?' I stare at her in confusion.

'Kelsey. Kelsey Roberts.' She studies me carefully. 'I'm so sorry, Maddie. I thought you knew. Me and my big mouth. I thought that was why Cole had been—'

'Tara, *what*?' I implore her.

She looks at me with a mixture of sympathy and wariness. 'She's dead, Mads,' she tells me finally.

'Dead?' I say incredulously. 'But... she *can't* be.'

'I'm so sorry, Maddie.' Tara looks devastated for me. 'I know you and she were close. You must be so shocked, and here's me banging on about it and all.'

'How?' My voice emerges a dry croak.

'I'm not sure.' Tara's gaze flicks awkwardly down and back. 'Rumour has it she was murdered, but you know how gossip runs rife in this place. The police have set up a cordon around the storage room where she was found, but I don't know anything for sure.'

'I have to go,' I mumble, my gaze darting around frantically. 'I have to find Ellie. She's here somewhere. She came to see

Cole, but…' I falter, pressing a hand to my mouth to suppress the sob climbing my throat.

'She's with Alex.' Tara wraps an arm gently around me. 'I saw him with her when Cole was… He asked Alex to look after her. He's probably taken her to the department staff room. It will be quieter there.'

Relief crashes through me. Alex will take care of her. I know him well enough to trust him to do that. 'Thanks,' I murmur.

'You know where I am if you need me,' Tara calls after me as I pull away from her.

Nodding over my shoulder, I hurry on. As I turn into the corridor that leads to Neurology, I slow, my heart jarring as I see people in white suits approaching the cordoned-off area around the storage room.

My eyes fixed down, I take the marked route around it, trying very hard to avoid looking towards the door behind which Kelsey's body might still lie. I'm a yard or so past the cordon when I see something that stops me dead in my tracks: the 'I Love You Unconditionally' charm from Ellie's bracelet. Fear slicing through to the core of me, I glance quickly around and then bend to scoop it up.

SIXTY-FIVE

Approaching the staff room, I see Ellie through the viewing pane in the door and almost wilt with relief. Her gaze snaps towards me as I go in. '*Mum*,' she cries, crashing her mug down so haphazardly Alex only just catches it before it falls from the table. Flying towards me, she throws her arms around me and squeezes me fiercely. 'What's going on?' she mumbles into my shoulder. 'Why have they taken Dad?'

'I don't know, sweetheart.' I hug her tight, then take hold of her shoulders and ease her away. 'But we'll find out. It will be okay, I promise you.' I look straight into her eyes as I lie. I don't know what else to do. How can I tell her the truth? I will. I will have no choice but to. But not now. Not yet. Not until I know whether Cole's being charged, and what with.

'But *how* can it be okay?' Her eyes are petrified, terror emanating from every pore in her body as she looks at me. 'Kelsey's dead. She's fucking well *dead*, Mum.'

'I know, sweetheart. I know.' My voice catches and I try to draw her back to me.

Ellie resists. 'Did he do it?' she asks, her voice tremulous. 'Did Dad kill her, Mum?'

'No,' I answer sharply. 'I don't believe he could ever be capable of such a thing,' I add firmly.

Glancing down, Ellie nods, but hesitantly.

'He didn't, Ellie,' I try again to reassure her. 'We'll hear from him soon and this will all be cleared up. Meanwhile, we need to pick up the twins. The police sent a car to the school for them, but I don't want to leave them for too long.'

Snapping her gaze back up, she pulls in a shaky breath and wipes her arm under her nose. 'I need the loo,' she says.

'Use the patient toilet in the department, Ellie,' Alex suggests as she starts towards the door. 'It's probably not a good idea to be wandering around out there with all that's going on.' He gives her a warm smile as she glances back at him, and I'm so thankful to him for being there for her when she needed him.

She answers with another small nod. I note her downcast gaze as she leaves and wonder what horrors must be going through her mind.

'She overheard someone talking,' Alex says, as I turn my gaze to him. 'I wasn't going to say anything, but...'

'She would have found out anyway.' I manage a smile. 'Thanks for looking after her, Alex.'

'No problem.' He gives me a small smile back. 'She's a good kid. I only wish she didn't have to go through all of this.'

'Me too.' A sudden icy shudder running through me, I wrap my arms around myself. It's my fault. I should never have exposed the children to any of this. I so wish I'd taken them to my mother's, as Kelsey... My thoughts grind to a halt as a sudden wave of grief crashes ferociously through me, forcing the air from my body.

Alex is across to me in one stride. 'Come here,' he says, circling his arms around me and pulling me close.

As I cry quietly into his shoulder, he tightens his hold and I lean into him, grateful for his being here for Ellie and me both.

'Sorry,' I murmur, trying to stem the useless tears that spill from my eyes.

'You've nothing to be sorry for.' He strokes my hair. 'I have no idea what Cole has been playing at. I can't fathom why the hell he would do it when he has everything a bloke could wish for.'

'Do what?' I pull away, eyeing him quizzically.

Alex looks awkward, and an uneasy feeling creeps through me. 'You knew, didn't you?' I ask in bewildered disbelief. 'About him and Kelsey. You knew.'

He glances down. 'Not until recently, no.' He breathes out a sigh as he looks back at me. 'I saw them arguing in the hospital grounds. I didn't get the whole gist of it, but it was a pretty violent argument. It was obvious they were in a relationship.'

'They *weren't*,' I insist, some instinctive reaction driving me to leap to Cole's defence.

Alex studies me, his look one of pity. 'She's pregnant, Maddie,' he says softly. 'Was. That was one of the things they were arguing about.'

I say nothing for a moment. I'm too stunned that Alex knew this and didn't tell me. 'Why didn't you say something?' I ask him. 'When I last spoke to you, why didn't you say something then?'

'What, and crucify you more than Cole already was?' He eyes me with a mixture of guilt and regret. 'I didn't know everything then, Maddie. I still don't know all of it. I do know that if he thinks he has a right to treat you so abysmally, then he doesn't deserve you.'

I have no idea what to say. He's looking at me with deep concern, and I know he cares, but if only he'd said something, perhaps I could have tackled Cole and things might not have gone this far.

'He's manipulating people, Maddie,' Alex goes on, a flash of fury now in his eyes. 'You. Me. Like I say, I don't know all the details, but if he treated Kelsey the way he appears to have done, if he's bloody well killed her in a fit of rage, then he also deserves everything that's coming to him.'

His words take my breath away. 'You don't believe that,' I say shakily.

He shrugs, telling me he does believe it.

'I have to go.' Seeing Ellie coming towards the door, I turn swiftly away from him.

'Maddie.' Alex follows me, catching my arm. 'I'm sorry,' he says quickly, clearly upset, and as confused as I am. 'I didn't mean to say all that. I shouldn't have. I just... Look, I'm here for you,' he offers, moving away as Ellie reaches the door. 'I always have been. You know that, right?'

SIXTY-SIX

COLE

'Tell me about the bruised knuckles, Cole,' Ingram said. 'The blood we found on your shirt. Can you explain that?'

Cole covered his knuckles with his other hand. 'I hit something,' he answered calmly.

'Animate or inanimate?' Ingram picked up his pen, watching him steadily as he tapped it on the table.

Cole met his gaze. 'Animate,' he told him truthfully, figuring it would come out anyway, possibly already had.

'Oh?' Ingram raised his eyebrows. 'Would you care to expand?'

Cole's gaze didn't flinch. 'He hurt my daughter.' Again he answered truthfully, but that was as far as he was prepared to go.

'So you resorted to violence to, what, teach him a lesson?' Ingram eyed him narrowly.

Cole didn't comment.

Another irritating tap of the pen. Cole guessed it was designed to rattle him. 'And your daughter will corroborate your story, will she?' Ingram asked.

Cole tugged in a terse breath. 'I'd rather she wasn't brought into this.'

'You might want to rethink that, Mr Chase.' DS Conner spoke at last. 'You see, you have a problem. A woman is dead. A woman you were overheard having an argument with in the grounds of the hospital. There's also an interesting photograph on your phone, which would corroborate the volatile nature of your relationship.'

'No comment.' Cole kneaded his forehead. Had Alex told them about the argument? Had to have. Recalling his open disdain, the scathing advice he'd imparted – *Sort it out, Cole. Do the right thing by the woman you promised to love and cherish for life, or else get* out *of her life* – he wondered whether his *friend* might even now be moving in on Maddie.

'According to the pathologist, Kelsey Roberts was injected with a lethal substance,' Conner continued. 'We think toxicology will confirm that substance to be ketamine, possibly mixed with an opioid. And right now, given what we found in the boot of your car, you're looking like our prime suspect.'

Cole cautioned himself to remain calm. 'You don't have any evidence,' he pointed out, sure that anything they did have was circumstantial. They hadn't mentioned any relevant CCTV footage. Then again, the hospital was ancient. The security systems not fit for purpose, cameras often out of action.

'Yet,' the detective countered. 'Your shirt has been sent off for forensic analysis, as you might expect it would.'

'It won't yield what you're hoping it will,' Cole responded. 'I didn't kill her.'

Conner studied him carefully. 'You don't look very bothered by the fact that she's dead,' he observed.

'Was that a question?' Cole asked, eyeing him levelly.

'You realise our forensics team are searching the crime scene?' Conner went on. 'You'd be surprised what microscopic evidence they might find: fibres, hair, the minutest particle of skin.'

'I'm a doctor,' Cole pointed out. 'I actually wouldn't be surprised. And since I've very probably been in the area in which she was found and have undoubtedly had occasion to come into contact with her, I'm not sure what any such evidence would amount to.'

Conner dragged his gaze away. On a scale of one to ten, Cole reckoned the detective's contempt for him was about a ten. 'You recently lost your father, I gather?' he said, after consulting his notes. 'Condolences.' He looked back at Cole, no trace of sympathy in his eyes. 'Your relationship with him was also volatile, wasn't it?'

That *had* to have come from Alex. Cole swallowed back the bitter taste of betrayal.

'I gather you didn't like him very much?' Conner went on.

Cole said nothing.

'He died on the operating table, we understand.' The detective paused. Cole felt his anger tighten inside him. 'Were you carrying out the procedure, Mr Chase?'

Cole breathed in deeply. 'I had cause to step in.'

Conner nodded contemplatively. 'Did you kill him?'

'No comment.'

'You have a lot of anger inside you, don't you?' Conner asked.

Cole held his gaze. 'No comment.'

'Were you angry with your father because he was a bully? A man with misogynistic tendencies?' Conner continued, clearly on a roll. 'Or were you angry with yourself, because you realised you were like him?'

Cole wiped the sweat from the back of his neck. Resisted telling the man to go fuck himself, just.

'Did you decide it was time for your father to pay for his

sins?' Conner pushed it. 'Were you playing God, Mr Chase, the day your father died?'

Cole felt his jaw clench. He looked Conner over stonily, then, 'Sitting in judgement of other people, you mean?' he asked. He didn't expand, holding the man's gaze pointedly instead.

Clearly irritated, DS Conner looked away first.

Cole waited while he recommenced doodling on his pad and Ingram continued to tap his pen on the table, obviously looking for another approach. Cole was answering their questions, those he was prepared to, as amicably as he could, considering the circumstances. It must be seriously aggravating them that they were getting nowhere.

Ingram appraised him for a moment. 'How long were you away from the hospital before we made your acquaintance?' he asked.

'About an hour and a half,' Cole answered. 'Two hours maybe. I imagine the CCTV in the car park will confirm how long I was gone.'

'Doesn't mean to say you didn't slip back, though, does it?' Conner retorted. 'Either on foot or by taxi.'

'I didn't.'

'We will need to talk to your daughter, Cole,' Ingram picked up when Conner fell silent. 'Ellie, isn't it? I understand why you wouldn't want us to, but we will need to corroborate your story. It would be helpful if you simply told us what happened. Obviously, any witnesses to your whereabouts are crucial in establishing exactly where you were and when.'

He needed an alibi. Cole knew it. He couldn't ask his mother to provide him with one, since he hadn't been with her the whole time. There was no way either he was going to drag Ellie any further into this than he already had. Why hadn't he thought about the implications for her before involving her in the first place? Because he was exhausted, tired to the core of his bones. And they knew it.

'Ellie asked me to pass something on to you,' Ingram said after a moment. 'I'm not sure what the context is, but she said to tell you that she's made up her mind she will. I think she thought it might help you with any decision she imagines you might have to make.'

Cole's heart hitched. Had she actually said that, meaning she'd decided to report Wainwright? He eyed Ingram warily. The man looked sincere, but Ellie had told him what she had in confidence. He couldn't break that confidence without talking to her first.

'I'd like my phone call now, please,' he said, praying Ingram would understand.

'We'll get something organised.' The DI nodded, a contemplative frown creasing his forehead.

Cole waited again, his patience growing paper-thin, as the man made a note on his pad, taking his time.

Eventually Ingram's gaze came back to him. 'Did you go back to the hospital, Cole?' he asked. 'I mean, after what Kelsey Roberts did to you, the subsequent harassment, you must have been angry.'

'Furious, I imagine. I would have been,' Conner chipped in.

Cole kept his gaze on Ingram. 'No,' he stated emphatically.

'You go back and find her. She denies what she did. She pursues you,' Ingram went on, hypothesising. 'Taunts you, maybe? You see what she's doing to your family, your temper reaches boiling point and—'

'No!' Cole slammed his hand on the table. 'That's not what happened!'

SIXTY-SEVEN

MADDIE

'Will you play interactive dancing with us, Ellie?' Lucas asks, tugging on Ellie's hand as we approach the house.

'Later, maybe.' Ellie smiles distractedly down at him.

'Your sister's tired,' I tell him, glancing at her in concern as I step around them to open the door. 'Why don't you two go and play a computer game for a while,' I suggest, ushering the boys in, 'and then maybe we can watch a film after your tea?'

'Cool,' Jayden enthuses, dropping his rucksack and charging towards the lounge. 'Come on, Lucas. We have to craft some armour to protect against our enemies,' he calls behind him.

'Not until you've changed out of your school clothes.' I stop him, wanting to give Ellie a little space.

Jayden sighs and trudges back, then hurries up the stairs, Lucas close behind him.

'Fancy a coffee?' I ask Ellie, dropping my keys and handbag on the hall table and shrugging out of my coat.

'Actually, do you mind if I go up and have a shower?' she asks.

I notice how pale she is as I turn to her, the tears brimming perilously close to the surface. Her body language is stiff, her arms folded tightly across her chest, as if she's trying to keep all her emotion stuffed inside. My heart bleeds for her. She's clearly worried to death for her father, petrified and confused by all that went on at the hospital. What that animal did to her. I want to ask her about the charm, but decide it can wait until Jayden and Lucas are in bed, when we'll have more privacy.

Once the boys are occupied with crafting armour, I take my phone and go to the kitchen, where I work to keep my emotions in check. I have to stay strong for the twins. For Ellie, whose reason for being at the hospital I still have to establish. My chest constricts as I wonder again whether she knows more about what happened today than she's telling me. *I went to see Dad* was all I got from her when I asked her on the way to pick up the boys.

Food, I instruct myself, and with little enthusiasm and nil appetite, I wander across to the fridge. A cold shiver runs through me as I notice the open bottle of wine there, a stark reminder of the night Ellie was drinking and I began to believe my husband might be having an affair. My thoughts swing to Kelsey and my breath stalls. She will be completely on her own now, laid out on a cold mortuary slab, as lonely in death as she must have been in life. In a way, I can understand why she wanted Cole so badly, a man she saw as loving and dependable where so many men had failed her. *He was mine, Kelsey*, I whisper silently. *You should never have tried to take him away from me.*

Desperately trying to erase the image, I attempt to focus on my family. Ignoring the wine, which I would very much like to drink, I go to the freezer. I'm pulling burgers and chips out, which I know at least the boys will wolf down, when my phone rings. Dumping the ingredients on the worktop, I hurry to grab it up. Not recognising the number, I hesitate, then cautiously answer. My heart leaps into my throat when I hear Cole's voice.

'Can we talk?' he asks tentatively. I hear his sharp intake of breath, as if he's bracing himself for my answer.

'How are you?' I ask, no idea what else to say to him.

'Not great,' he says, sounding exhausted, his voice hollow, yet achingly familiar. 'You?'

'Staying strong,' I reply. Telling him how I really feel will achieve nothing other than to make him feel worse than he must already. I can't do that, kick a dog when it's down.

'Ellie?' he asks quietly.

'Distraught.' I don't lie. He would guess she would be. 'She's coping. The boys don't know anything. They're fine.' I keep it short and get to the question I need to ask. 'What did they find in your car, Cole?'

'Ketamine,' he says, after a pause. 'Several ampoules.'

My heart twists in confusion and fear. 'You realise I received a message implying you were going to harm me?'

'They told me.' He tugs in another sharp breath. 'I had no idea the ketamine was there, Maddie. I swear on my life I didn't. You *have* to believe me.'

I don't know what to think. I've swung from not believing him to be capable of being anything but what he appears to be, to not believing a word he says. This, though, something that he could never hope to get away with, something that would rob him of his life, his career, it's too obviously calculated. 'Kelsey,' I breathe.

He hesitates. 'I'm not sure. I mean, why would she, knowing I would be arrested?'

Because if she couldn't have him, then she was going to make damn sure I didn't either. Surely he must realise how twisted her thinking was? 'Did you kill her?' I ask, because I have to.

'*No*,' he denies vehemently. 'You can't think I would have, Maddie. Please tell me you don't.'

'Someone did,' I point out shakily. 'Someone put those drugs in your car, Cole. If not Kelsey, then who?'

Again he hesitates. Then, 'Alex,' he answers cautiously.

'Alex?' I gasp in disbelief. 'But that's ridiculous.'

'Is it?' Cole asks. 'Like you say, someone did.'

'But he's your *friend*,' I remind him. 'You've known each other for years. He's angry with you, yes, but why would he—'

'He's still in *love* with you, Maddie.' Cole cuts across me. 'He's always been in love with you. I just didn't see it. I wish to Christ I had.'

I'm too stunned to speak. It's incomprehensible.

'Think about it,' Cole goes on. 'He's never married. Never really had a relationship that went anywhere. He's decided to live in his mother's run-down cottage where he's totally isolated. Doesn't that strike you as odd?'

'I don't know.' I try to process. 'I've never really spoken to him about it.'

'He passed up the opportunity of a job in the private sector, which was far better paid,' Cole continues, 'because his heart lay with the NHS, he said, and he didn't want to abandon me. It was bullshit. He wanted to stay close to me to be close to you.'

I laugh, incredulous. 'Even if that were true, why would he risk his own career? His freedom?'

'Love can drive people to all sorts of madness,' Cole points out.

Is he talking about Kelsey, or himself? 'I still can't believe it,' I reply, more confused than ever.

'He heard me arguing with Kelsey,' Cole says awkwardly, 'about the insane messages she'd been sending, her false accusations, the whole terrifying campaign to destroy our family. The police know about it. It could only have come from Alex.' He pauses while I digest his words. 'They also know about my relationship with my father, the way he died. I doubt my mother would have said anything, so unless you did…'

'No.' I shake my head. 'I haven't been asked about your father. Why would I mention it anyway? Why would anyone? Unless...'

'To convince the police that I'm capable of murder?' Cole finishes.

'But he wouldn't, surely? Not Alex.' Even as I say it, I'm recalling his readiness to condemn Cole without knowing the facts, what he said to me as I left – *I'm here for you. I always have been. You know that, right?* – the way he held me, stroked my hair. Uneasy foreboding creeps through me.

'Any more than I would do what I'm being accused of?' Cole asks.

It's a loaded question. One I can't answer.

'If he wanted me out of the way, it worked, didn't it?' he points out – and I have a sick feeling in the pit of my stomach that he might be right.

'But what about Kelsey? Are they saying you did it?' I ask, clutching my phone tight.

'They're questioning me about it, yes,' he answers, his voice strained.

'Do they have any evidence against you?' I ask, hardly daring to breathe.

'I had blood on my shirt,' he answers after another excruciating pause. 'Look, it's going to come out anyway, so I should tell you before it does,' he goes on quickly. 'I found the guy Ellie told us about.'

My breath lodges in my throat. 'The bastard who raped her,' I seethe, anger almost burning a hole inside me.

'I hit him,' he says. 'Hurt him. I didn't intend to, but when I saw him, when he had the nerve to actually smirk... I lost it.'

'Good,' I say, immense satisfaction surging through me. I probably shouldn't condone what he's done, but I do. He did it for Ellie, because whatever he's done or not done, he's her father and he loves her with his bones. That's indisputable.

'It felt it,' Cole murmurs, relief obvious in his voice.

'Do they have anything else?' I ask, my heart banging.

'Nothing but the messages, the witness account of the argument and the ketamine, which is all circumstantial as far as I can tell. It looks like I'll need a solicitor, though. I was hoping you might contact one for me. Mike Andrews. He's located in Solihull. I don't have my phone, so...'

'I'll find his details,' I assure him. 'Are they going to charge you?'

'The jury's still out on that one,' Cole jokes wearily. 'The blood won't prove anything, obviously. They're waiting on phone data to come back to establish my whereabouts. Whether they'll dream up anything else, I don't know.'

'They won't,' I assure him.

'I'm glad you still have some faith in me,' he says.

I hear his voice crack. And I want to go to him, protect him. Have him protect me. We need to look out for each other, as we've always done. We were a unit until Kelsey tore us apart. There will be no further evidence, I'm sure of it. Not unless it's planted, which it might be, I realise. In which case, I have to do something about it.

SIXTY-EIGHT

Hearing Ellie moving about upstairs, I will Alex to pick up. Relief crashes through me when he does. 'Hey, I'm glad you called,' he says, sounding so normal, so like the amiable Alex I know, I almost waver. 'How are you doing?'

'Not very well,' I answer truthfully.

'No, I guess you wouldn't be.' His voice is filled with concern. 'Look, if you need a shoulder, I'll be heading home in an hour or so. You're welcome to come over.'

'No,' I say quickly. Recalling how isolated his cottage is – the lane it's located on pitch-black and with no neighbours close by – I'm not sure I would feel safe going there. 'Actually, do you mind if I come to the hospital?' I suggest. 'I don't want to leave the children too long. I could be there in half an hour.'

'No problem,' he says. 'Is Ellie doing okay?'

'As well as can be expected,' I answer truthfully. 'I'll be heading off shortly.'

'Great.' He sounds pleased. 'Give me a call when you arrive and I'll get the coffee on.'

'Thanks, Alex.' Ending the call, I glance up as Ellie comes through the kitchen door.

'Was that Dad?' she asks, such hope in her eyes I want to hug her to me and never let her go. I can't let any harm come to her ever again. I won't.

'It was Alex,' I tell her, 'but your dad called,' I add quickly. 'He couldn't talk for long, though.'

'What did he say?' she asks, ice-cold fear in her voice. 'Are they saying it was him who killed Kelsey?'

I hesitate. How much should I tell her?

'Mum, *tell* me,' she urges, clearly desperate for news.

I take a breath. 'They're holding him for questioning, but—'

'Oh God, no.' Her face drains of colour. 'He didn't do it, Mum,' she says, tears springing to her eyes. 'I *know* he didn't.'

'I know, sweetheart. I know.' Hurrying across to her, I wrap my arms around her and pull her close. 'Please try not to worry.' I attempt to reassure her as she buries her face in my shoulder. 'I'm going to contact a solicitor for him.'

She snaps her gaze up. 'You believe him then?' Her voice is hopeful, her eyes scanning mine, willing me to say that I do.

I prevaricate for a second. Then, 'Yes,' I say firmly, aware that she needs to know that I haven't given up on him, that we are still a unit. That we *will* fight this and whatever else we have to. Together.

Her body wilts with relief and she leans back into me.

I hug her hard. 'Your dad said to tell you he loves you.' Then, lying a little, because I have to, 'He asked if you still had the charm he bought you.' I found it so close to the storage room and I'm worrying myself sick wondering how it got there. 'I think he was hoping that you still love him unconditionally too.'

Ellie freezes for a moment, then shakes her head. 'No,' she murmurs, and pulls away from me. 'I lost it somewhere.'

She's not looking at me, I notice, her eyes downcast, one hand twisting anxiously around the wrist of her other. 'But you don't know where?' I probe carefully.

Again she shakes her head.

'At the hospital?' I press her gently.

'Possibly,' she says, and turns away. And I know that she knows something. I know my daughter well enough, too, to know that she's not ready or willing to say more.

SIXTY-NINE

COLE

Cole lifted his head from his hands as he heard metal clanging against metal, bolts being drawn and keys turning. As the thick steel door that felt like the seal to his coffin opened, he got unsteadily to his feet, his heart rate slowing to a dull thud as he wondered whether he was about to be arrested for the murder of Kelsey Roberts.

'So, Cole,' DI Ingram said, and paused for a long, blood-freezing moment, 'it looks as if we might have to let you go.'

It took Cole a second to comprehend. When he did, relief crashed through every cell in his body. 'You mean you're not charging me with...?'

'Murder?' Ingram scrutinised him carefully. 'Apparently not. According to the CPS, we don't have enough evidence.'

'Yet,' Conner chipped in with his usual sarcasm.

Ingram shot him a look, telling Cole that even he was getting bored with his sidekick's lack of original wit. Emitting a despairing sigh, the DI turned back to Cole. 'There's no CCTV or dashcam footage placing you in or around the vicinity of the hospital before you were arrested. No mobile data.'

'Although you did switch your mobile off at one point,' Conner picked up. 'Any particular reason why?'

Cole heard the derision in his voice and ignored it. 'I went from my mother's house to visit my brother's grave,' he answered calmly. 'Wouldn't most people turn their mobile off in a cemetery?'

Conner shook his head in disbelief. 'We'll be asking her to corroborate that,' he muttered.

'Obviously,' Cole answered with a tight smile. 'And the drugs charge?' he asked, sure they weren't just going to drop it.

'That sticks,' Ingram said, with an almost apologetic shrug. 'You'll be released under investigation. You'll receive a summons in due course informing you of what you've been charged with and requiring you to attend the magistrates' court at a future date. Naturally you'll be informed if any other evidence comes to light.' He gave a terse smile and turned to walk out, followed by Conner.

As the custody officer beckoned him, Cole wondered if his legs would actually hold him up. He was half expecting to be taken back to his cell as he was being processed to leave, particularly when Ingram reappeared to give him the news about Kelsey's pregnancy.

With his personal belongings returned, it was only once he was outside, heading away from the station, that he allowed himself to relax. He'd never appreciated the freedom to do the most banal things in life, such as breathing fresh air. He did in that moment. Never again did he want to go back there, feeling the hollow hopelessness as the cell door slammed shut on him. Quashing the rage that burned inside him as his mind went to Alex and the reason he'd been arrested, humiliated, every aspect of his life scrutinised, he pulled out his phone to attend to his first priority. Quickly he called Maddie. He had no idea what reception he would get, but he had to know she and the children were safe.

Apprehension crept through him when she didn't pick up. He tried again after a minute, and then called the landline, another surge of relief running through him when it was answered. 'Hi, Ellie, it's me,' he said, recognising her tentative, 'Hello.'

'Dad?' She emitted a disbelieving gasp. 'Are you all right? What's going on? Are they charging you?' Her questions tumbled out, her concern all for him, and Cole was reminded how much he loved his daughter. He hoped she knew there was nothing on this earth that could change that.

'I'm fine,' he assured her, 'and no, they're not charging me with anything to do with what happened to Kelsey.'

'I knew they wouldn't,' Ellie murmured emotionally. 'I know you didn't do it.'

Cole heard her catch a quiet sob in her throat and his chest constricted. 'Are *you* okay?' he asked her gently.

'I'm all right,' she assured him, though she couldn't possibly be.

'The boys?' he checked.

'Exhausting,' Ellie joked. 'They're all tucked up in bed now.'

Cole smiled.

'Where are you?' she asked worriedly. 'Are you coming home?'

'I've just left the station,' he said, and hesitated. He couldn't tell her he was coming home without checking with Maddie. 'Is your mum around, Ellie? I need to talk to her.'

'No, she's out,' Ellie answered.

'Oh? Out where?' Cole asked warily. His heart stopped dead in his chest when Ellie told him where she'd gone. He doubted very much she would have taken a night shift under the circumstances.

'Dad, *are* you coming home?' Ellie pressed him.

Cole thought fast. 'I have someone I need to see,' he said.

'It's important, related to my job,' he explained, not wanting her to think it was more important than seeing her. 'I'll call you back, okay? As soon as I can.'

She sighed disappointedly. 'Okay.'

'See you soon,' he said softly.

'See you soon. And, Dad?' She stopped him before he hung up. 'Thanks.'

'For what?' Cole frowned, confused.

'What you did to that wanker,' Ellie enlightened him eloquently. 'Mum told me.'

He drew in a breath. 'I didn't go there with that intention,' he said carefully. 'Violence isn't something I condone, you know that, right? I lost control. I'm not proud of myself.'

'No, I get that,' Ellie said, after a second. 'But *I'm* proud of you.'

After ending the call, Cole dragged a hand over his eyes and attempted to compose himself. He hadn't lied about that. He *didn't* condone violence. Alex, above all people, should realise how hard he'd worked over the years to keep his emotions under control, which really should have been warning enough of what the consequences might be if he failed.

SEVENTY

MADDIE

Ellie was shocked when I told her about Cole seeking out the animal who'd hurt her. She was worried about her dad, what the consequences for him would be, scouring her phone for the inevitable social media fallout. There wasn't any, and we both breathed a sigh of relief. All we can do now is wait. When I asked her to look after the boys while I went to see Alex, she agreed, offering to take over and cook their tea. She clearly thinks I need to talk to him about her father, and that Alex will be there for him. I didn't mention Cole's suspicions. I didn't want to heap more worry onto her shoulders.

Checking the time, I hurry through the hospital reception, giving one of the women on the desk a wave as I go. I'm halfway along the corridor, heading for the neurosurgical department, when I see Alex coming towards me.

'Good to see you, Mads,' he says, smiling when he reaches me. I'm taken aback as he wraps his arms around me, holding me a little too close, hugging me a little too tightly. 'You still wear the same perfume,' he says, smiling as he steps away. 'I always liked it.'

Now I'm really taken aback. Do men remember the

fragrance of a woman they dated so many years ago? I'm not sure I can read the look in his eyes as his gaze travels over me. Nostalgia? Regret? Either way, it doesn't sit comfortably.

'Sorry.' He shakes his head, as if snapping himself out of a daydream. 'Miles away. So, do you fancy going somewhere a bit less clinical? The pub, or a restaurant maybe? I'm guessing you haven't eaten, and there's a decent Italian not far from here. I could call and book—'

'Alex, no.' I stop him, now utterly bewildered. He's acting almost as if this is a date. 'I'm really not in the mood for public places,' I say as diplomatically as I can.

'Oh.' He looks slightly crestfallen. 'Yes, of course. I wasn't thinking, sorry. It's been a long day.'

For you and me both. I look him over cautiously. 'I'd rather talk in private.'

He frowns thoughtfully. 'The relatives' room in Neuro is free,' he suggests.

'Perfect.' I force a smile and turn to walk with him along the corridor.

'At least we can have a decent coffee there,' he says chattily. 'Do you still take yours sweet and black?'

He's remembered that too? As he leads the way to open the security doors into the department, I squint after him, feeling as if things are slightly off. He was furious when I last saw him. Far from that now, he seems almost buoyant. I note the jauntiness of his walk as I follow him, and I wonder what he thinks I've come to talk to him about other than the dire situation my husband's in.

I'm barely through the door, him following and closing it behind us, when he slides his arm around me. My wariness turns to anger. Does he not realise how inappropriate this is – in every sense of the word? I whirl around to face him, causing him to step back. 'I came to talk about Cole,' I inform him, hoping that will make him realise it is, extremely.

'Ah,' he says with a short smile. 'I suppose I should have guessed that.' He actually looks annoyed as he walks past me to the coffee machine, and my anger intensifies.

'Did you put the ketamine in his car?' I ask him outright, even though I was intending to approach the subject a little more subtly.

'What?' He turns back, his expression incredulous.

I hold his gaze. Alex is the first to glance away. 'Did you?' I demand.

'No, I did *not*.' He looks back at me, a flash of fury in his eyes. 'Did he put that idea into your head?' he asks, a deep frown creasing his forehead. 'He did, didn't he?'

I say nothing, but keep my gaze locked on his.

'Bloody hell, Maddie, don't tell me you believe him?' He shakes his head in astonishment. '*Why* would I?'

'Because you want him out of the way,' I suggest bluntly. 'Because you still have feelings for me.'

I fully expect him to refute that, to tell me I'm flattering myself. He doesn't, studying me for a long, hard moment instead, then averting his gaze and turning away. 'Of course I still have feelings for you,' he says agitatedly as he fetches mugs from the tray next to the machine. 'Did you imagine I wouldn't have?'

He's still in love with you, Maddie. He's always been in love with you. Cole's words ring loud in my head and my stomach turns over. 'But we went out a lifetime ago,' I point out. 'I've moved on, Alex. You surely don't think—'

'I *know*.' He crashes a mug down and spins back to face me. 'You moved on pretty fast, didn't you, Maddie?'

'Alex.' I glance quickly at the door, not sure whether to feel relieved when it appears no one has heard us. 'What in God's name are you talking about?' My blood races, my mind racing faster as my thoughts swing to what Cole said. *He's never married. Never really had a relationship that went anywhere. He wanted to stay close to me to be close to you.* He's right, isn't he? A turmoil of emotion churns inside me – shock, confusion, fear. Alex was trying to frame Cole to get him out of the way, but surely not for murder?

'You didn't give me a chance to catch my breath before you started sleeping with him,' he goes on, completely staggering me. 'What I did was stupid, idiotic, but I was drunk, for fuck's sake! Would you accept my apologies, though? No,' he answers for me. 'You saw a better prospect and that was it, you *moved on*, straight into the great Dr Chase's bed. Of course I wanted him out of the way. I've wanted him out of the way ever since you two got together.'

'Did you plant the drugs?' I ask him again, my heart beating wildly.

'He killed Kelsey,' he says, his face tight, his eyes filled with disdain. 'He *murdered* her, Maddie, yet you're still taken in by him. All this caring doctor and husband routine is absolute bullshit,' he growls, growing steadily more agitated. 'He's been having an *affair* with her. Right under your nose. And you still *care* for him?'

I feel the blood leave my body. 'You did, didn't you?'

He studies me a second longer and then looks mutely away.

'*Why?*' I stare at him in sheer disbelief.

He doesn't respond for a long moment. Then, 'Do you really have to wonder why?' He looks back at me, his expression now one of scorn. 'Because I wanted some contact with my daughter.'

I feel the ground shift beneath me. 'You're insane,' I murmur shakily.

'Am I?' He reaches into his pocket and extracts a slip of paper. 'Ellie's mine, Maddie,' he says flatly, handing it to me. 'You know she is.'

SEVENTY-ONE

My world stops turning as I stare in horror at the piece of paper that confirms Alex Evans is Ellie's biological father.

'You must have suspected I knew.' His voice reaches me as if from a distance. 'I can't believe Cole didn't realise. Then again, I guess a guy can forgive anything when he's in love. It was one way of making sure you stayed with him, I suppose. He was besotted with you then, bound to do the gallant thing, the *caring* thing, and marry you. The gloss obviously wore off for him, though, didn't it? He doesn't give a damn about you, Maddie. You need to wise up to that fact.'

My heart rate ratchets up, my blood pumping so fast my head spins.

'I care about you, Maddie,' he says softly. 'I've never stopped loving you. I never will.' Smiling, he moves towards me and holds out his hand, waiting for me to give back the damning evidence.

As I feel his other hand sliding softly down my back, I freeze. I'm too stunned to speak, to make my brain or limbs function.

'I should have told you I intended to do a test,' he goes on as my mind whirls. 'I collected her DNA from her glass when you invited me round at Christmas. I hoped you might tell me about her, but you never did, and I guess I thought I might need it one day.'

He did *what*? Anger unfurls inside me, and I bunch the paper up in my fist, press the heels of both hands against his chest and shove him hard. 'Stop. Just *don't*, Alex,' I warn him.

'Don't be like this, Maddie.' He looks at me in bewildered shock. 'I did this for *you*. You're trapped in a toxic relationship and you just can't see it. You don't need him,' he continues inanely. 'I can be there for you and our daughter, if only you'll give me a chance. That's all I've ever wanted.'

Dread pooling in the pit of my stomach, I scan his face. 'I *love* Cole,' I point out forcefully. 'I will *always* love Cole, no matter what. I love my daughter. I won't let you rob her of the man who absolutely *is* her father. Do you honestly think I would ever allow that to happen?'

'I see,' he says quietly after a moment. 'What's he got that I haven't, Maddie?' he asks, tipping his head curiously to one side. 'Is he good in bed, is that it? Better than I was? Or should I say, *was* he good in bed. I imagine he's been too distracted to fulfil his marital obligations lately.'

Disgust ripples through me. 'I've heard enough. I'm leaving,' I say, as calmly as I can.

'Don't go, Maddie. Not like this,' he implores me, looking hurt and confused, which only destabilises me further. 'Look, I'm sorry. I didn't mean to sound so scathing. We can still be friends, at least, can't we?'

'I need to go,' I mumble. 'I need to think.'

As he moves towards me again, his eyes almost pleading, I whirl around and fly for the door.

SEVENTY-TWO

It's dark when I get home, and I come quietly through the front door, lest I wake the twins. Realising Ellie is in her room, possibly sleeping or else listening to music, I decide to leave her awhile, making myself a coffee and taking it to the lounge, where I try to get my chaotic thoughts in some sort of order. I passed a group of teenagers while I was driving aimlessly around attempting to gain some control over my emotions. They were spilling from a pub they possibly shouldn't have been in, laughing and joking and doing what young people do, despite the pouring rain. It brought the stark reality of the damage I might do to my daughter into sharp focus. I realised then that I had no choice but to make it all stop.

Weary to my bones, I finish the dregs of my coffee, which has gone cold while I've been contemplating what the consequences of my actions might be for all my children, what damage will be caused by the stability around them being rocked to the core. I have to be here for them. Stay strong for them. Whatever happens, I will.

Going to the kitchen, I deposit my mug in the sink, then

head upstairs to shower. My clothes feel tainted after my encounter with Alex. *I* feel tainted.

I'm in the bathroom when Ellie taps on the door. 'Mum?'

'Yes. Won't be a sec.' Peeling off my jeans and top, I drape them hurriedly over the bath and tug on my dressing gown, forgoing the shower in favour of making sure she's okay.

I find her sitting on her bed when I go to her room. Attempting to compose myself, I give her a smile. 'Sorry, I should have let you know I was home,' I say, not quite able to meet her eyes. 'Are the boys okay?'

'Yes, asleep. Where've you been?' she asks. 'I was so worried when Dad didn't come straight back. I tried to call you, but then I realised you hadn't got your phone and—'

'Your dad?' My heart jolts. 'He called?'

She nods, a deep frown in her forehead. 'He rang on the landline. He said he'd tried to call you. I told him you'd gone to see Alex and...' She stops, her eyes snapping to the bedroom door as Cole calls from the hall, 'Maddie?'

Ellie is off the bed and through the door in a second flat. Shaking myself, I follow as she flies along the landing and thunders down the stairs to throw herself into his arms.

Squeezing his eyes closed, Cole hugs her hard. His gaze meets mine as I stand uncertainly on the stairs, and the look I see in his eyes – a combination of pure love for his daughter and raw, unguarded vulnerability – touches the very core of me. I don't say anything, simply nod, and hope with all of me that he will realise how much I need him right now. How much I still love him, will always love him.

Ellie pulls back as I reach the hall. 'Where were you?' she asks Cole, her voice small. 'You said you'd call back.'

'It took a little longer than I thought it would,' he says. 'Then I thought I would just come straight here and—' He stops as the doorbell rings jarringly behind him.

As his gaze shoots again to mine, his eyes hold a warning, and my stomach clenches. Does he know something?

I watch as he visibly steels himself and then reaches to open the door. My blood turns to icicles in my veins as I see DI Ingram standing there, along with a uniformed officer. 'Cole, Mrs Chase,' he says, with a short smile. 'I thought I should come personally. It's regarding Alex Evans. Do you think we could come inside?'

I clutch the neck of my dressing gown tightly to me, my mind ticking feverishly as Cole hesitates for a second, and then steps back to let them in. 'What about Alex?' he asks, his forehead creased in consternation.

Ingram glances towards Ellie, and it's clear that he doesn't want to speak in front of her.

'Do you think you could go up and keep an eye on the boys, Ellie?' Cole asks her, giving her a reassuring smile.

Ellie looks from her dad to the detective with trepidation, and then nods, albeit reluctantly, and turns to go back upstairs.

'Come through,' Cole says, exchanging cautious glances with me as he turns to lead the way to the lounge. He's scared, I can see it in his eyes, and the knot of fear that's been permanently lodged inside me since I saw that first message twists itself impossibly tighter.

Ingram waits, allowing me to go ahead of him, and I wish fervently I'd had time to get dressed.

Once we're in the lounge, I close the door then go and stand next to Cole. 'So?' He eyes the detective curiously.

'I'm afraid I have some bad news.' Ingram's expression is grave. 'I'm sorry to tell you that Alex Evans was found dead this evening.'

'*Dead?* Oh God, no.' I slide my hand quickly into Cole's.

'Jesus.' Cole sucks in a shocked breath. 'How?' he asks, incredulous. 'Where?'

'A dog walker found him,' Ingram provides. 'He was lying in the lane a short distance from his cottage.'

Cole stares at him, speechless for a second. 'Had he been injured?' he asks, his voice hoarse. 'Attacked? What?'

'A post-mortem examination will need to be completed to establish probable cause of death,' Ingram informs him, 'but he was certainly attacked – in a manner of speaking.'

Cole squints at him in confusion.

'We believe Mr Evans died from fatal injuries sustained in a hit-and-run accident,' Ingram goes on. 'Where did you go once you left the station, Mr Chase?' he tags on quickly. 'You can understand why I would need to ascertain your whereabouts.'

'I... Yes, of course.' Cole wipes a hand over his face. 'I was at the hospital.'

I don't dare look at him. Was he really there?

'And can anyone verify this?' Ingram asks.

'I spoke to one or two people,' Cole confirms. 'I can provide you with names.'

Ingram narrows his eyes, looking at him with deep suspicion, I note.

Cole obviously does too. 'You'll find my car was in the car park. And my phone was with me, switched on at all times,' he says wearily.

After a moment, Ingram nods. Satisfied? I'm unsure. I squeeze Cole's hand more tightly.

'Do you have any ideas about the vehicle involved?' Cole asks.

'As yet, no,' Ingram replies with a regretful sigh. 'We'll be combing the area and checking his bike for anything it might yield. Unfortunately, with the torrential rain causing the canal to overflow into the lane, we have little to go on there as yet.'

'I see.' Kneading his forehead hard with his thumb and forefinger, Cole falls silent for a moment. Then, 'So why are you here?' he asks. 'Wouldn't you normally inform the next of kin?'

'His mum died,' I remind him, my throat catching, my head reeling.

'Would you like to sit down, Mrs Chase?' Ingram asks as I feel the floor tilt dangerously beneath me.

'No.' I shake my head and wipe away the tears from my eyes with my fingers. 'I'm okay.'

He gives me a small smile. 'We found a message sent from his phone. It was sent to you, Mrs Chase.' He pauses, scrutinising me carefully. 'I'm assuming you haven't seen it?'

My phone. I haven't even looked at it. 'My phone's in the kitchen,' I mumble. Snapping my gaze to Cole, I pull away from him and hurry to fetch it. My eyes darting frantically around, I find it on the island. Quickly I select the message and read it, and a mixture of raw grief and excruciating guilt kicks sharply in. *I'm sorry, Maddie. I never meant to hurt Kelsey. The last person in the world I would ever want to hurt is you. Please accept my apologies.*

The tears come then, hot, fat tears of regret spilling down my face. 'He killed Kelsey?' I turn, looking in bewilderment from Cole to the detective, who's followed him in. 'But *why*?'

'Our guess is to incriminate your husband,' Ingram offers. 'We think the last threatening message you received may possibly have come from him too.' Noticing my confusion, he explains, 'After a brief search of his home, we found another phone. One belonging to Kelsey Roberts. Plus, there was evidence in his saddlebag that leads us to believe that he might have been responsible for her death. Obviously we'll be checking that forensically.'

He doesn't say what evidence, but I gather he means the syringe. I nod and lean into my husband, never more grateful for the solidity of him as he circles me with his arms.

SEVENTY-THREE

I glance at Cole as he turns from the front door after seeing DI Ingram out. He meets my gaze, his striking blue eyes seeming to look right down into my soul. He doesn't say anything for an excruciatingly long moment. Then, 'I'll go and check on the kids.' He nods towards the stairs.

With no idea what to say to him, I watch him go before wrapping my arms tightly around myself and heading for the kitchen. I feel cold, my limbs trembling, my whole body shaking. I don't feel I'll ever be warm again. Switching on the kettle, I freeze as a blinding image of Alex making coffee crashes into my mind, his eyes ablaze with fury as he turns to hold mine.

A raucous sob escapes me, and I work to stifle another. I have to compose myself. My children can't see me like this. Swiping the tears from my face, I pull in a breath and go to the stairs to follow Cole up. As I quietly approach the boys' bedroom door, I see him sitting on the edge of Lucas's bed, his head bowed, his thumbs pressed hard to his forehead. I want to go to him, to try somehow to reassure him. But how do I?

Carrying on to our room, I stand in the middle of it, and my gaze goes to the bed, where just a short time ago I was nestled close to my husband. Even if things weren't right between us, the intimacy lacking, I felt my world was safe. Will it ever feel safe again?

As I glance around, my eyes snag on the jacket Cole was wearing draped over the chair, and my heart jars. Spinning around, I race to the bathroom. I'm scrabbling through my jeans pockets when I sense him standing behind me. Slowly I turn to face him.

He watches me silently, his eyes scanning mine curiously. 'Is this what you're looking for?' he asks eventually.

My gaze snaps from his face to the crumpled slip of paper he's holding, and my heart stops stone-cold dead.

He studies me a second longer, a troubled frown creasing his brow. 'Love really can drive people to all sorts of madness, can't it?' he says, his voice ragged. 'You clearly went to great lengths to stop me finding out. I do wonder why, though. I thought you realised I knew when I swore to love her unconditionally.'

'Cole...' I start.

He turns away. 'Oh.' He stops at the door and glances back at me. 'Kelsey wasn't pregnant, by the way. I thought it might help ease your conscience, but somehow now I very much doubt it.'

'He planted the ketamine,' I whisper as he walks through the door.

His step falters briefly. He doesn't speak, doesn't look back, but goes quietly to the landing and down the stairs.

I stay where I am, rooted to the spot, unsure what to do. I'm wondering whether the choice will be taken out of my hands as I make my limbs move and go quietly into the boys' room. I don't disturb them, looking down at them instead as they lie in identical positions, looking like perfect little angels. I simply want to take a mental snapshot of them and etch it on my mind.

After a moment drinking in the miracle of them, I brush the

tears I don't deserve to cry from my cheeks and go to Ellie's room. I find her scrunched up on her side on the bed, facing away from me. As I approach her, she uncoils herself, springing up and tugging her earphones out.

I lower myself to sit on the edge of the bed. 'I need to give you something,' I say, smiling to reassure her.

As I unfurl my hand, Ellie stares down at the charm that lies in the palm of it. 'I wasn't sure where I lost it,' she murmurs. 'I didn't kill her, Mum.' Her terrified eyes snap back to mine. 'I wanted to, but I didn't, I swear.'

My heart wrenches with unbearable guilt. 'I know you didn't, sweetheart. I know.' I reach to pull her close to me, hold her tight, possibly for the last time. As I close my eyes, I can still see the image that will never leave me. The deep gash in Kelsey's flesh, her deceitful eyes growing empty as she draws her last breath.

EPILOGUE

ALEX

Earlier that evening

Alex cursed the rain that dripped from his cycle helmet and somehow managed to find its way under his waterproof jersey, sending an icy shiver the length of his torso. It was bucketing down. That was a given considering how the day had gone thus far. God was obviously pissing on his plans – again, he thought irritably. Or rather Cole, who everyone seemed to think was some kind of god, simply by nature of the fact that he was a top neurosurgeon. He wasn't a god. He was human. Flawed. And Maddie had never been able to see it. There'd been times when he could have left emergency procedures to lesser mortals and gone home. He'd chosen not to. In Alex's mind, that was a clear indication that he didn't want to, that he didn't rate his wife and children above his *crucial* work at the hospital.

'*Shit.*' He cursed out loud as he navigated around a puddle only to hit a pothole, which jarred the vertebrae from his coccyx to the cervical joints in his neck, and most probably damaged the rim of his wheel. Blowing out a despairing breath, he cycled on through the slush and mud that passed for a lane towards the cottage where there would be no one to welcome him home. Cole had all that, a warm glow at the window, a family waiting for him, and he'd taken it for granted, risking it all for the thrill of illicit sex with a woman who was transparently a gold-digger.

Alex had had enough. The man had taken Maddie from him. Okay, Alex had been a prat, but he'd *loved* her. And he'd had to stand aside and watch Cole Chase waltz off with her. He'd kept his mouth shut, figured Maddie must be happy, but the thing with Kelsey... A gold-digger she might have been, but she didn't deserve to be treated with the blatant disrespect Cole was showing her, denying that he'd fathered a child with her, even though it could be easily proven. That had been the proverbial last straw. Alex had felt obliged to do something about it, to stop Cole Chase thinking he could have it all, destroying Maddie in the process. And Ellie... Watching her grow up without him had almost crucified him. *He* was her father and there was no way he was going to stand by and watch Cole destroy her too. Cole didn't deserve his freedom to abuse women. Alex hoped fervently the police would find enough evidence to convict him of murder. He might not be guilty of the drugs charges, Maddie had guessed right about that, but Alex was positive he'd had some kind of mental aberration and killed Kelsey.

Wishing he'd handled things differently with Maddie, he cycled on, trying to figure out a way to apologise to her, to explain that his emotions had got the better of him, because, unlike her shit of a husband, he actually did have feelings. Maybe he should send her some flowers. Something special. Red roses maybe? he mused. He wasn't aware of a car approaching until he heard the swish of tyres on the wet road behind him, the low whir of the engine indicating that it was powered by electricity. So what was it doing on a largely uninhabited lane in the arse end of nowhere used mainly by farm vehicles?

Alex glanced over his shoulder, ready to move over, and felt uneasy trepidation creep through him. Where were its lights? He felt marginally relieved a second later as it appeared to draw to a stop. Lovers courting, probably. Or more likely some bloke of the same ilk as Cole Chase getting his kicks from cheating on his wife.

Shaking his head, he pushed on. Then slowed, his heart slowing with him as the lane was suddenly floodlit around him. Headlights. On full beam. *What the fuck?* A lurch of fear gripped him as he heard not the low whir of an electric car but the grinding rev as it switched to traction. Alex stopped. Dropping a foot to the ground and twisting around, he splayed a hand in front of him and peered through his fingers. Cold foreboding clenched his stomach as the engine revved throatily again. And again. For a blood-freezing second he was petrified, unable to move even a muscle as the vehicle rolled towards him.

Fear ripped through him as it picked up speed, and he remounted fast, pedalling with every reserve of energy he had. He didn't feel the impact, he thought obliquely as he landed, his cheekbone hitting the potholed road with a nauseating crack. Lifting his head a fraction, thanking God his neck wasn't broken even if he couldn't feel his legs, he was surprised when he recognised his own number plate reversing sharply towards him. *Maddie.* He almost smiled at her ingenuity. She'd obviously remembered where his mother had kept her spare key, allowing her access to the cottage and his car keys.

He felt it when the car rolled over him a second time, with every pulverised bone in his body.

A LETTER FROM SHERYL

Thank you so much for choosing to read *My Loving Husband*. I can't believe this is my seventeenth book published with fabulous Bookouture! I really hope you enjoy reading it as much as I enjoyed writing it. If you would like to keep up to date with my new releases, please do sign up at the link below, where you can grab my FREE short story, *The Ceremony*.

www.bookouture.com/sheryl-browne

I was once asked the question, 'Do you scare yourself when you're writing your thrillers?' The truth is, I do a bit. In writing psychological thrillers, I'm exploring the darker psyche of some of my characters, looking at the nature vs nurture conundrum. Is badness in the genes? Is it brain function that creates a killer? Childhood experience? A lethal combination of all three? The driving force linked to most murders, I'm reliably informed by a former DCI, is humiliation or the need for revenge. Love can drive us to all sorts of madness, even murder. A lover spurned, a husband, partner or wife cheated on might be seething with jealousy, deeply humiliated. Seeking revenge.

I was also asked, 'What part of you is included in your books?' The answer to that is my heart. Coming from a large family myself, my writing tends to gravitate towards family, where there is always a rich vein of emotion to mine. I like to look at the dynamics within that family. Personally, I am fiercely protective of my loved ones. Is the desire to protect someone you love, though, an understandable motive for murder? I'll leave that question with you, my wonderful readers.

If you have enjoyed the book, I would love it if you could share your thoughts and write a brief review. Reviews really mean the world to an author. They not only help a book find its wings but they really are hugely inspiring. I would also love to hear from you via social media or my website.

Happy reading, all!

Sheryl x

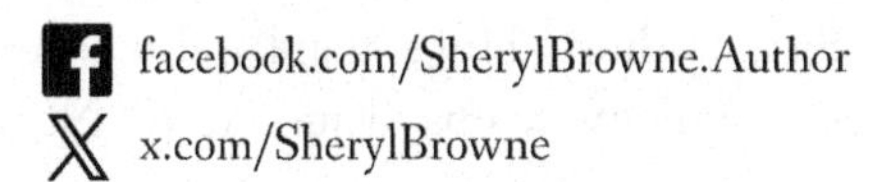

ACKNOWLEDGMENTS

Heartfelt thanks to the fabulous team at Bookouture, whose support of their authors is phenomenal. Special thanks to Helen Jenner, who has an uncanny knack of steering my stories in the right direction when I might be in danger of going off the rails. To everyone in our wonderful editorial team, too, who work so hard for all their authors. Huge thanks also to our fantastic marketing and publicity teams. Kim Nash, Noelle Holten, Sarah Hardy and Jess Readett are always enthusiastically behind us and are just amazing. To the other authors at Bookouture, thank you for your support, which is always there when one of us might need it.

I owe a huge debt of gratitude to all the fantastically hard-working bloggers and reviewers who have taken time to read and review my books. It's truly appreciated. You do an amazing job shouting out to the world when we might be too nervous to. Special thanks, too, to the amazing book groups out there who get behind us. When we're flagging or doubting ourselves, as we often do, you can positively uplift us.

Final thanks to every single reader out there for buying and reading our books. Knowing you have enjoyed our stories and care enough about our characters to want to share them with other readers is the best incentive ever for us to keep writing.

PUBLISHING TEAM

Turning a manuscript into a book requires the efforts of many people. The publishing team at Bookouture would like to acknowledge everyone who contributed to this publication.

Audio
Alba Proko
Sinead O'Connor
Melissa Tran

Commercial
Lauren Morrissette
Hannah Richmond
Imogen Allport

Cover design
Aaron Munday

Data and analysis
Mark Alder
Mohamed Bussuri

Editorial
Helen Jenner
Ria Clare

Copyeditor
Jane Selley

Proofreader
Shirley Khan

Marketing
Alex Crow
Melanie Price
Occy Carr
Cíara Rosney
Martyna Młynarska

Operations and distribution
Marina Valles
Stephanie Straub
Joe Morris

Production
Hannah Snetsinger
Mandy Kullar
Ria Clare
Nadia Michael

Publicity
Kim Nash
Noelle Holten
Jess Readett
Sarah Hardy

Rights and contracts
Peta Nightingale
Richard King
Saidah Graham

Made in the USA
Las Vegas, NV
27 April 2025